SINS

OF

BLEEDING GOLD

S. S. NIGHTSHADE

Second edition paperback ISBN: 979-8-9913670-3-5
Nightshade's Writing Desk LLC

FOR THE READERS WHO'VE FELT LIKE
THEY'RE SIMULTANEOUSLY TOO MUCH,
YET NOT ENOUGH.

KEEP FIGHTING.

Trigger Warning

- Religion: this text does not claim to represent accurate records or teachings of any religious histories or practices

- Kidnapping

- Explicit sexual scenes; allusions of rape

- Graphic violence; war; death

- Substance abuse

- Violent/emotional outbursts

- Blood drinking

PROLOGUE

A burning church should not look beautiful. But there it was, so out of place on a mountaintop thick with pine forest. For a moment, the pale steeple reflected the light of the moon, and flames, before releasing a groan of protest and caving in.

The double doors flung open with a spray of red embers, and out stumbled a young girl. She was covered in soot, and blood that was not her own, but she didn't look back as she raced down the short staircase and bolted for the cover of the trees.

The dagger she swiped before she fled drummed against her thigh as she ran. Half the blade was made with cursed obsidian, a metal that could bring no harm to her. But the other half was forged from Holy metal, the same purified silver which made up Heavens gates. A well–placed attack with that edge would be enough to kill most dark entities. Perhaps even herself.

A sharp crack rang through the night as the rest of the building gave way to the flames. The girl just ran faster, away from the life burning behind her.

'You will not have my daughter, I forbid it.'

'Come now Mary, she will only grow darker if you continue to suppress her power.'

'I need you to run for me. Run and never stop.'

The darkness was a welcome blessing, the silence of the trees somehow dampening the echoing screams inside her skull. Unfortunately, that darkness was crawling with other monsters besides herself.

She panted a curse as she noticed a ghostly blue glow weaving towards her between the trunks. Her footfalls were nearly silent on the carpet of pine needles, but silence would not save her from a soul-searching spell.

Suddenly, the forest floor turned to slick rock, and the thick cover of trees gave way to cold, open air. Her pumping legs swung helplessly, and she tucked her head as she found herself tumbling through the night. The dark had made it impossible for her to see the small cliff she just took a dive over.

Branches tore at her hair and clothes, and with a profound thud she landed on her back in a clearing far below. If she were human, she would be dead.

The girl lay still for several silent minutes. She steadied her breath before she finally braved opening her eyes. Surprised, she saw a starry night sky above her rather than the swords and teeth she was expecting. She had fallen straight into a clearing in the woods. The tall grass sprinkled with foxglove and poppies could almost be tranquil, but it gave her no place to hide.

Her breath floated away from her in hot steaming clouds as she sat up, the breeze tickling her hair across her cheeks. Getting to her feet she turned and stared up at the cliffside she had just crashed down. Vines and thorns clung to the rock, fighting against the rivulets of water that steadily trickled down. The pool at the base was vibrantly blue, bubbling away into a stream.

The snap of a branch sounded.

She ripped the dagger from its perch on her hip, brandishing it with a snarl that turned into a choked sob. In the trees around her she could see the stars above reflected in the eyes of the Hellhounds who had been tracking her.

The faint wisps of blue light skittered between the pack members, before bursting into the clearing to circle her. Her soul had been tracked, there was no convincing them she wasn't their target.

"She has Holy metal," one observed but none stepped from the trees.

Hellhounds were an interesting breed of dark creatures. They had the ability to shift between a humanoid body and a wolf, and with that ability could speak in either form. Born from the darkness, shadows were their hunting grounds. The voice sounded again, "How are we supposed to get close to her while she's holding that?"

"Well, we can't simply ask her to hand it over, though that would make this whole ordeal much easier." A snicker echoed from the trees.

"There is no time for chatter with this delay. Focus on getting the blade." The girl swallowed a scream as she watched a gigantic white wolf calmly step into the clearing in front of her. To her shock, this Hound was a she-wolf.

It was very rare that a female Hellhound would be in an army, let alone be a commanding officer. Most of the time they would be locked away and pampered, their existence revolving around their ability to breed. Her coat shone like the moon and her eyes gleamed like its light on the sea. They were the same shade of blue as the spell which had chased the girl through the woods.

"Now is not the time to play warrior, girl." Though her muzzle didn't move, her gravelly voice rang in the girl's head, "You are coming with us."

"Coming with us?" The first wolf interjected, sounding confused, "I thought our orders were to kill her?"

"Those were your orders." The she-wolf's voice turned malicious, "Mine were quite different." The Hound turned away from the child and faced the woods baring her teeth. "Now is the time to change the course of this war!"

Howls filled the night as Hounds began attacking their comrades hidden within the trees. Any who dared to charge the girl were cut off and struck dead by the she-wolf, who now circled her in a defensive manner.

As suddenly as it started, the mutiny was over.

Slowly, three more Hounds stepped from the trees. Blood dripped from their lips and the stench of death clung to their fur. They were a few feet taller and wider than the she-wolf but dipped their heads in respect.

Two were gray, one like charcoal and the other ash. Together, they supported a smaller, auburn Hound between them who was limping.

"It is done, as you asked, Luna." The ashen Hound spoke while urging the injured Hound to sit.

"I don't understand," the girl whispered, eyes glued to the she-wolf, Luna, still beside her. "If your army has been ordered to kill me then why is this happening?"

"Because your death will not end this war any more than your mothers would." Luna answered simply. The girl stilled.

"What do you know of my mother?" Luna shifted her gaze to the girl, pity replacing the menace in her eyes.

"She was lost in the church, child. To save you we did not have the luxury of saving her." The Hound bent her head down, genuine empathy in her eyes before the same arrogant voice from earlier interjected.

"Speaking of which, we are on a pretty tight schedule. We need to get going if ya don't mind."

"Silence Akashi." Luna snapped but looked immediately back to the girl. "Child..."

"I'm not going anywhere with you," the girl whispered out. The smell of smoke filled her nostrils again, the clanging of swords echoing in her mind. She flipped the blade in her palm, silver edge out, "I'm not going anywhere with you until you tell me why my mother is dead!" She screamed, lunging for Luna with her blade raised.

Flames burst to life on her forearms and Luna darted away, narrowly missing the column of lavender fire erupting towards her. From behind, a solid block of muscle knocked between the girl's shoulder blades and pressed her into the dirt, smothering the flames. Furious she fought the weight, flipping herself over before freezing. Above her crouched Akashi.

He was the embodiment of the word Hellhound. His coat was dark as the inky night, shining with vivid streaks of red. She couldn't tell if it was blood or not which made it all the more sinister with the scene of death around them. Gray claws ground into the dirt beside her head, his bared teeth merely inches from her face.

Out of the darkness embodying him though, he had stunning green eyes. They burst with different hues of the growth and rebirth of spring. Much like his eyes, beneath the scent of blood and death lay something more comforting: rain and pine and smoke.

She found herself drifting, feeling calm for the first time that night as they lay there, eyes locked on each other. If not for the growl rumbling in his throat she might have forgotten how dangerous he truly was to her.

"I came here to steal whatever war device our previous Master was set on claiming for himself. I don't fancy watching you spill my Mother's blood with it."

"Your Mother?" The girl asked, eyes flicking to Luna placing her immediately.

"Akashi no," Luna growled. "This is not the time or place. Bring her." Akashi didn't move, eyes not shifting from the girls. He was staring at her so intensely she felt as if she would break.

Finally, he shifted back onto his haunches, removing the claws from beside her head and uncaging her from beneath him. Without hesitation he lowered his nose to her hand, nudging against the fingers that still grasped the knife. The other Hounds stood stock still, preparing to pounce in between him and the blade if it came to that.

"Instead of a weapon, we found you. A kid filled with power, craved by both sides of this war. You'll have to live your entire life on the run, alone and untrusting. Until you're finally caught and kept like a bird in a cage." He lifted his head, face hovering above hers, "Now if that's what you want, I'll walk straight out of this clearing, and you'll never see me again. But something about you makes me think you're not fit for a cage, Raven."

Raven's breathing was ragged. Silent tears slid down her dirty cheeks, but despite her worn state she struck with more rage than Akashi accounted for.

There was the singing of metal and then a short yelp before Akashi leapt away from her. One of the grey Hounds growled and lunged towards them but Akashi whirled, snapping his teeth.

"Back off! Do I look like I need help?"

"If I wasn't exhausted, you'd definitely need help," Raven muttered, still flat on her back against the dirt. "You don't get to call me by name. I don't want to hear it from you. Ever."

Akashi grumbled in annoyance, turning round to face her again. Blood dripped from his left eye, a clean cut from north to south. Raven flashed him a smirk, before abruptly bursting into sobs as her pitiful triumph faded. The knife fell from her hand as she reached up to cover her own eyes before curling into a ball. Fire in her veins, vines tickling her back, breath on her face.

"Hey..." A hand gently closed around her wrist. When she tried to yank away, it held firm and tugged her upright. Her cheek hit bare skin, and Akashi's scent flooded her nose making her freeze. She could hear his heart pumping in his chest, the only sign of his nerves as he reached behind her with his free hand to toss the blade away. Then he just held her till her cries died into soft whimpers and the shaking of her shoulders subsided to weak shivers.

Bleary eyed, she twisted her head, shocked that he didn't look much older than her. Tousled dark hair and chubby boyish cheeks had replaced the black fur and sharp teeth that were poised over her just a moment ago. The only sign hinting towards his ferocious wolf was the dazzling green of his eyes.

Blood dripped from the cut she gave him, a lazy river of red staining his pale skin. Guilt immediately tore through her. He shifted as she stared at him, his eyes averting self-consciously before asking, "Do I seem less scary to you this way?"

"I promised her I would run," Raven whispered as a reply. "I promised her I would run and never stop." Akashi cocked his head, something like humor flickering through his gaze.

"Funny. You act like you promised her you would fight."

Raven shook her head, before sagging forward against his shoulder again, her body finally giving in to the stress. Wordlessly Akashi rose, cradling her in his arms and turned to his mother.

"Now what?"

Lunas voice was as solemn as the night, "We keep our promise."

CHAPTER 1

I don't have any memories of before the Hounds. As far as I'm concerned, that night which revisits me in my dreams was when my life began. The night was decades ago, but time for immortals passes slow. And boy does it drag sometimes.

As fate would have it, half-demons half-angels aren't all that common, so I live hidden away in the human realm full time. Considering that the night the Hounds rescued me was when my Father was trying to kill me, perhaps hiding myself and my powers wasn't such a terrible idea. Even though those powers would give me one hell of an advantage while sparring with my stepbrother.

I duck as Akashi tries to knock my head off with a punch I barely avoid. With my rushing thoughts thoroughly eliminated, I roll across the mat and spring for his back. Too slow. He flips over me, hands snagging my waist and I end up pinned under him.

"Hah! That's ten pins for me, and zero for you Little Bird." Akashi taunts.

He's refrained from calling me by name
all these years. In the beginning, it
provided some type of undefinable relief,
like a cushion between the girl I was and
the monster I could be. Now, the pet
name just nags at me like a scab. I huff,
annoyed.

"Oh please. If I didn't let you win,
your ego would surely never recover."

"Ouch, someone's in a pissy mood
this evening." Despite our first encounter,
Akashi became like an older brother to
me. The kind of hot and cocky older
brother I never wished for.

That once scrawny pre-teen who
couldn't compare to the bulk and strength
of his wolf form, grew into a mass of
smooth muscles and sly grins. His black
hair reflected his Hounds coat with a
single streak of red through the bangs,
which were just short and tousled enough
to not hang in his eyes.

His eyes... they remained the
same. Glittering pools of green as bright
as a leprechaun's clover, constantly
teasing and baiting me to fight. Though
staring at them for too long brings a
lingering pain to my heart.

A thin scar cuts a perfectly straight
white line down from the center of his
eyebrow to the top of his cheekbone, the
remnant of when I attacked him with the

knife. I drag my eyes off it as he releases me, rolling before my fist can connect with his jaw.

"Too slow again." He grabs a handful of my hair and wraps it around his wrist, snagging me in place. "You know, maybe we should cut this. Someone grabbing it during an actual fight would be an unfair yet completely possible tactic."

"Don't even think about cutting my hair!" With a swift turn I landed a kick to his knee, resulting in a satisfying crack. Any other opponent would have surely crumpled where they stood but Akashi barely took a step back to regain his balance. A satisfied smirk graced his lips.

"Now that's more like it."

"Masochist." I mutter.

"Time!" A short bout of clapping interrupts us as our oldest brother Hikari climbs onto the mats.

Unlike Akashi's wide frame of ochre muscle, Hikari resembles a modern surfer. Being tall and lean makes him an especially deft sparring partner. His bleached blonde hair is cropped short, leaving ample room to display his ocean blue eyes.

"I swear you fight almost as well as some of the Hounds I trained."

"Remind me why I need to fight like a Hound again?" I ask. Brushing him off I retreat to the corner for a drink. "It's not like I can say a magic word and grow fur like the rest of you." Possible, but unlikely.

"You know what mother says," Hikari answered.

I sigh. Yes, I do indeed know. I can repeat the speech in my head: 'If you learn to fight like a Hound, you can beat a Hound. One on one combat helps settle your emotions as you focus on the task in front of you. And your emotions must be settled since your power is ruled by what you feel.'

I rub my temples in frustration, already feeling the familiar prickle of sparks threatening to leap from my fingers.

"I just want all this training to pay off one day. Instead of just sitting in here and not putting it to good use," I say gesturing to the space around us.

The sparring area resides in the basement of the house, though they both know I'm referring to the entire property. Beyond having Heaven's support, I never learned the particulars of how we came to live here. We certainly didn't skip out on space and privacy though.

The home is a three-story colonial farmhouse, set deep in the country of northwestern New Jersey. Twenty minutes from the nearest town gives our unique family all the privacy we need to be ourselves. For the Hounds, it's transformation and hunting purposes, and for me it's practicing magic. Magic Luna had forbidden me from using off the property.

"Well today is your lucky day Little Bird," Akashi announces, interrupting my strained thoughts once more. "Ma said it's time to 'broaden your horizons'. So maybe you'll get the opportunity to whoop someone's else's ass besides mine or Anzen's."

"Oh yes, I do remember her mentioning that the other day. This will be so exciting." Hikari said and clapped his hands again, "Right! Out of this basement and into the shower you go," he commanded, ushering me towards the staircase.

"Wait." I grip the banister looking back and forth between my brothers, "What's going on? I'm confused."

"Nothing too special," Akashi's mouth drops into a crooked, sly smile. With a twist in my gut, I had a feeling I'd be enjoying my freedom the least.

"You've got to be kidding me," I say through a mouthful of bread. Luna pauses, glass raised halfway to her lips, and looks briefly taken aback by my tone. The quietest of growls rumbles in her throat as she slowly lowers the glass back to the table. My own throat constricts, and my brothers shrink back in their seats.

It was hard sometimes. Having an Alpha Hellhound as my mother figure. I didn't know the full story of how they all came to be together, but I'd gathered bits and pieces through the years.

Anzen is our youngest brother. Where he doesn't pack as much of a punch as some of the others, he makes up for it with that Einstein brain of his. I feel his doe eyes on me, always studying everything from beneath his wild copper hair.

Kuma is the second oldest and our strongest brother. His long black hair is braided back from his face. Built like a mafia thug, he carefully controls the pressure he applies while cutting his pancakes and pays us little attention. Hikari is the oldest and Beta of the pack, and then there's Akashi.

No matter what the rest of us do to get ahead, Akashi somehow produces the desired result with ease. He's skilled and intelligent, and even able to hold his own against Kuma which has given him an alpha complex. That is until Luna snaps her only surviving pup back into reality.

The only signs of her age are the sporadic grays amongst her otherwise ebony hair, and the few wrinkles gracing her ochre skin. Her eyes, usually dark like Anzens, now reflect the same pale blue as her soul-searching spell. She clears her throat, the color fading.

"I don't think there is any reason for that tone missy, but if you believe there is, I require a swift explanation." I scoff.

"You think I'm being overdramatic?" I glare at her over my plate until her eyes narrow.

For years, I wallowed in the anguish and pain of losing my birth mother, Mary. After her human life, she rose and became one of the Lords Angels. But because of my Father, because of my half demon blood, we could not stay. I couldn't help but feel that her blood was on my hands, and I vowed to avenge her.

I took a breath, attempting to steady myself but my voice still came out bitter, "I've been training to kill the Devil.

Not play damsel in distress for the sake of the family business."

"The family business," Luna spoke with equal bitterness, "is what you and everyone at this table should thank for everything provided around here. Your beds, your meals, your clothes."

"Our lack of social lives?" Akashi drawls, earning a snicker from Kuma.

The family business, as Luna calls it, is essentially an extermination team which targets supernatural entities who cross the border into the human realm. It's similar to what duties the Hounds had while serving in the Devil's army, so the task of tracking and killing is a familiar and easy job for them to do.

Back in their army days they would be hunting Angels, holy and fallen alike. Since committing a mutiny to save me, they avoid hunting entities such as those and demons. I'm not sure if they would see it as hypocritical to raise me yet kill my kind, but either way the business is sketchy and, in my eyes, a waste of my abilities.

Luna drums her fingers against the table, "I am trying to provide you the opportunity to actually engage in a supernatural fight—"

I slam my fist down on the table, my frustration boiling over. Whatever she has to offer, it won't be a big enough challenge. It won't prepare me enough. And I already know using my magic and testing its limits won't be an option she allows.

I feel Akashi shift beside me, his voice hushed against my ear, "Watch the tablecloth."

Looking down at my hand I see wisps of smoke starting to rise. I yank my hand off the table and clamp it between my thighs as Luna clicks her tongue.

"It's errors like that which is why I am having you practice on lesser beings rather than throwing you into the world of fighting Angels and Demons." I feel my temper flare.

Errors, that's what me using magic is always seen as. Errors and dramatics. Weak. I grit my teeth, throwing out a halfhearted attempt to defend myself.

"I'm strong enough to fight any Angel or Demon that attacks me if I'd be allowed to not hold myself back. Kuma has even said so." Luna whips her head to gaze sternly at my older brother who suddenly seems fascinated by the salt and pepper shakers sitting in the middle of the table. She drags her eyes back to me.

"You cannot keep mistaking constructive criticism and praise for permission to stalk your father."

"If my skills are not ready for that type of praise then maybe people should learn to not over exaggerate." I shot back.

"*Vapulabis,*" Luna mutters, rising from the table, "It is not that your skills are weak but your brain. You cannot handle any adversary if you cannot manage your emotions!" My gaze drops from hers and she takes a heavy breath before adding, somewhat hesitatingly, "Raven, your abilities are beyond measure and comparison. But in your current state, it would be all too easy for your Father to break your spirit, and then your mind shortly after."

The mounting pressure in my head explodes and I bolt from my seat. My fingers feel like they're melting as I push past Akashi and disappear down the hall in a blur. Night air hits my face, shocking my body into action and soon I'm sprinting, flying through the yard to the trees.

I'm sick and tired of this back and forth. Every conversation turns into warnings or ridicules about how my Father could catch me. Reminders that he would probably let me live and use me to his advantage; make me hurt everyone I care about. And then to finish, she would point out the opposite threat. That if I don't behave, the Angels could seek me out to destroy me as well.

So, for my own safety, I need to sit still and be quiet. Do nothing, or Angels and Devils alike will try and kill me. Over, and over, and over again it's drilled into my head until I relent. Or run away, like right now.

Though I'm far into the trees by now, it doesn't take long for hot breath to hit my ankles. The induced adrenaline of being chased kicks in and I splay my fingers out like a star.

Vines burst from the ground, warm and green, vibrating with magic and life. They gather around me until I'm lifted away from my pursuer and swung into the canopy of needles and pinecones above my head. Wrapping my arms around a passing trunk I snap my fingers and the vines recede, leaving me squatting on a thin branch about thirty feet above the ground. I shut my eyes and press my face against the bark, breathing in the scent of sap until my heart steadies into a steady rhythm.

"You should know not to chase me," I mumble, just loud enough for my pursuer panting at the bottom of the tree to hear. "Especially in the forest. You know what it does to me."

"You don't really leave us much choice Little Bird." It's Akashi's voice that filters up to me, but I know they're all here. Except for Luna of course. She's never followed when I've run, and I don't know if that makes me feel better or worse.

"If it's worth anything, I think you should take the job." I hear Anzen call up, "It's not like it's in a terrible place. New York City might be a fun experience for you!"

"And I think we all would agree that it would be nice for her to direct her physical fury at something other than us." Hikari adds with a chuckle. I hear them muttering back and forth between themselves as I sit there and collect myself. Eventually, I make the branch bend to my will, drooping until I can slide off to sit on the trees protruding roots.

"Hey Kuma?" Their chatter dies, and I can feel Kuma's eyes on me like he already knows what I'm about to ask. "Was it only praise, or do you really think I could beat him?"

"I think you would stand a fair chance alone. But if you let us help you, you'll definitely be victorious." He answers without hesitation.

His words carry a heavy weight though and I drop my head. He knows I won't let them help me. They know I'm consumed and have made it my purpose to defeat my Father, avenge my Mother, to not fail like I did before. Or worse: put anyone else in danger again.

"You were a child," Akashi says, reading my mind. His green eyes study me calmly. The scar I gave him is even more visible with the lack of inky fur. It reflects what little moonlight filters through the trees, making him look older, "Now, you're not. When the time comes, he won't be ready for you." His words lift some of the weight I feel, and I nod. He's always been there for me. The first one to come for me and bring me home. Despite his annoying personality I owe him everything, so I stop this fit.

Slowly I stand, rubbing my thumb and forefinger together in small, practiced circles just long enough to coax a small orange flame to appear.

"You're right. He won't be."

CHAPTER 2

Somehow all the glamorous movies about New York failed to mention the rancid smell of rot protruding from every grate in the sidewalk. I stifle a gag passing what seems like the hundredth overflowing dumpster and avert my eyes back skyward to the towering buildings. This whole place seems devoid of natural life yet has a surplus of waste.

Anzen, seemingly set on making this trip enjoyable for me, keeps pointing out tourist traps and monuments hoping to catch my interest with one. For his efforts I force light smiles onto my face and let him ramble about the "fun" facts he knows about each place.

Seeing my brothers in public was weird. At this time of day, we would typically be in the woods covered in dirt and sweat but today they wear street clothes and buy trinkets from vendors.

Anzen looks like a Pinterest hipster, with his graphic tee and stressed jeans. On his head was a floppy beanie purely for style and not the weather. Hikari played on his California boy looks with white pants, a blue button down and sunglasses (with the tag still attached) perched in his hair. Kuma somehow managed to squeeze his muscles into a silk dress shirt, which made precisely seven women walk into a pole or a bike. So far.

Akashi's outfit choice clashed with the rest of us. Despite the relentless sun, he was dressed head to toe in plain black: t-shirt, jeans, sneakers, and jacket. He looked more like his Hound form than human, and irritatingly I found myself glancing at him far more times than necessary. Eventually he caught me looking, and that arrogant smirk of his knocked out any sense of admiration I had.

"I thought you preferred me shirtless in the sparring ring?" He raised an eyebrow. A challenge. I roll my eyes in return.

"You look like a brooding Emo who's ditching class," I mutter, poking his arm. He shrugs, giving me a quick once over.

"And you look like the popular rich girl." I groan, eyes snagging on my reflection of one of the wide glass windows lining the street. Indeed, I do.

My layers of dark hair were pulled up into a high, *high*, swishing ponytail. My legs felt like they were losing circulation in skinny jeans Luna forced me into. She paired them with heeled boots that I could barely walk in. After much arguing I was permitted to choose my own top: my favorite band t-shirt. I pursed my lips and glanced up at my face. My river water eyes were traced with liner and stared back at me with a bored expression, the trained cool neutral I was used to adapting.

At my silence he nudged my shoulder, "I didn't even know you owned those butt huggers." Believe me, neither did I.

"The majority of my outfit was completely non-consensual," I muttered, suddenly self-conscious. My nerves had been running high since we got to this city, and Akashi's nit-picking only aggravated them further.

"Well, I think she looks great." Hikari chimed in, dropping his arm over my shoulders.

"Only because for once she doesn't have dirt on her face and twigs in her hair." Akashi smirked again, "Or mud on her—"

"You're just brooding because men are looking at her and you can't kill them for it," Kuma mused and sent a wink towards a blonde who had just dropped her pizza on the sidewalk. Akashi tripped off the curb, a flabbergasted look on his face. Then he launched his fist towards Kuma's smirk and the pair started to rough house it right there on the sidewalk.

"Even if they were looking, they aren't doing anything so what's the big deal?" Exasperated, I step forward to put myself between the two. Hikari laughs and drops an arm around my shoulders, gently tugging me back.

"They're not doing anything because you are surrounded by four large and devastatingly handsome men." He drops his voice before adding, "If you were alone, at least one of them would have definitely approached you by now."

"Can we just focus on the task at hand please?" I ask, pushing away as I feel a rush of heat coating my cheeks. Curse these jeans, curse this day!

"Absolutely." Hikari cleared his throat and began to run through the game plan. Somehow, I thought my role would be a lot more exciting, but I was disappointed once I was labeled as vampire bait. At my burst of protest, Hikari shut me up with one of his rare glares.

Apparently, a group of vampires had been preying on young women clubbing down by the harbor. Local authorities, knowing they couldn't handle this type of job, sent word out to Luna asking for our services. Luna had insisted she was far too gray for the vamps to take any interest in her which was the only reason I got to come on this trip at all: stand still and look pretty.

I huffed and rolled my eyes, zoning out as Hikari continued talking of flanking positions the rest of them would take, where to bite to kill blah blah blah. The fun part did not pertain to me.

"Raven, are you listening?" Hikari tapped my nose and I flinched.

"Hmm? Yep. You guys get to kick ass while I play damsel in distress. Though I think playing stripper would get their attention easier." Akashi stopped dead in his tracks, causing Anzen to collide into his back. Kuma cleared his throat loudly, shifting his weight from foot to foot before Hikari grabbed my shoulder, swinging me around with a stern look in his eyes.

"This isn't a game Raven–"

"Oh, I'm making it a game, so I don't tear anyone's tails off. This is humiliating," I shot back. Hikari sighed but relented slightly, the edge in his gaze dampening.

"We're not using you or limiting you. We just need you to lure them into privacy so normal people don't see and become scarred for life." I grit my teeth looking down. He did make it sound better with the luring part.

"Fine. But I get to play the floozy role my way." Hikari opened his mouth again, but I cut him off, "I won't go overboard but they need to feel like they're actually hunting right? One girl wandering away from a throng of women with better assets won't be enough."

Hikari set his mouth into a thin line but didn't argue. I cracked my knuckles, studying the women strolling the streets. Their designer dresses and heels made bold statements against the city's concrete shell, and for the second time today I feel self-conscious.

I might not know much about this side of life, but even I wouldn't give a second glance to a woman in a club this covered up compared to those walking past. I needed to make some adjustments so the vampires would take the bait. Eyeing the glass storefronts of the boutiques surrounding us I thrust out my hand.

"Hikari, give me your wallet."

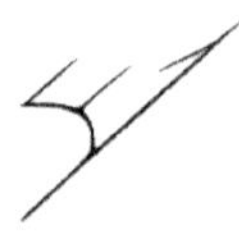

Three hours later the soles of my feet were aching in those damn booted heels. I found myself irritably thankful for the makeup Luna had forcibly applied as I peered around me, taking in the faces and bodies of the women outside the *Marquee.* They were gorgeous. Their flawless skin, curves and silk-like hair made me feel like I was a janitor amidst models despite the strides I took in acquiring my new outfit.

Glittery black fishnets rose from my boots and disappeared under the skirt of a matching skintight dress. At least the tag claimed it was a dress. Its slight length did not back that up and did even less to hide my tanned legs.

Kuma was in line with me. Almost all the buttons on his shirt were now undone and he didn't bother trying to hide his exposed chest while standing there with his arm draped over my shoulders.

The original plan was for Akashi to be my escort, but after he tried decapitating me for the length of my skirt Hikari decided it would be best to not send us in together. That said, I knew Kuma was in no way pleased with my attire either.

"Is it really that big of a deal?" I asked quietly while we shuffled forward following the line inside.

"Is what a big deal?" He muttered, hand dropping to my waist to steer me around the curve of the door into the hall.

"The other women are dressed precisely like me. I thought blending in was the goal?" Kuma released a heavy groan.

"It IS the goal," he growled. "But you're also my little sister. And now we are preoccupied with keeping normal men off of this as well." He yanked the back of my skirt down causing me to let out a startled yelp. I felt my cheeks warm realizing it still barely reached the middle of my thighs.

"I can keep men off me just fine," I mumbled, spinning a lock of hair between my fingers. Kuma barked out a laugh.

"Says the girl who's never interacted with one before."

"It wasn't my decision to be locked on that property my whole life, so yea. I say I can handle myself out here with a guy who can't turn into a wolf," I muttered with a frown.

The bouncer, or at least I'm guessing he was a bouncer, swiped my ID and grabbed my hand to press a stamp down on the back of it. Receiving it back I read over my alias name once more. Megan Turner, 23. That's who I would be tonight. Once Kuma was through, he grabbed my shoulder, spinning me to face him.

"Is that really how you view it? That we locked you up?" I glanced away, biting my tongue. "It was for your own safety." Kuma hissed, "In case you forgot your father—"

"Yes, that's what it felt like sometimes," I snap, cutting him off. "And if you want me to do my job right and not lose control, do not mention my father again."

Kuma just stared at me and with pride alone I held his gaze until he walked off towards the bar. There was a crackling noise as someone plugged something in, and then the throng of men and women roared as the DJ began spinning his music. The lights were flashing, and people were dancing. The whole atmosphere was enough to get me drunk and disoriented, but I smiled and walked directly into their sea.

CHAPTER 3

I don't know how long I was there, dancing, letting myself go. I danced against men and women, sharing skin and sweat. Hands were everywhere, and people were laughing and smiling. I could not see Kuma or any of my brothers, but I could smell them.

I smelled Hikari on a woman with purple hair. Anzen on a man in a suit. Kuma on practically every woman in the club. I could not smell Akashi though. It was this which made me pause and swirl my way out of the bodies towards the bar at the edge of the crowd.

Plopping myself on a barstool I ordered myself ice water before circling back around to face the crowd. My eyes scanned heads and tables but I still couldn't pinpoint him. Damn him for wearing all black.

"You look bitter." I jumped hearing an unexpected voice in my ear, "Boyfriend problems?"

A woman leaned against the counter next to me, her piercing blue eyes studying me from head to toe. She had blonde hair slicked back from her face to cascade over her shoulders, coming to a halt just above her waist. Her dress was similar to mine, black and low cut with a slit in the skirt from her knee to her hip. The fabric there was held closed by swinging silver chains.

"No boyfriend problems." I swivel away, "I just can't seem to place my— oh." I stop short, finally seeing Akashi at the far side of the dance floor. The woman follows my gaze and together we watch Akashi grind against his dance partner, hands roaming over her unchecked. A rock dropped into the pit of my stomach. The blonde whistles.

"Damn, if he's not your boyfriend can I snag him?"

"Feel free to," I mutter and turn my back on the dance floor. I gulp down my water trying to settle my stomach.

"So, there's got to be a story there." The blonde edges closer, "I'm one who loves drama but doesn't spread it. Care to make my night and fill me in?"

"There's not much of a story. I live with his family, that's all."

"What are you, an orphan or something?"

"Something like that I guess," I mumble. She studied me for a minute before taking the seat next to mine.

"I happen to know ways to steer a man's attention elsewhere," She chitters, tapping her nails on the bar. "Advice comes cheap, the price is only your name." She smiles, dark red lips parting to reveal straight white teeth.

"And why my name?" I bristle, but my panicked thoughts are cut short as she tilts her head back releasing a shrill laugh.

"Damn you're uptight. I'm Rebecca." She holds out a hand and I stare at it a moment before taking it, shaking it once.

"I'm Megan."

"Megan," she repeats, nails slightly digging into my skin. "You're a pretty woman, surely, he's not blind to that. Would you like to make your roommate over there jealous?" Before I can answer she's off her stool and dragging me back into the sea of swinging bodies. "Oh Silas! Where did you go pretty boy?" She calls out.

"Who's Silas?" I yell over the music, and she gives me a wicked smile.

"Trust me Megan, you don't know how good you can be taken care of until you meet this guy."

"Should I feel pride or itemized by that statement, my beautiful Rebecca?" A voice like honey spills over my shoulder and I freeze. Everyone in this club is sweating but the hand that slips into mine is eerily soft and cool.

"Shut up." Rebecca beams, "We need to show my new friend Megan here a good time. The dumbass boy she wishes would give her attention has been focused elsewhere for the evening."

"No, that's not what I said, you're jumping to conclusions." I quickly interject and pull my hand out of the cold grip.

"Darling there's nothing shameful about a crush." I was on the verge of pointing out that my so-called crush was my *brother,* but a finger slipped under my chin, tilting my gaze to meet burgundy eyes gazing at me so intensely that I'm silenced.

Exquisite was the only appropriate way to describe the face looking down at me. He was pale in a stunning way, face framed by black locks of hair drifting to his shoulders. Prominent cheekbones and a strong jaw accentuate his full pink lips, which were twisted into a soft smile. I freeze as Silas rubs a thumb over my bottom lip, leaving snowflakes dancing in its wake.

Momentarily I felt myself lose my cool. Shots of electricity bounced across my skin where his body brushed mine in the tight space and I couldn't stop the automatic shiver which ran the full length of my spine.

Those lips spread into a wide, knowing smile before Silas asked, "Now where is this naive young man exactly? We need to give him a good view of the show we are about to put on."

I snap out of it, ripping my eyes from his mouth to stare at his chest, trying to calm my nerves. I reminded myself I was here for a job, and judging by the slight metallic tang permeating the air I was fairly certain I had found my target.

I let a shy smile creep onto my face while tucking a stray lock of hair behind my ear, before lifting a finger to point back in Akashi's direction. I'm only pointing him out because I can't see the others, I affirmed to myself.

My nervous heartbeat though, ticks unchecked. Silas' eyes glaze over, undoubtedly sensing the reaction my body gave to both his touch and Akashi's presence.

I force the embarrassment from my mind. What should I care if he reads it as love, lust or whatever else motivates a vampire to hunt? He hears my blood pumping and has decided I'm his prey.

This is my job tonight after all isn't it?
Hunt the hunter.

 I didn't have the luxury of feeling
self-conscious about what I was doing. I
had to let this play out, needed Silas
completely convinced I would submit
under his will. That's how I found myself
up on one of the mini dance stages with
him.
 He held me facing the crowd, back
to him, and swung my hips back and
forth against his body in slow, lazy
arches. His hands would occasionally
skim the insides of my thighs, popping
individual strands of my fishnets. When
his hands weren't on my legs they were
curving around my hips, gliding up my
arms, tracing the shape of my breasts.
His lips left sporadic trails of kisses
against my neck and shoulders. His
tongue soon followed.
 Doing this it was easy to see how a
human woman could fall directly into a
vampire's trap. Only knowing what he
was had kept me self-aware to this point.
We danced until my legs and back ached,
until somehow both my shoes

disappeared, and I was swirling against his rock-hard body barefoot.

Part of me felt shame, this was my first experience with a man after all. It was a form of vulnerable and dirty I never imagined enduring. Or wanting.

The lights were flashing pink when I finally asked him if we could come up for air and take a break. My legs wobbled as he led me through the club, out the side door into the crisp night air. I leaned against the side of the building, head bent and hands on my knees as I gulped in oxygen, my nose flaring at the stank of the alley.

Alley.

Immediately I straightened and whipped around. I was alone.

"Silas?" I asked, taking a step backwards towards the club door. "Rebecca?" Maybe she had come outside with us? Someone had to have seen us leave, plenty of people were watching. I took another step back.

"What's got you so frightened darling?" That honey voice swept over my shoulder, and I spun around just in time to have my back pinned to the wall. Silas' eyes were no longer burgundy− they were glowing scarlet.

"Now, wasn't that thrilling? Letting him see what a lewd woman you truly are? I wonder what sorts of delicious thoughts he had while watching you." My mind screeched to a halt as the obvious dawned on me.

"He was watching?" Akashi had been watching. All my brothers had. This time my blush was real as I reimagined everything I had just done. I shuddered in embarrassment and Silas let out a dark laugh.

"My darling, even the bouncers and gays couldn't keep their eyes off you as you pleasured yourself against my body. Isn't that what you wanted?" Silas expertly wound a hand behind my neck and tilted my head to the side, "Megan..." He purred. I locked eyes with him.

Looking surprised, he leaned backwards, some of the glow to his eyes ebbing away before he shook his head and set a glare on me. "Megan" he purred again and this time I felt it. The wash of warmth swirling around my body but not sinking in.

'The price is only your name...'

So that's how he did it. He needed his victims' names to control them. I slowly grinned, before doing something really, really, stupid.

"My name," I said leaning forward, baiting him, exhaling on his lips, "is Raven."

Silas lunged for my throat, infuriated once he realized he had been played. I screamed as I felt his teeth sink in but had been prepared for that.

Concrete split at our feet, thorny vines shooting out and twisting around him from the earth. He hissed, yanking his teeth from my skin but I wasn't done.

Flames licked life on my hands, and I clocked him across the head with a right hook. I landed a kick to his stomach, and he dropped to his knees giving my vines the leverage they needed to sink into him and pin him down.

I went to strike again but slipped. My head slammed into the side of the building, and I sank to my ass with a groan. I pressed my hand to my neck where he had bitten, my head foggy.

"Well, this is a first, but unfortunately you won't win this." Once my eyes refocused, I saw the patch of ice I had slipped on. I followed the trail of it to Rebecca's feet, her outstretched hand still raised towards me.

Her fingers had been replaced by silver claws and ice slowly seeped outwards from her in every direction. It climbed its way up my vines, cracking them, killing them, allowing Silas to start shaking loose. Where the hell were my brothers?

"Why the fuck did you bring her to me?" Silas snapped. Rebecca's gaze turned to him, and she glared.

"You said you were in the mood for a slutty brunette. She was the most vulnerable."

"You bring him women to eat?" I choked out, hand dropping to my lap.

"It's part of a deal we have." Silas grinned and got to his feet. "She provides her lover proper meals in exchange for asylum. Not to mention, how else would I be able to perform to her expectations if I were starving? Speaking of which, where were we, Raven?"

This time, the heat that had been circling me ruthlessly plunged into my body. It was hot, so hot it burned but didn't hurt. My eyelids were heavy. He was on top of me, and I was limp, the heat had weighed me down. I felt him inhaling the scent of my blood, felt the hair on my neck be brushed away. Felt him freeze.

"What the hell?" Silas breathed. Our eyes met.

He looked terrified.

Suddenly he was off me. Hands were under my arms pulling me up. Hikari's frantic gaze was in my field of vision. Blood was dripping from his lip. Beyond him I saw Akashi, his Hound tearing his clothes to shreds as he transformed. The fury in his eyes he chased Rebecca and Silas down the alley. Silas was a blur as he ran, Rebecca a blonde flash perched in his arms as they made their escape.

Kuma's Hound appeared at the other end of the alley, teeth bared. Silas stopped running, eyes meeting Rebecca's, lips colliding with hers. Then they dropped into the shadow at their feet, disappearing.

"How did they do that!?" I didn't realize that I too had been running until I dropped to the spot where they had just vanished and began beating the pavement with my fists. "How did they shadow jump?! Luna said only I could do that?! What the fuck is she?!"

"You're bleeding, Little Bird." Akashi's bare body yanked me backwards, but I slammed my elbow back into his chest, a blast wind following the blow and throwing him off me. I launched myself back towards the dip in the pavement, black vines by my side and cracking the asphalt to reveal... nothing.

"Raven, you're bleeding gold!" Akashi yelled, my name on his lips freezing me and my vines in place. I gazed at my knuckles, at the glittering blood oozing from them.

"What's happening to me?" I choked out a sob and squeezed my eyes shut. The horror of my mother's death replayed in my head. A torn apart body lying in a pool of gold.

"It's just blood Little Bird. Yours. You're okay. Everyone is okay." Akashi's voice was soft, but it hit me like thunder, knocking me from the vision and I felt my legs go limp. The last thing I remember was his steady breath on the back of my neck before I drifted into the black.

CHAPTER 4

Hikari was driving. Kuma and Akashi were arguing. My blood soaked dress was nowhere in sight. My head was in Anzen's lap, his soft voice repeating each time I woke that everything was going to be okay, fingers stroking my hair until I would fall back asleep. And finally, we pulled up to the house.

Groggily, I sat up and pressed my face to the window. The house's lights were on, a small pocket of warmth in the middle of the woods. To others the ivy climbing the stone wall would look romantic. The soft wisps of smoke rising from the chimney homely. The randomly assorted deck chairs and couches inviting. But something in me shuddered and made bile rise in my throat.

Even after the past few hours, I'd prefer to go back to the city and be at Silas' mercy than return to the confines of this place. And with what happened, who knew if Luna would ever let me out again at all?

Kuma had tried carrying me from the car but, delirious as I was, I was on my feet and marching towards the house before any of my brothers could protest. The grass withered where I stepped, and my hair danced in the growing winds circling me like a small cyclone. Promptly, a column of it whistled past me and reduced the door to splinters on impact.

I could feel my ragged breaths, but my rage was eerily calm as I marched up the steps and into the dining room. With a flick of my wrist the wind flipped the table out of my way and left me standing chest to chest with Luna.

"Who is she?" I asked, voice like steel. My hair blew about my shoulders and the curtains swished on their rods, but Luna paid no mind to my rampant powers and kept an even gaze on me.

"Anyone mind telling me what went wrong out there?" She asked, eyes not leaving mine. Her composure just pissed me off more.

"We were ambushed in the club once Raven was taken outside." It was Hikari who broke the silence. He went on to explain, "At least a dozen vampires swarmed us as soon as she was out of sight. We couldn't change forms in front of a crowd like that, so it took us longer than we liked to work our way out. She was...bitten." That final word hung in the air like a bomb waiting to go off.

"They must have known you were there," Luna said, eyes flashing blue as she looked beyond me to my brothers. "How?"

"They didn't bother covering their scents," I interrupted, my fury momentarily diverted. "So many humans reeked of them it was hard to keep a track of who was where."

"That was sloppy, and you nearly got your sister killed!" Luna stepped past me and slapped Hikari across the face. I winced, but all he did was blink once in shock before looking at me regretfully. He opened his mouth as if to say something, but stopped short as Luna now addressed them all. "Were you too busy trying to find whatever you could to hump like a pack of wild dogs instead of protecting her?! Being this irresponsible I can never let her out!"

My feet were moving on their own, arms wrapping around Luna's waist, and before I knew it, I had tackled her out the empty doorway into the yard. Aged as she was, she still rolled away and hopped to her feet spry as a cat before my vines could ensnare her. She growled as I lunged at her again, but Kuma intercepted me, locking my arms behind my back in a viselike grip.

"You're acting out of rage–"

"I feel like a prisoner!" My voice shook the trees, and everyone froze. Luna's mouth hung agape. Kuma's arms went slack around me. I could feel Akashi's gaze searing into me, but I refused to look at him. Instead, I pushed Kuma off me and stalked a few feet away putting some much-needed distance between us all as I added, "I've been locked in there for years, constantly under supervision, constantly restraining my power—"

"And for good reason! Look at what almost happened to you." Luna's voice was cold, judgment coating every word.

"I handled the vampire," I snarled, and flames burst to life on my arms. Tree branches began groaning as the storm under my skin grew stronger. Lightning skittered between vantage points in the clouds, chased by low booms of thunder. Violet flames danced to life on my arms, wild and untamed.

Luna faltered for a moment and took a single step back. The look on her face told me she was finally sensing the rage I had bottled inside me through the years, and registered it was threatening to break its seal.

"What I couldn't handle," I hissed, "Was their flirty little friend shadow jumping them to safety." Luna paled slightly, gaze jerking to Hikari for confirmation and I smirked satisfied. "You can't lock me in here anymore. I'll break out to find her. Especially since she has a power that you claim that only I possess."

"Are you sure she wasn't using teleportation?" Luna asked, so quietly I could barely hear her over the brewing tempest above us. I raised a brow.

"Do I look like I doubt it?" She gave a nod of acknowledgment to that before asking,

"Were you the only child born to your mother?" My storm collapsed in my shock, the fire on my arms dying with it. All was still, silent as death.

"Of course, I was," I tasted acid on my tongue and fought the urge to retch. "If I had a sibling, you surely would have brought them here with me."

"Shadow jumping," Luna mumbled stepping toward me, "is a power only demons have. Specifically, demons who had been created by falling. Children born of your father." My knees buckled as my head started to spin again.

"So what? You think he raped my mother twice?"

"I think your mother might not have been his only powerful victim." The world tilted sideways, and I shut my eyes, focusing every atom of my being on keeping my balance.

"You think?" I spat out a laugh. "He kills all his children. I'm only alive because you turned on him. I have no siblings. So, you wanna know what I think?" I reached out grasping Luna's shoulder to keep myself upright. "I think this bitch is mine to hunt."

"Are you okay?" Akashi's voice filtered up to me through the leaves. I had been perched on an oak bough for the better part of an hour trying to ease the swelling of my stomach with the fresh scent of sap and air. It was moments like this where Akashi's insistent teasing actually subsided. Out of fear or respect, I was never quite sure which. I don't think I'll ever truly know.

"Physically I'm divine," I mused, shifting my weight forward so I could peer down to the dark forest floor trying to pick him out. "You've turned, haven't you? All I can see is your eyes."

"I went for a run," he mumbled. I nodded and shifted my weight back against the trunk. Slowly, I slip through the cracks between here and there, wading through the darkness before finally gliding back into the physical world through the roots on the forest floor.

Shadow jumping. It made me feel giddy. Teleportation was a rare thing, but this? You needed a raw, unmuted type of power to use the dark and not get lost in it.

"You know Luna doesn't like it when you do that," Akashi muttered, now only a few feet from where I stood. I suppress a sigh.

"Because I could be lost in space forever if I'm not clear about my destination," I say, monotone. He drags his claws across the dirt uncomfortably.

"Yes."

"You don't think it's that dangerous either do you?" I ask. Silence is his answer. Annoying.

I hesitate for a moment, before copying Silas' action from earlier and dipping my fingers under Akashi's chin to raise his head. His fur was wet; he definitely had run the full hour. "Do you?" I repeat, searching his eyes.

"There are times I think you are just as capable using your powers as that girl in the alley." He sounds more decided than I was expecting. "That my mom has become so blinded by her duty to protect you that she tries to fit you in a box she's labeled as safe and forgets exactly who you are. We all do, sometimes." He sighs, "But then you let loose and cause a tempest as you did earlier. When you're completely out of control I understand why she limits you."

"I wouldn't need limits if I was able to practice. If I could just work out the kinks and be in control, I think we would all feel better because truth is," I pause, dropping my hand back to my side before adding, "we really don't know what I can do."

"The less you can do, the less your father can use." Akashi's words were sharp, and I averted my gaze.

"You think I would willingly become a pawn for him?" I asked, anger flaring beneath the hurt.

"I think he wouldn't give you a choice."

I stepped back, away from the weight of it. As much as I hated it, Akashi was right. I didn't know Lucifer, beyond the obvious. The Hounds had been in his army. They worked for him. They guarded him. They knew what he was capable of. Frustrated I turned back to the tree, settling into a nook in the roots and changed the topic.

"So, what was with all of you back at the club?" At his blank stare I rolled my eyes. "Come on, you guys never really get any lady time." Akashi snorted and shook his head but still said nothing. I shifted back and forth on my feet uncomfortably, pressing slightly further, "It was very...involved."

I had wanted to say feral, but I bit my tongue. They were my brothers, it unnerved me to see them like that. Finally, he sighed, lowering his snout to my shoulder as he sat down beside me.

"Involved indeed," he muttered, tail flicking about as he considered his answer. "Hounds mate for life. We never got the chance to even court a female, we were too young. So given the opportunity, surrounded by them like that... we're driven on autopilot you could say."

"So essentially you're drugged by instinct to find your mate because you've been repressing it for so long?" His claws dug into the dirt again.

"Yes."

"I'm sorry." The apology flew out of my mouth before I could even think of it. Akashi sat back, head cocked. Quickly I wipe the broken look off my face replacing it with a snarky grin. "You might have had a better chance getting laid if you didn't decide to go rogue and hide me."

"Finding our mates has nothing to do with you," he snapped. He and I both seemed stunned by the tone, but he only shook out his fur and laid down, averting his gaze. "You don't have to be in a certain place or time for it. It just happens. Now can we stop talking about my lack of it?"

"Yep."

His head settled in my lap, and I stayed still. Feeling him start to drift into sleep, I allowed myself this moment to curl my fingers through his fur and inhale his scent unchecked. I traced his muzzle and his ears, wondering if I would ever be so bold to touch him if he weren't a wolf.

I felt a tingling ripple flow through me again and this time didn't deny what it was. Jealousy. How he danced with that woman in the club. So unchecked, so loose. Burden free. And then after the rush of jealousy: shame. He was my brother and though we didn't discuss it at length the snap of anger moments ago was proof enough.

They all threw away their chances for love, for a life, because of me. Their life's work. Their burden. If I could one day not be his burden then maybe, just maybe, he would dance with me too.

CHAPTER 5

At some point throughout the night Akashi had shifted out of his Hound form, leaving me to wake cradled against his hard, naked body. My cry of shock sent all the morning birds to the air in a panicked frenzy and I'm sure the laughter erupting from Akashi was confirmation of my scarlet face. Luna had barreled into me halfway back to the house, the panic on her face subsiding as soon as she saw her naked son in hysterical pursuit.

At breakfast, thankfully with everyone clothed, Luna proposed a new hunt for us down in New Orleans. I was surprised when she said I would be joining, but grateful nonetheless. Perhaps something positive would come from the disaster that was New York.

My mind flashed to Rebecca and Silas, wondering if our trip to the Vampire Capital of America would allow me to cross paths with them once more. Though my vendetta was subsequently crushed for the time being upon learning we were to seek out a misplaced gargoyle wreaking havoc in an elementary school.

I didn't know much about gargoyles. What I did know was that they could shift forms like my brothers, and usually went into a frenzy if their protectee released them from a contract. That seemed to be the case here. The church across the street from the school happened to have a priest leave abruptly and had yet to find a replacement. No wonder the creature was having a meltdown. Its purpose was taken away. Somehow, that thought was relatable.

"Can we construct a plan that doesn't have Little Bird posing as a street whore?" Akashi muttered around a mouthful of bacon.

"Excuse me?" Luna and I exclaimed at once. Kuma was having trouble hiding his laughter behind his coffee, Anzen kept his eyes trained on his empty plate and Hikari gave me a sympathetic smile. I grit my teeth, trying to avoid meeting Luna's eyes which I could feel grilling me for an explanation.

I had nearly forgotten she didn't know about the change of clothes. How should I introduce the subject of fishnet leggings? And beyond that, what of the dancing?

My gut screamed out a warning signal that she would not appreciate the knowledge of my actions in that club. She wouldn't see the logic of my approach, just view it as me being careless and naive.

Instead of letting my panic get the best of me, I squared my shoulders and leaned back in my seat locking eyes with Akashi. Damn him, bringing this up now. His mouth quirked into a half smile, the situation clearly unfolding as he liked. Well let's remedy that, shall we? Before I lost my nerve, I lowered my voice and asked,

"Would you like me to dress like a whore at home rather than in public?" Coffee shot out of Kumas nose. Hikari's jaw hit the table. Poor Anzen turned red as a beet. But I kept my eyes on Akashi, not missing the subtle clench of his jaw, the quick flit of his eyes from my face to my chest, darker once they rose to meet my gaze again.

"Nobody here wants to see what you don't have," he replied, voice flat.

I growled clenching my fork in my fist. Akashi pointedly stared at my hand, and our conversation from last night popped into my brain. I couldn't lose control. Luna would revoke the offer of another chance at freedom. And he knew it. He knew it and was using it to his advantage to rile me up. The bastard. So, instead of stabbing him with my fork, I released a dramatic sigh and used my words instead.

"I think you're just upset because I cock blocked you in the club. Couldn't get too dirty in front of your little sister now, could you?" Kuma was full on howling now. Even Hikari was chuckling a little. Poor Anzen excused himself from the table muttering something about orange juice.

This time Akashi's cheeks flushed, and he just sat there silently. I was surprised, expecting a comeback about how I was the one up on a stage, but his jaw remained clenched, nose flaring as he glared at me in his fury. No, not anger: hurt.

Immediately I drop my gaze, guilt sweeping away any sense of victory. He had pointedly said he didn't want to discuss his lack of affairs with me. It was my fault for his loneliness after all.

Luna warily rose from the table shaking her head, "Children, I'm beginning to get too old for this."

"Apologies, mother," Hikari called after her as she began making her exit. Kuma's howls had finally begun to subside as I too rose from the table, following my mother outside to the front lawn.

"Can I speak to you for a moment?" I asked after the new screen door creaked shut behind me. Luna peered up at me from the grass, spread out in her stretching ritual before her morning run.

"I take off in two minutes. Can you fit it in?" I take a breath before I answer.

"I think I may have inadvertently hurt Akashi." Luna chuckles,

"No offense sweetie, but you two are known for verbally abusing each other."

"He is so much worse than me and you know it." Luna gave me a knowing smile and I sighed, "Fine. But we know who I got my sharp tongue from."

"Now that I have no argument against. But how do you feel as if you actually hurt him this time?"

"Well last night, after..." I averted my gaze.

"Yes, after our discussion in the yard," Luna prodded casually, "now continue."

"He came to find me–"

"As per usual," she commented with a snort. A warm flutter took place in my chest, but I ignored it as I continued.

"The conversation was so abrupt, and I don't even know how we got on the subject of this, but he pretty much stated how he never got the opportunity to find his mate because of me." Luna sighed,

"Yes well, everyone here including yourself has had to make sacrifices for our safety. The boys haven't been able to thrive as young Hounds. And I had to leave my mate behind."

"You what?" I breathed out, my head snapping back in her direction. Luna had the briefest faraway look in her eyes, before it morphed into a blank expression.

"Oh, my dear please don't focus on that. I was an adult Hound and capable of making my own decisions." She stood, "I believed saving you served a higher purpose than remaining on the inside trying to crumble the system. My mate didn't agree."

"So, this was—"

"Akashi's father." Luna smiled, a true genuine smile I rarely see from her. "He is the spitting image of his father. Structure, colors, foul mouthed and ill tempered. But their devotion, I've never met anyone more loyal than the two of them." I was barely able to keep up with the influx of information let alone process it all, but Luna slapped her hands together. "Alright I'm off. I'll be back for lunch. I expect a full comprehensible plan by then."

Without further delay she shifted, a flash momentarily blinding me before her moonlike Hound stood in her place. A sense of comfort washed through me. This was the image in my head that I clung to, the white wolf in the woods. I mustered a smile for her,

"We will do our best to not disappoint you."

We definitely disappointed her. By the time Luna had gotten back, the only thing we agreed on was when we would enter the school. We decided on the weekend, the least likely time we would encounter any human interference. We laid out our options for her, which she critiqued and combined without mercy until we had a plan (and carefully chosen outfits) she approved of.

Now three days later, we found ourselves in New Orleans historic French Quarter, awaiting our impending death caused by heatstroke.

"I'm sweating my balls off." Kuma grumbled, his mood worsening the longer we trudged through the humid streets. I adjusted my shirt collar, safely assuming that if I had balls I would be feeling the same way right about now. I was melting and it was 6pm. I could only imagine how bad off we would have been in the heat of the day.

Still, I was enraptured by the city. New York was all rough edges and modern flare, promising an exciting future with the glam to go with it. I much preferred the vibe of this dead city, and I mean that as the highest compliment.

The city reeked of things have-been. Of what people had seen, art that had flourished, music which had played. In every corner store or chipped cobblestone of this quarter, some ghost of history clung, and I was drinking every drop my senses could accommodate. If we were here on a sightseeing trip my brothers would have lost track of me immediately as I had been fighting the urge to melt into the crowd and explore since we arrived. It was taking every ounce of self-control I had to not flock to the nearest cemetery, bookstore or jewelry cart. And it became increasingly harder as I eyed the latter, the gems still shimmering brightly in the evening light.

"Now if one of us had that look on our face, you'd poke fun by telling us to stop frothing at the mouth." Hikari playfully chides, slowing down beside me as I greedily reach out to check the price tag of a dangling amber locket.

"Please we all know she has the brain of a crow." Akashi calls back towards us, "See shiny thing: want shiny thing." Quieter he added, "And yet crows are intelligent."

Before I can retort Hikari chuckles, gently guiding me forward while adding, "Another day. Birthdays are a thing, remember?"

"You know I don't like celebrating mine," I grumble but my stomach does a happy little kickflip at the thought of receiving one of the small shiny things anyway. He arches a brow,

"Then I guess I'll just have to give you a present on mine, and you'll have to open it."

"That's cheating."

"I've done it before."

"And I'm still mad." We share a grin before catching up to the others. Kuma had finally reached his limit with the heat, slinging his t-shirt over his shoulder. Anzen had his head buried in a tourist map seemingly confused. I tried not to take that as a bad sign since he was the one with the address of the school. I wrinkled my brow,

"Where's Akashi?"

"Blockhead ran off up ahead to make sure we didn't miss our turn and need to back track." I frown.

"We were supposed to not split up today."

Kuma gave me an odd look, "It's five minutes Raven." Right. He's right.

"Well, where are we exactly?" I ask, peering over Anzen's shoulder.

"We're on St Ann Street. We need to go northeast on Bourbon, or we'll end up walking straight into Jackson Square by mistake."

"Would that really be such an awful mistake?" I ask, fluttering my eyelashes.

"Nice try."

I faked a pout and within minutes bribed my way into a small tea shop for the promise of air conditioning while we waited for Akashi to return.

My brothers sat at the makeshift bar at the front window, but after ordering a drink I wandered a bit further into the shop. Just like everything else in this city, this shop had crevices that could only be found in a place that was old and I perched myself in a window seat behind a pane of blue stained glass. Blessedly, I was below a jet stream of air conditioning that fell from the ceiling.

I freed my tangled hair from its tie, combing through it with my fingers while watching tourists flock bye. After a few minutes my drink arrived and I cradled the cup in my hands, grateful I ordered something hot despite the temperature outside. As I took a sip and let the strawberry flavor cascade over my tongue, I laughed at myself a little.

As otherworldly as I was, here I am experiencing hot and cold shocks just as a human would. Made me wonder if with my fire I could regulate my body temperature in the cold. And if I could somehow learn to manipulate ice like Rebecca, then maybe the heat wouldn't weigh on me as it had today.

I felt myself scowling at the thought of her. As enraged and frankly, scared as I was, I was also intrigued. I wanted to know everything about her, but I also wanted to kill her. Outwardly I cringed at the thought. That was a process I'm sure my father would have. I set my cup down with a frustrated clack.

"Is this seat taken?"

"Does it look taken ya smelly– oh." I had begun to reply before I turned, assuming it was one of my brothers but was greatly mistaken.

I grit my teeth staring at the vampire standing before me. I shouldn't be shocked really; we were in New Orleans after all. But my mind was stuck in that alley with Silas, so I immediately got to my feet.

"Now I can't claim a young lady had ever addressed me in this way before." A warm chuckle slid from the man's throat as he shifted, clearly blocking my path. My nostrils flared in annoyance, catching the metallic tang which clung to his kind, before warily giving him a onceover.

The only thing vampiric about him was the burgundy of his eyes and other than that, he was a stark contrast to Silas. Where Silas was gothic and pale, this man was modern and warm. His cream suit complimented the rich tones of his skin. Golden hair fell down his back, neatly braided away from his face and secured at the nape of his neck. He smiled, lips parting to freely show his fangs as his back was to human patrons.

"No tricks love, my name is Finn." At my silence, another warm chuckle seeped from him. Any more warmth and I would begin sweating again despite the air conditioning. He gestured back to my seat once more, "Please miss, there is something I wish to discuss."

"Can't you discuss it with another stranger?" My eyes jumped beyond him, where I noticed Hikari materialize. I give a subtle shake of my head, and reluctantly lower myself back to my seat. I didn't wish to entertain a vampire, but I needed to start fending for myself. I couldn't be my brother's problem forever.

Finn sat across from me and folded his hands in front of him, "Now just because you don't recognize me doesn't mean I don't recognize you my dear." My heart paused.

"You were at the club."

"I was not." His red eyes dimmed, "However unfortunate that may have turned out for you."

"Who is Rebecca?" I demanded, voice dipping an octave lower. Finn didn't respond for a minute, before abruptly laughing. I was so fed up at this point I picked up my cup, downed the contents, and once again stood to leave, but his hand darted out to snatch my wrist.

"Please forgive me." My glare bounced off his gentle gaze as he calmly explained himself. "It's not every day I meet a lady as strong willed as you. I'm afraid I'm enjoying the moment for too long. Allow me to explain my business with you."

"We have no business with each other," I growled, now close enough to catch the underlying scents of honey and clove seeping from him. Did everything about this man radiate heat?

"But we could." His thumb arched up over the back of my hand, leaving pops of electricity in its wake. I felt the tension in my arm ease at the caress, before he dropped my hand and left it feeling disturbingly empty.

"That's not what I wanted to discuss with you though. I wanted to apologize for my brother's behavior." My brows furrowed. A vampire apologizing? I've never heard of THAT before.

"Your brother?" I asked, thinking it would be better to not continue insulting him. This meeting, as odd as it was, was pleasant...which was why it was odd.

"Silas." Finn says, pointedly looking at my neck. Well forget all the sunshine and rainbows about him then. Anyone related to Silas was bound to be just as twisted. I barked out a laugh and turned away.

"Have a nice life, Finn. Or not life."

"You have a nice life as well, Raven." I froze, a bolt of panic going through me. I waited for the paralyzing heat. I waited for the powerlessness. But it didn't come.

I heard Finn's chair scrape the floor behind me as he stood and felt his

hand drag across my shoulder blades as
he passed me,
  "I do hope we meet again."

CHAPTER 6

Like a schoolgirl I retreated to the bathroom. I walked, I'm sure because I fought the muscles in my legs that wanted to sprint, but I still barely got there in time to slam the door in my brother's faces with a clipped 'I'm fine' before locking it between us.

And it was fine. It was just a conversation. I didn't lose control, and to his slight credit Finn remained civil. But still it was clear now: vampires had my name and my scent. It was safe to assume that I wouldn't be meeting them in passing anymore, they would seek me out. And this could not become my brothers' problem.

I turned on the sink and splashed my face once, twice, three times. Was my heartbeat this rapid out there? Did I let that beast know he unnerved me so much during that meeting or did I do good at keeping my cool? I couldn't remember.

"Raven, you're not the only lady that has to use the restroom. Unlock the damn door so this poor woman can get in there!" Kuma pounded his fist on the door for emphasis.

"Sorry!" Did my voice just squeak? At least this bathroom was large so I could stay in here stalling, grounding myself before facing them. I spun the lock out of place and turned back to the sink.

The door swished open behind me. Hikari's gentle voice filters in, followed by a laugh and heels clicking into the room before the door swings shut again.

"Oh honey, all those boys out there belong to you?" A thick southern accent greeted me. I glanced in the mirror eyeing the woman. She was probably in her late fifties and wore a sundress that matched her rosy cheeks. She pulled a powder swatch from her purse and started tidying up her face.

"Please don't get the wrong idea, they're my brothers." I clarified and she nodded her head.

"I have big brothers. I understand the need to hide out, have a moment of ladies' time." She smiled and gave me a knowing wink.

"Yes." I didn't know what else to say other than that.

My head was spinning, and my legs were shaky. The heat that had radiated from Finn somehow had penetrated my belly and I felt sick. But a weird sick. I didn't know what was happening. I turned the sink on and splashed my face again. Upon standing straight again I found the woman staring at me, a questioning look in her eyes.

"I don't exactly know what's happening to me right now," I say, aware she hadn't asked for an explanation, but the words were tumbling out of me. "I'm just really overwhelmed, and I feel weird. There was a guy here earlier, and now my brothers won't back off. I'm fine." To escape her gaze, I turned and locked myself in a bathroom stall.

"Did the man hurt you?" Her voice was thick with genuine concern. Great. Now I was burdening a stranger too.

"No. I'm fine. I'm sure I'll–" I pulled my pants down and sat on the toilet seat, stifling a cry as I noticed some type of clear liquid pooled in my underwear. I hadn't pissed myself had I!?

"Pardon me if I'm prying." The woman said, "I just want to make sure you're okay."

"I said I'm fine!" I groan, ripping at the toilet paper and frantically rubbing between my legs to dry myself off.

"You spoke with a man," she continued as if I hadn't snapped at her, "and now are all flushed up and feel weak between the legs, yes?" I froze, humiliation creeping in but she spoke as if this was a normal conversation, "I know it's embarrassing, especially with that lot of boys out there. But there is nothing shameful about attraction."

I cocked my head. Attraction? At my continued silence I heard her release a long sigh, "My advice, use a wet paper towel. The cold will ease it away."

There was not another word exchanged between us and a few moments later she left the bathroom. When the door swished shut, I thought back to the brief discussion with Finn. The heat that he himself wasn't causing, I was just experiencing. From the caress on my hand, grip on my wrist, palm pressed between my shoulders. I leaned my head against the stall and shut my eyes. I didn't need this now on top of everything else.

I didn't meet any eyes or answer any questions when I finally worked up enough courage to exit the bathroom. I walked straight back outside into the humid evening air and scanned the crowd looking for Akashi. He should be back by now. We should already be headed into the school not still looking for it.

"I don't like that it's taking so long for him to get back. Let's go." I demanded. Kuma fell into step beside me immediately as I knew he would. Sitting around and waiting wasn't his style. Hikari and Anzen followed us through the crowd, directing us which turns to make.

It only took about five minutes to reach our destination and Akashi had been gone for nearly thirty. I took a deep breath at the gate. He was inside. I could smell him. I could smell *them*. I knew my brothers could too.

"How many do you think there are?"

"I'd say at least three," Anzen mumbled. "Vampires are skilled, but Akashi is a fighter. Less couldn't hold him here." I nodded and kicked in the gate. It was dinner hour now, no one was on this attraction-less street. And I didn't care if the security footage caught it because I would never be coming back here anyway.

I reveled in watching the metal tear under the force of my wind, rip from its station, and fly halfway across the schoolyard before skittering to a stop.

"You could have just unlocked it," Kuma grumbled but nevertheless bolted for the door, the three of us hot on his heels. I wondered if Akashi went inside looking for the damn gargoyle himself or if the vampires caught him and dragged him in.

No. He came inside of his own accord. Akashi would not be dragged.

Kuma took his turn kicking in the actual school door, making my move look like a weak slap as the door split in two and flew down the hallway ripping lockers apart. Briefly I wondered if Luna would care about the damage. Considering the circumstances, I don't think so. The plan went to hell as soon as Akashi struck off on his own anyway.

"We stay together," Hikari demanded as we flew into the hall. A glance to my left showed the alarm system completely unwired. The vampires at least handled one problem for us.

"We need to split up, it will take too long otherwise." I argued, "I'll stay with Kuma but there's no other option. Go." Hikari seemed satisfied enough with that so nodded to Anzen. Both took off in either direction from us leaving Kuma and I to bolt ahead down the main hall. As soon as they were out of earshot I skidded to a stop.

"Wait."

"What the fuck do you mean wait–"
Kuma whirled on me.

"Shut up!" I held my hand up and
shut my eyes. "Please just give me ten
seconds. Ten *seconds,* Kuma." He
remained silent, but I could feel him
bristle as I called upon my power.

I dropped to my knees, pressing my
palms to the floor, and let my senses flow
outward from me. They traced every wall,
every tile, every damn dust bunny in this
building, climbing higher and higher until
I completed the map in my head to the
roof.

I felt the vibrations of Anzen and
Hikari's footsteps pounding through the
floor. Anzen's were heavier, he had
already shifted.

I grit my teeth when I felt Akashi's
heartbeat pounding against the floor. He
was on his back, ragged breaths echoing
through the foundation of the school. And
beside him I could feel the light taps of
feet, graceful like dancers. Vampires. My
hands balled into fists.

"He's in the gym. West side of the
school," I choked out but didn't stand. I
shouldn't do what I was about to do. But
the memory of Rebeccas smug grin in the
alleyway paired with the danger my
brother was in was too much for me to
hesitate.

"Run to the gym," I muttered, shifting my body to face Kuma. "Now." Before he could respond I lunged toward his feet and disappeared through the faint shadow he cast.

"Raven no!" His shout was a frantic echo, but too late. I was in the shadow realm, between existence and dreams.

Darkness swirled around me, and I reached ahead for something tangible. With a gasp I fell back into the world underneath the sink in the girl's locker room. I had done it! I had no time to waste on the victory though.

I stood and stalked for the door to the gym, no plan in mind other than getting to Akashi who I could hear growling on the other side. This time I kicked like Kuma, putting all my wrath into it and the door exploded outwards into the gym raining splinters.

The laughter that had been erupting around the room ceased immediately as I stalked into vision. Five vampires bared their fangs at me. Momentarily, I was shocked to see they were all female, but the scene unfolding before me had me seeing red in no time.

Akashi was splayed out on the floor, shirt gone. His hands and legs were bound in what I assumed were the gargoyles chains, and he had a petite vampire straddling his hips. Her hands were poised on his belt buckle.

"You have a lot of nerve interrupting me while I get ready to eat." She sneered in my direction. Her four colleagues were all various categories of flawless, but she was immaculately beautiful. Her blonde hair was cut in a sharp bob, lips painted as red as her eyes, and her breasts were swaying freely, just mere inches from my brother's face. He had already been bitten; I could see the puncture wound on his neck.

Something flared in the pit of my stomach, hot and twisting, the sick love child of my rage and misplaced jealousy.

"Did you also eat the gargoyle you slut?" I sneered right back at her. The gym floor began to crack as I slowly made my way into the middle of the room. Two of the other girls had already circled behind me, but this was a waiting game now. Who would spook and jump first?

The blonde released an annoyed groan, dropping Akashi's belt and stood stalking towards me. I braved a quick glance at his face and was somewhat pleased to find him staring at this beauty with utter hate and disgust in his gaze. I met her eyes again. "Didn't your mommy ever tell you it was rude to play with your food?"

"Didn't yours ever tell you to mind your own fucking business?" She lunged for me, and I dodged just as the gym doors exploded and the rest of my brothers ran in all transformed into Hounds.

I didn't hesitate to attack her; I got a couple good punches in but didn't quite know what else to do. I didn't want to set the school on fire, there was already enough damage to it. Same with calling upon the earth, if my vines could even burst through all the floors and walls of this school. Frustrated, I grabbed her by the hair and swung her into one of those walls, putting it to some good use. She jumped right back up unscathed.

"You'll need a lot more than fists and feet to knock me out, little girl. Don't tell me you're useless and all you can do is box?" She giggled right in my face before flipping me over and I gasped in pain as her knee connected with my throat.

She was toying with me now, beating me down to a useless pulp. She lunged on top of me then, knees squeezing either side of my throat and ripped her nails down my face, licking up the glittering gold blood that spurt free.

"Oh, a rare meal! It's not every day we get to devour an Angel-born. Perhaps I'll eat you first in front of your puppies?"

I screamed out in rage and blasted her off me with a focused channel of wind. I didn't know how my brothers were faring and didn't get a chance to look because she was already back on top of me fangs poised and ready to strike. But they didn't.

Thorny vines burst from my arms and hoisted her off the ground. My veins were screaming, I couldn't tell where my skin ended and vines began. A collar of thorns dug into her throat, and she yowled in agony. As I stood, I watched two of her companions bolt out the door. Cowards.

"Looks like you're being abandoned," I wheezed. "Maybe because they know you're going to end up a corpse." I hurled her across the gym, vines whipping her from behind as she collided with the brick wall.

I could hear the chains behind me rattling, my brothers breaking Akashi free. I should go help. I should let her go. Instead, the thorns from my left arm grabbed her by the ankle and dragged her back to me. Her perfect skin was punctured from my attacks, her eyes were glazed with pain. I was about to beat a vampire.

A desire in me rose to puncture her own flesh with my teeth. Kill her in the way she had undoubtedly killed hundreds of others. I pounced on her as she had on me, pinned her with my hands on her wrists and vines paralyzing her legs. Those legs that had been so greedily wrapped around Akashi's waist. "This is what you get for hurting my family–"

"Are you an Angel?" A soft voice broke through my murderous haze. I looked up, away from the spent monster below me. Beneath the bleachers curious black eyes peered out at me.

"What?" I rasped, my vines retreating from the vampire's legs but my grip on her wrists not letting up.

"She called you Angel-born. And you are bleeding gold, but your eyes are black like mine." Slowly, a boy crept out from under the bleachers. Ashy gray bat wings were tucked in tight against his spine and his skin was a translucent gray.

"Yes," I said quietly, "I am part Angel."

"You must have been sent by my priest's spirit to save me!" The boy ran across the room to me without hesitation and threw his arms around my neck. I stumbled backwards, pulling him, and myself, away from the vampire I was just about to kill.

"Y-you're the gargoyle?" I sputtered. He nodded against my neck, and I could feel his tears slicking my skin.

"Those vampires came and killed my priest. Then made me come to this school and do all types of weird things with them and to humans. She won't make me hurt anyone anymore, will she?" He asked, trembling.

I didn't know how gargoyles aged, but the common trait among immortals was if they looked like a kid, they were a kid. And I could tell this kid had been through a version of hell.

My arms felt raw but as sore as I was, I gently hugged him back. Slowly I stood, keeping him perched in my arms and taking extra care not to pull his wings.

"No, she won't hurt you anymore. You're safe now, and we will find you another priest to keep you safe. I promise." He pulled back with a huge smile on his face, but the look immediately morphed into confusion.

"You have color changing eyes?" He asked.

"My eyes are blue..." I said softly and he shook his head.

"No, they were black a minute ago. And now they're green."

I turned around looking to my brothers for some sort of explanation, but I was met with three very empty stares. The only one who was expressing anything at all was Akashi who was still kneeling on the floor. His mouth was agape, and his eyes were glowing brighter than I had ever seen before, like green cauldrons of fire.

"Hey, can you turn your eyes blue? I want to see that too!" The boy gargoyle asked. I shook my head while tearing my eyes from Akashi and started walking towards the gym doors.

"Where are you going?" Hikari called after me, his voice sounding strained. I turned and as confidently as I could replied,

"To the church. Surely, they have another priest for this boy to watch over."

Once Raven exited the gym, all four of the Hounds gasped for a breath they didn't know they had been holding. Kuma, Hikari and Anzen all transformed back to human form and started speaking at once.

"Vines came out of her damn skin did you see that?"

"Oh my GOD she was about to kill that vampire! Do you think she would have actually done it!"

"Luna needs to know. We need to tell her everything! Kuma, what did you do with our clothes?"

"Hallway. And no, we can't tell Luna. For one, Raven fucking shadow jumped to a destination she couldn't picture she'll get her ass beat for that alone despite everything else!"

"Wait, she SHADOW JUMPED too?"

"Shut up–"

"That's more of a reason we need to tell–"

"I said SHUT UP!" Akashi bellowed and slammed a fist into the floor. His brothers silenced themselves immediately and he groaned trying to compose himself. He dragged his hand across his neck, his blood coming with it, and he sighed, "Before you ask, they injected me with wolfsbane. I couldn't transform after that."

"Well, that explains that." Kuma squatted and slid his arm around Akashi's back, hoisting him up, "Anzen get my pants. I'm not carrying him outta here while I'm naked." Akashi shoved him off and staggered away.

"I don't need it."

The blonde vampire was still unconscious on the floor where Raven left her. Deep penetrating wounds covered her body from the thorns. Akashi thought for a minute that perhaps a few would even scar.

"Hikari what do we do with her?" He asked, voice grave.

"Well, her friends ran off, perhaps they'll come back for her?" Hikari considered as he dressed himself.

"So, we just leave her here for the school janitor to find in the meantime?" Akashi asked sarcastically and gave his brothers a onceover, "What took so fucking long anyway?" Hikari paused, as did Kuma. Akashi's gaze fell on his youngest brother.

"Well?"

Anzen gulped, "Well... Raven was having a conversation and then went to the bathroom."

"Vague." Akashi drawled.

"U-uh a private conversation...with a man...and then hid in the bathroom."

"Would hardly call a vampire a man." Kuma muttered, beginning to re-button his shirt.

"She was talking to a vampire alone and you let her?" Akashi growled and started stalking back towards them.

"Easy. I was right there." Hikari held up his hands. Akashi's nostrils flared.

"Oh yea, then what did they say?" Hikari glanced away and Akashi cursed.

"So, I'm taken hostage, and you let Raven talk to a vampire alone."

"It was only five minutes—"

"She was in the bathroom for about twenty." Kuma reached for his shoes, "and when she came out, she reeked of arousal."

"Kuma!" Hikari hissed.

"What?" Kuma gestured towards Akashi, "He's the one fucking pushing for details. Well, there ya have it. Hot vampire, aroused girl. Move on."

Akashi's entire body was rigid. He wanted to punch someone. Kill something. He didn't care, this rage had to go somewhere. He turned back to the vampire on the floor, a deep rumbling in his chest.

"Akashi..." Anzen was at his back, pleading, hand gripping the hair on the nape of his neck. An enraged growl ripped from Akashi's throat as he turned away instead of delivering the killing blow, and he bolted from the gym.

CHAPTER 7

    I never thought I would enter a church again. Despite the tremor that racked down my spine, there was no hesitation in my stride as I scaled the concrete steps. The gargoyle lay cradled in my arms, his excited heartbeat pattering against my rampant one. I kept my focus on him. I would not allow my splintered memories to prolong his return.

    The priests, one of the very few human organizations made aware of the supernatural kind, nearly cried in relief when they saw he had been rescued. He was now assigned to a very kind, and young Father Ethan. The two of them would have many decades to work with each other, possibly enough time for the gargoyle to mature as well.

    Thankfully the boy was so excited to return home that nothing about my gold blood or black eyes had been brought up in conversation. Respectfully the priests didn't question me at all, they were just grateful I had brought the boy home.

By the time I exited the building it was dark, and the oil lamps lining the staircase were in full flame. Humidity still clung to the air, amplifying the silence of the evening. Which was why I jumped as I suddenly heard Akashi speak.

"Were you okay in there?" He asked, back leaning against the building just outside the door.

"Are you okay?" Immediately my hands flew across him, searching for any other wounds besides the bite on his neck. He shrugged me off.

"My question first," he said, keeping a level gaze on me. I rolled my eyes.

"If you're indirectly making sure I'm not having a mental breakdown because the last time I was in a church it was on fire, then you have nothing to worry about. I'm good. Your turn."

"Wolfsbane." Akashi diverted his gaze, "So I hear you got chummy with a vampire and that's why I was shackled up for so long."

I should have expected his disappointment, but the suddenness of the accusation had me tasting bile in my throat. Surprisingly, I even felt tears spring into my eyes. His smirk instantly fell from his face.

"Oh shit, no. No, stop. It's okay– I mean I am concerned about the vampire part but that's not the point." His hands gently swiped below my eyes before resting on my shoulders. His gaze we serious as he amended, "I'm not pinning this on you Little Bird. I went in by myself. I did this to myself."

"But we were late because of me," I admitted and turned away. "I didn't do it on purpose. I didn't know you hadn't come back yet, and I didn't want to embarrass myself in front of you guys–"

"Embarrass yourself?" Akashi sounded genuinely confused and I groaned.

"Oh, come *on,* don't make me spell it out for you," I groaned. "If you don't want to share your lack of lady action that's fine, but don't force me to highlight my lack of anything on the subject."

A long silence stretched out between us, and I could feel my face beginning to burn. I stepped back, freeing myself from his grip that I could have sworn he tightened before letting go.

My whole life I felt complicated around Akashi, and I'd be lying if I said I didn't know what it meant. I'd only been able to ignore it this far because of how he clearly viewed me as just an annoying little sister. At least until recently…

I shook my head, knowing I was deluding myself into noticing imaginary signs that I couldn't allow myself to entertain. And now to add on top of it, an encounter with an entirely different man made me lock myself in a bathroom stall because my body reacted to him on its own.

Exasperated, I leaned my forehead against the church wall, the cool stone providing relief against the heat threatening to take over my body. It was all too confusing, and I didn't have the energy for it.

"I don't like that it's a vampire. That did that to you," Akashi said, voice void of emotion. "In lieu of recent events, you should be avoiding them. Not flirting."

"I didn't flirt!" I snapped, so sick of them thinking the worst of me. "And for your information he was the brother of Silas, the vampire from the alleyway." I spun around to face him, finding him much closer than I expected. Whatever else I'd planned to say evaporated into thin air.

We were chest to chest with barely an inch of space between us and my back was plastered to the wall. The scent of pine and rain hit me, causing me to automatically suck in a breath. Akashi's eyes noticeably darkened at the reaction, and I forced myself to look away.

"I stayed put long enough to try and get information on Rebecca, the girl." The explanation came half-heartedly. "But I got nothing. Other than confused, and moderately humiliated."

"It's what vampires do," he said with a sigh. "They make people react in ways they normally never would. Play on desires people don't even know they have."

"Is that how you ended up getting tied up on a gym floor and stripped?" He winced and I immediately regretted saying it.

We stood there like that for a few more minutes, sharing space with our breaths going in and out of sync with each other. I desperately wanted to look at his face to try and read what he was thinking. Maybe find something reassuring to say. Even something stupid to get him to laugh would be better than this silence, but I didn't want to start another fight so kept my head down and my mouth closed.

"Your eyes are back to normal," he finally mumbled, one outstretched finger suddenly tracing the curve of my cheek bone. He took one last breath, then turned and started walking down the

stairs to the sidewalk so fast it was like I
had burnt him.

"It's time to go home. We all need
to talk to Luna," he called over his
shoulder. I ignored the slamming of my
heart against my ribcage, like a wild
animal trying to break free, and hurried
down the steps after him.

"You did WHAT?" Unsurprisingly
Luna was various levels of displeased by
my displays put on in New Orleans, the
shadow jumping most of all. I said
nothing as she ridiculed me and didn't
react when she banned me from leaving
the property for a month.

However, I was shocked to hear my
brothers argue in my favor. According to
them, it was my power which located
Akashi fast enough to prevent a worst-
case scenario type of situation. They
advocated for 'shadow-searching',
comparing my ability to Luna's soul-
searching spell.

Silently I beamed with a little bit
of pride. During the encounter at the
school, I was in complete control of my
power, and did new things with it that
none of us knew were possible. If I was

going to be locked at home, I would be practicing. Whether Luna wanted me to or not.

"Can I ask a few random questions that have nothing to do with each other?" I finally interrupted the bickering Hounds after what seemed like hours.

"What?" Luna snapped. Her tone was anger, but her eyes were scared. I breathed, staying calm as I shared what was on my mind.

"My eyes turned black, and I experienced bloodlust, or at least what I'm assuming was a type of bloodlust. My Father?" I questioned, brows raised. Luna paused, expression blank other than a strained type of calmness.

"He created vampires and modeled their eating habits off of one of his more, acquired tastes." Her voice was sharp as a knife. I couldn't tell if it was more so because of him, or me. I tapped my fingers along the table,

"What happens if I engage in that?" Luna's eyes narrowed, so I clarified, "I mean, if it's something natural, how much punishment would I face?"

"It's not natural."

"For you," I retort, and sit up straighter. "Frankly, we have no idea what's natural for me because it's all *too dangerous*. Perhaps vines should have been coming out of my skin this whole time? My control of them was flawless that way, even with my raging emotions." Luna fell quiet, taking my point into consideration.

"I won't condone blood drinking in my house," she finally stated. "Or of the innocent."

"Understood," I said and released a breath I hadn't known I'd been holding. They were trying to hide it, but I could practically feel my brother's eyes bugging out of their heads. I sighed, addressing the room as one,

"I'm not saying I'm going to do it. I just wanted to make sure I wouldn't be kicked out of my family for giving into it one day. If it comes to that," I added at the end. Luna's expression seemed less strained after that comment. But unfortunately, I wasn't done yet.

"I have more questions," I added quietly, "and I would appreciate privacy from the rest of you for this subject."

Akashi's foot tapped mine under the table. He knew, of course. I didn't look at him, knowing if I did my shame and embarrassment would get the better of me, and right now I needed rage.

I remained silent until Hikari all but peeled him from the table. Begrudgingly, he followed the rest of my brothers out of the house. I only spoke when the screen door gently slapped shut behind them.

"I became aroused because of a vampire." I didn't sugarcoat it.

"I heard."

"I didn't even know that's what it was. It had to be explained to me by a human in a tea shop." I clenched my fists, "You never prepared me for these things. And it happened so fast I couldn't even hide it. They all smelled it, Luna. It was humiliating." I hissed, feeling a blush creep back onto my face. Luna swallowed and folded her hands on the table.

"Truth be told, I didn't think I would have to have a talk with you about that for several more years. I've actually been trying to prolong it, but it's like your body is in a full sprint towards maturity. Plus, you're not a Hound. I didn't know exactly what would happen to you or when." At my scowl she held up a hand.

"It's not an excuse. I waited too long. But in a house full of men that you technically aren't related to by blood... I was just trying to avoid the inevitable I guess."

"What do you mean?"

"What I'm trying to say is I thought you would start experiencing these feelings because of one of your brothers." I blinked, before cautiously adding,

"And if I do one day?" Luna didn't flinch at the question and didn't express anything other than her normal cool, neutral tone.

"We mate for life, Raven. So, if you choose one of them and then change your mind..." she trailed off and sighed. I nodded slowly, understanding.

"If I change my mind, I doom them to an eternity of loneliness," I whispered. She didn't correct me.

Frustrated, I stood from the table having asked enough questions for today and left without another word.

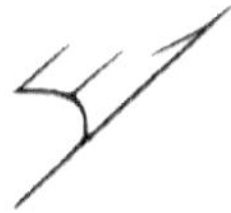

It was dark again by the time I finished isolated training. Not only were the vines sprouting from my wrists easier to control, but they were stronger too. I needed less of them to pin or pull apart a directed object and they formed into a flexible rotating shield around me as well. It was nice finally having something to defend myself with which didn't require attacking. If needed, I could just stand in the center of this dome and catch my breath.

Now tired and laying out in the dirt I experimented with what I could make of them: thorns, leaves, flowers. That's two more than I could make before, as blooming wasn't an option. I almost would have felt giddy if the conversation with Luna hadn't brought me down so much.

"You know, training this hard would pay off more if you had an opponent." I bolted upright, the metallic scent of vampire flooding my nose just as sudden as the voice had appeared.

"Who–"

"Relax Angel, it's only me." Finn emerged from the undergrowth beneath the trees, looking completely out of place in a designer suit like he had just left a business meeting. He offered me that trademark sunbeam smile and I frowned.

"Angel?" I asked warily, shifting my weight to prepare to sprint. He chuckled,

"Considering you looked mortified when I used your actual name, I decided an appropriate pet name would be best to call you by. Now, would it kill you to look happy to see me?"

"How did you find this place?" I ignored his question and took a step backwards. "I can scream once and within seconds five Hellhounds will be ripping you to bits."

"Oh, we always knew the dogs lived here." I scowled at the derogatory remark and slowly a smirk replaced his smile, "We just weren't aware something so delicious lived with them. They kept you well protected here."

"What do you want?" I snarled and took another step back.

I should have been gone by now, but I couldn't help myself– he was the first person I've socialized with besides my brothers. Silas and Rebecca didn't count. And I didn't have any friends. The Hounds never have house guests. So long as I wasn't being attacked, I wanted to entertain this. The night was his domain, but I was a child of the Devil. I had just as much of an advantage as he did, and we were on my territory.

Finn released a measured sigh, seemingly unbothered by my agitation. Casually, he popped open the buttons of his jacket and slipped it off. Automatically, my eyes drifted to his torso. His physique was evident despite his choice of attire. How annoying.

"I'm interested in you my dear, so I guess you could say I want your attention. You reek of dog but your scent," he shivered, *he actually shivered what a creep*, "it's intoxicating."

"Okay it's been a nice chat but time to go. Goodnight Finn," I said defiantly and gestured to the woods behind him. He was still like a statue for a moment, before erupting into laughter. My skin crawled with goosebumps and heat. God what was happening to me?

He was a flash before my eyes, crossing the space between us and gripping my chin. Instinctively, vines sprang from my wrist. He eyed them wondrously, actually grabbing at my hand to study them closer. Slowly, he ran a finger along a sprouted leaf.

Still in his grip, his gaze tracked upwards from the foliage to where it disappeared under my skin. That finger traced its way up to my elbow, before turning it slightly for a new angle and I felt laid bare. He was studying this...studying me. Not shying from it. Not yelling at it. His eyes were glowing a deep ruby when they met mine again.

"I meant it when I said you're intoxicating Angel. I can smell everything." His words washed over my skin and suddenly it struck me. My brothers weren't the only ones who got a whiff of my reaction yesterday, he too knew exactly what his presence did to me. Just as he probably did now.

He chuckled again and another wave of those goosebumps crossed my skin. I yanked my wrist out of his hands turning away.

"Either try to kill me or leave," I spat out and began walking. In another flash he was ahead of me again, arms spread wide blocking my path.

"Kill you or leave you? Well, I despise both of those options."

"That sounds like a you problem," I said and ducked under his arm and continued walking. "I'm going to bed, so again, goodbye."

"Is that an invitation?" His breath curled against my neck. I stiffened, feeling his hands slide along both my shoulders and down my arms. He wasn't pinning me there, but I didn't dare move.

"I can't believe you actually have the nerve to ask that," I choked out. I was enraged and embarrassed and I wanted to hit something, but he wasn't hurting me. Yet at least. God, I wish he was, it would give me something to fight back against. It would make this encounter make sense.

As if he read my mind his fingers dug into my skin a bit deeper, and he dipped his mouth towards my neck.

Immediately my vines swarmed him, no thorns, and swallowed him in a restrictive cocoon.

I took several paces away, leaving him wrapped up and dangling. His breath came in short pants though his eyes once again marveled at my power. I wish I could sink into a shadow and disappear. I want to get out from under his observation. I felt like a specimen in a lab.

"How are you doing that?" He managed to croak out.

"I think I've always been able to," I said, cinching the vines tighter for emphasis but he shook his head, pointedly staring towards my feet.

It took me a minute to register, but I found myself standing in a hazy fog of shadows. Tendrils of them wafted up from the dirt to me, partially obscuring me from his view.

My heart skipped a beat at this new sense of power. Could I control shadows or just call upon them? Is this what made shadow jumping so easy? Finn released a cough, reminding me of my restricted audience.

"Oh please, you're fine." I released my vines all at once, dropping him to the ground. He remained on his knees coughing and catching his breath, hand on his throat but kept that gaze on me as I turned away again.

"You never answered my question, Angel," he called out behind me, voice raw. "You gave me a snarky comeback and then diverted to violence. Cute, but insincere." I didn't turn around or stop this time, but I was a foolish girl with a pounding heart on the verge of lighting up the woods, so I answered.

"Because I don't know how to. Violence however, that I know."

CHAPTER 8

The next several weeks of house arrest passed by quite similarly to that first night. On most evenings throughout the week Finn would show up and taunt me, sometimes fight me, sometimes just flirt. The fighting was beneficial at the very least. I could feel the difference practicing against someone besides my brothers. I wasn't used to Finn's moves or attacks, or the distraction pounding in my chest or occasionally between my legs. It was a new environment, and my skills noticeably improved.

The only bad thing was I was beginning to enjoy having Finn around. Every night when he showed up, I braced myself for more vampires to be with him, or for Silas to come instead and drag me away as a useless paralyzed doll. He always came alone though, and other than that first night never made a go for my throat.

I was getting curiouser, which was why I knew I needed to cut this off for good. It was already a miracle that I hadn't gotten caught but I worked my ass off to cover up his scent so I could regain what tiny freedom I had before and at least get to leave our property.

"Alright I yield," I gasp out, heaving myself up into a tree and out of his reach. "I've been circling it for weeks but can't figure it out. Tell me, what's your endgame here?" I asked and plopped myself down on the branch.

Finn was splayed out on the ground, golden hair unbound and spread around his head like a halo. Forget looking like the sun. Like this he had the same aura as a Greek God. His shirt was pulled up over his abdomen slightly, showing off a sliver of a V line. I looked away.

"Other than making it my life's mission to have your heart skip a beat like that, I actually have been trying to figure out how to introduce you to a friend of mine." I tilted my head. I couldn't meet a friend of his even if I cared to. He sat up, "She lives with Silas and me. She and Silas are actually a pretty steady thing."

"Rebecca?!" I spat. Finn's eyes widened at the venom in my voice before releasing an uncomfortable chuckle,

"Ah yes, I forgot she was at the club that night. Wait, is that how you ended up on stage with him?" My face flushed,

"I thought you said you weren't there."

"Security footage." He winked, "We Vampires own that club ya know, so it's fair hunting grounds. We looked over the tape to figure out how a bunch of Hellhounds got in, and instead found you front and center."

I wanted to evaporate into nothingness imagining how many vampires must have seen that tape.

"You can forget about me meeting Rebecca. If I do, I'll probably try to kill her on sight."

"Ever consistent with that violent streak of yours," Finn mused. "Aren't you interested to know if you actually are siblings?" He grinned but I wasn't having it and waved his question off. I leaned my head back on the trunk of the tree and shut my eyes.

"You're wasting your time, Finn. Go home and stop coming back here."

The branch under me dipped so I knew he was sitting with me before I felt his breath wash over my skin. At this point I could slip into the shadow against the trunk, pull him with me and leave him in that realm as I made my way out. So, I remained calm and didn't open my eyes, satisfied with ignoring him until I felt his mouth on mine.

He wasn't kissing me exactly, wasn't touching me anywhere other than the thin line of contact between our lips. I should punch him, fall backwards into the shadows, call my brothers and let them rip him to shreds. Instead, I sat there with my eyes wide open in shock, heart hammering in my chest. He leaned back.

"You're not breathing." I blinked and realized he was right. I gasped, sucking the air back into my lungs greedily. He chuckled, "So you were being honest about not knowing how to answer. You really know nothing at all."

"What?" I rasped and felt his slender, cool fingers slide under my chin and around my throat.

"How to kiss for example." Finn's eyes shimmered in the dark, "I'll teach you."

There was a crack from the forest floor beneath us and I stiffened.

"I believe she told you to leave." It was Kumas voice. I nearly cried in relief. If it was Akashi–

"Start running before I eat your heart." A rock dropped into the pit of my stomach. Akashi was in the tree behind Finn. And he was glaring directly at me.

"I told you I didn't like it! Why a damn Vampire!?" Finn was long gone, any chance of our encounters ending in death or something more pleasant gone with him. I could hear Akashi stalking back and forth in my room, the rage rolling off him was wild enough to penetrate the bathroom door shut between us. I had been ordered to wash the 'foul stench of vamp' off me immediately.

We had all agreed not to tell Luna. I would undoubtedly be locked inside the house and forbidden to ever exit if she knew a vampire fancied me. Not getting to go outside, I'd wither away in days. However, there was now a strict policy that I was to not go anywhere alone. Even bathing, as I was now, would require a very close chaperone.

"I kept telling him to leave!" I argued back as I wrung my hair out in a towel, "and he never attempted to kidnap, rape or kill me so I didn't feel like manslaughter was an appropriate reaction to an unwanted guest no matter how annoying they might have been."

"Didn't try to pull anything huh? Then what was with the kiss?" Akashi pounded a fist on the door, and I jumped before releasing a sigh.

"Not kiss. I didn't engage with it."

"But you wanted to."

"Your point?" I pulled on the sweats and t-shirt I brought in the bathroom with me, then opened the door. Akashi promptly tumbled in as if he was leaning his whole weight against it.

"Oh my god, this is ridiculous! Why are you making this into such a big deal?" I pushed him out of the way and crossed my room, whipping the towel into his face to keep him back. "I was actually having fun, you know? That's not a concept I usually get to partake in."

"We would train with you—"

"Training isn't fun!" I yelled. Something previously buried deep exploded out of me and I closed the distance between us getting in his face. "Training is stale and painful and limiting because around here no one thinks I can do anything! None of you even know the new capabilities I've taught myself in the past few weeks because God forbid, I don't remain the fragile burden you all force yourselves to bear!"

Akashi stumbled back as if I'd struck him. Absently, his hand drifted to his eye, the one I had scarred. I choked on my next words, regret crashing through me as he glared at me.

"You have never been fragile, so quit the whiny bullshit," he growled. There was a soft knock at the door, and I lunged for the opportunity to get away from this, whatever it was, and engage in anything else. Hikari was on the other side, looking between myself and Akashi expressionlessly.

"Luna said you can join us on our next job. Petty vampire causing mischief not covering his tracks. We don't need to do anything but convince him to be more proactive. We leave in five hours, so get to sleep you two."

"I'm not sleeping here." Akashi's voice sounded like thunder. "She thinks she's fragile, so let her sleep with someone she hasn't defaced. I on the other hand, know better."

He pushed past me, his spine a rigid line as he stalked away from us and didn't turn back, didn't even slam his bedroom door once he disappeared behind it at the end of the hall. Hikari looked personally wounded for me, but I did what I had always done. I swallowed the hurt and looked at him with dead eyes.

"I guess I'll sleep with Anzen."

CHAPTER 9

I think this was the longest I had ever gone without speaking to Akashi my entire life and it hadn't even been a full week yet. We had stopped in many towns in the southern United States tracking the vampire further south. I don't know where we were going to end up today, but I knew we were somewhere in Texas as I spotted the border sign a few hours ago.

Apparently, part of my punishment for keeping my training sessions with Finn a secret was not being told anything about anything. It was clear in all their attitudes: I wasn't here to help. They were just too scared to let me out of their sight.

"You know I could just shadow jump home?" I muttered from the backseat.

"Be my guest." Kuma snorted, "Have fun explaining yourself to Luna." He was the only one who responded. Anzen had been my sleeping buddy since the night they chased Finn off the property, but even he had barely said a word to me other than good morning and goodnight.

The one silver lining was the minimal information that was shared between my brothers, and I was true: this vampire was easy to track. Partially because they never bothered to hide what they were in front of large groups of impressionable women. Partially because we just spotted him feasting on a girl on the street corner. And partially because it was—

"Stay in the car." All four of my brothers growled in unison and slammed their doors shut. Precisely two seconds later I was locked in the car for good measure, but I didn't object. Once releasing the girl from his arms (who disappeared down the street screaming) Silas beamed at my brothers in what seemed to be welcome.

I don't know what was with these vampire brothers, but I was over it. I'd live a satisfying life never seeing either of them again. Especially this one in particular. I got out of the car with a sigh, interrupting Kuma as he thrust his finger into Silas' face.

"Can we leave? There's nothing for us to do here." I tried acting nonchalant but inside I was panicking. The last time I saw him he tried to kill me. And I had been playing friends with his brother, even letting him try to kiss me. What had

I been thinking? I was almost as mad at myself as my brothers were now. Almost.

"Ah, just who I've been waiting to see." Silas beamed at me. In the daylight he was even more beautiful, those black locks of his shining nearly purple against the sun. It was a mystery how he and Finn could be brothers.

"You know where I live but sent your brother instead of coming yourself," I said flatly, then pointed a finger after the fleeing girl and smirked at him. "Whoa, have we moved on from grade school and know how to hunt on our own now?"

"I didn't want to interrupt your dates with my brother." He cooed. I felt each of my brothers stiffen and I kept my voice even in my reply,

"If he thinks getting his ass beat to a pulp is a date then I feel sorry for him." My body was rigid, ready to fly into action. I was ready to cut off my own ears if it meant Silas saying my name wouldn't paralyze me. "By the way, where's your better half? I have a bone to pick with her."

"No, you don't. Stick to business." Hikari stepped between Silas and I and launched straight into the 'get your act together' speech that Luna had me memorize in case my brothers let me handle this. As if they let me handle anything.

Silas was saying something along the lines of owning the club in New York, so he didn't have to be careful there. Kuma wasn't having it and was back in his face. Surprisingly, I almost stuck up for Silas since Finn had in fact mentioned they owned it, meaning that the club was a vampire sanctuary. We were actually in the wrong for invading it like we had.

Instead of speaking up I drifted away, meandering back towards the car. In the process of reaching for the door handle, the air shifted and I froze. He was here.

I whipped around, fist clenched and slammed it straight into the palm Finn had up in front of his face, ready to block me as always. He wore his trademark smile, but something was off. His eyes reflected a predatory gleam, similar to his brothers which I hadn't seen on him before. Something was wrong.

"Akashi...?" his name came out of my mouth in a silent scream. Finn's eyes grew even brighter, and his smile deepened.

"My sweet little Angel. I sincerely hope you did indeed wish to join me." Finn purred into my ear, arms wrapping themselves around my waist to fully block me from my brothers and violently I jerked back.

"Oh, let them go," Finn encouraged, planting a kiss into my hair with a soft sigh, "after all I've been the one helping you, they've been holding you back."

"Let me go!" I screamed. I could get out. I could light myself on fire and he would have to release me. Instead, I stood frozen like a deer in the headlights of an oncoming semi-truck with tears streaming down my face.

Useless. I felt utterly useless. Was this giving up? Giving in? Everything was spinning and briefly I didn't care anymore.

"Angel, I only wish to see you at your full potential." The grip on my waist tightened, "And I still have so many things to teach you before you reach it."

Too late, I began struggling in his arms. I spun around just enough to catch a glimpse of my brothers. The road was eclipsed by a black ring, but I still could see Kuma and Hikari in a full sprint down the street after Silas. Anzen had his arms cinched between Akashi's elbows holding him back as he thrashed in my direction.

I felt myself being pulled away into the dark abyss of teleportation. There was no gravity where I was standing. I couldn't hear Akashi screaming but I could see his desperation as I watched him fight against Anzen before slowly disappearing into the dark. In fact, the only thing I could hear was Finn's amused laughter as we disappeared from my life.

I don't know how to explain how teleportation is different from shadow jumping other than the speed. With shadow jumping you can wade around, explore alternative routes and creep back into the world of the living where you please. When you teleport, you crack from point A to point B like a whip. There is no way out of getting where you're going until you're already there.

As soon as our feet touched solid ground, I sagged against Finn resisting the urge to vomit. My head was spinning like a top and I was seeing stars.

"They'll find me you stupid son of a—"

"Yes, yes, I'm aware. However, even with her magic gift Luna will take quite a while to uncover this place. A month at least, perhaps even two."

Slowly the world righted itself and I found my sense of balance. I quickly took in the basics of my surroundings. Crumbling stone staircases and overgrown foundations of a civilization that once was. Quiet. Alone.

Finn sensed my intent too late, probably thinking I would take longer to recover from the shock. He dropped his hold on me, but thorns erupted from my body shooting outwards like bullets. He must have been weaker from the teleportation too because he was on his ass within seconds rather than putting up a fight like normal.

"You fucking kidnapped me." I hissed, lashing out with my vines and cinched him tight enough to cut off the blood flow of anything living. I raised him up a few yards and slammed him down into a stone foundation at our feet. Thorns the size of small boulders erupted from the earth to greet him as I slammed him again.

"You played me this entire fucking time!" Slam. "And for what? Am I some trophy that you're going to present to my father?!" Slam. "I'll kill you both!"

"We're trying to do you a favor Raven." Silas' voice was in my ear, and I froze. I released my hold on Finn and clamped my hands over my ears bellowing in rage.

It was a feeble attempt; his spell had already taken hold. I couldn't move or fight so instead I crumpled to the ground and covered my neck with my hands as the last unmanipulated act I had in me.

"That's cute and all but sit up," Silas commanded, and like a puppet I straightened my posture, clenching my hands around my throat so hard I was losing oxygen in defiance of his control.

Finn was bloodied but moved as if he were unscathed. He worked on untangling himself from the vines, cursing as he pulled jagged, red thorns from his body. Red with his blood I realized and swallowed a sob. If I had done that the moment he took hold of me in Texas this wouldn't be happening right now.

"Come on now," Silas drew my attention back to him, "let go of your neck my dear. I want my brother to get a look at your golden blood himself." My fingers shook against my throat, and I squeezed my eyes shut focusing all my energy on not giving in. Silas cocked a brow, "Ooh? How adorable, she's so into you she's shy Finn."

"You're making this worse," I heard Finn choke out.

"And here I was thinking I was going to be able to have some fun. Whatever. *Dimittis.*" I felt a weight lift off of me as Silas released the spell. I stopped entertaining them and just pulled a 180, bolting away. I didn't know where I was but getting away from them was a start.

"Whoa, wait." Finn, despite the beating I just gave him, was already back in front of me, "Are you injured? Have you ever teleported before?" He asked, sounding truly concerned and I nearly clocked him across the face.

"You STOLE me–"

"They were being reckless with you."

"They're my family you spawn of Sa–"

"They were going to get you killed!" Finn roared in my face, "They let you strut about in the mortal realm, traveling wherever you want, leaving your scent wherever you please. Believe me when I tell you the immortal world is overflowing with gossip about the girl that bleeds gold. Angel blood, Raven. They're letting you spill Angel blood wherever the fuck you please because for some reason no one can seem to tell you, 'No'."

Since I met him, he had been nothing but kind and flirty. This newfound anger, plus the information about my blood– I checked my temper. If people knew I existed and were talking…

"You see, those puppies of yours believe it's best to hide you away and take you out for dinner and a show once in a while." Silas interjected, cleaning imaginary dust off his jacket,

"However, that leaves you open, exposed, and weak on top of it. A month ago, all you could do was make shit grow out of the ground. Now you can shoot thorns out of your skin. Imagine what you'd be capable of if you weren't held back." His words struck a chord in me, but before I had the chance to acknowledge the truth to his statements, he went ahead and ruined it by muttering, "Instead, you're just a problem with pretty packaging, and a bounty on your head."

"Not. Helping." Finn scowled at his brother again, but I still found myself begrudgingly agreeing. Silas was an asshole, but he was right.

Deep down I knew the Hounds had my best interest at heart. It wasn't safe to be doing what I had pushed for, especially when I was younger. They had risked and lost so much in order to save me, and in return I had created this mess.

I was still wary of who I was receiving this information from though. Despite the genuine expressions Finn usually wore, vampires were master manipulators. I had to proceed carefully if I was to get out of here in one piece.

"Will my family be okay, or are they going to be found and killed?" I asked quietly to which Silas snickered.

"Sweetie, they're Hellhounds. I'm pretty sure they're the ones doing the finding and the–"

"What he means to say is," Finn cut his brother off, softening his glare for me as he said, "we're pretty sure they were in more danger with you."

I glanced between Finn and Silas. Day and night stared back at me as I weighed my options.

I could leave. Despite being dragged here, it was evident I wasn't being held hostage. There would have been no room for a fight and conversation if that were the case.

"You have two hours to get me physical evidence that anything that you've said is true. Otherwise, I'm going back to my family, and letting them kill you."

"I like our odds brother," Silas said, clapping Finn's shoulder with a palm. He winced, barely, but I saw it. Guilt chipped at the pride I had in my attack.

"Well let me stack them higher against you then." I glared at each of them in turn, "I want to know everything that you know about me. My father, my mother, my relation to Rebecca. My power. And why does everyone and their mother want me dead?"

Finn and Silas exchanged a look. Finn gave an imperceptible shake of his head. Silas rolled his eyes dramatically,

"That might take a bit longer than two hours. Good luck brother." He began to whistle as he walked off, turning a corner around a stone wall and vanished out of sight. I looked at Finn expectantly. He stared at me with eyes so sympathetic that I wanted to gouge them out.

"What?" I snapped.

"Well, I can't tell you why people want you dead, because they want you very much the opposite," Finn muttered and followed his brother's lead, leaving me no choice but to follow him around the corner if I wanted answers. A cracked staircase clung to the backside of the wall, and Finn paused at the top looking down at me.

"It might not be a shock that heaven and hell are at war. However, you are the key to one side prevailing over the other. Your unique heritage has made you quite a powerful weapon indeed. Everyone and their mother want their hands on you." He threw my own words back into my face.

"So, when you say you want to see me at my full potential, that just means you want to see me used as a weapon?" For which side, I wondered. Finn pinned me with his hot, burgundy gaze and I steeled myself, before climbing up after him.

CHAPTER 10

I took a more calculated look around at our surroundings. We had clearly landed in some type of ruin which was either protected from the masses or just wasn't preferred. The architecture appeared Roman, perhaps late Greek. Amongst the rubble of clay and stone rose a single standing wall of marble which seemed to be our target.

As we approached Silas slipped a key from his pocket, inserting it into a jagged crack in the wall. With a groan, a panel of marble slid to the side revealing a twisting staircase. I don't know what I was expecting as we descended into the dark, Silas ahead of me and Finn behind carrying a torch, but it definitely wasn't this.

There was a full city beneath the Earth, teeming with reapers, mages, fey, goblins, and some that I didn't know what name to attach to them. This was the largest number of supernatural's I had ever been surrounded by, not counting the night I lost my mother. The staircase continued to spiral away from us, lighting up the edges of a massive cave which plunged towards the Earth's core.

Each level blended seamlessly into the others, and all had their apparent purposes. One was full of blooming fields where food was being harvested. Another twinkled with flying sparks and popping metals of blacksmiths and engineers. There was even one that had a type of subway system connected to it. Tunnels channeled off of it into the Earth with no telling of what place they lead.

On our current level, restaurants and businesses littered the street. There was a massive crowd flowing in and out of shops, consumers pushing little carriages or hoisting bags onto their shoulders. I could hear music drifting towards us from further ahead and fought the urge to salivate as we passed a tiny shop selling sugary concoctions.

"Where are we going?" I shouted over the noise. Finn's hand found my lower back, and automatically I jerked away before his heat could seep into my bones.

"The housing district is seven levels below us. There's a platform up the street which will lower us down."

"So, a fancy underground elevator will lower me closer to hell? That's exactly what an Angel wants to hear," I mutter sarcastically. Finn grabbed my elbow and twisted me around.

"Do not say that here so casually." His eyes were serious. "These are my neighbors and my friends, but there are also strangers here as well." I averted my eyes but nodded, once again pulling myself from his grip.

"So, what is this place?" I finally asked as we stood in line waiting for the platform to reach our level.

"Believe it or not, Atlantis."

"Atlantis? The lost city under the ocean?" I asked slowly, my doubt clear.

"Think of it this way," Silas interjected, hands on my shoulders steering me forward into a seat. The platform might function like an elevator, but it was outfitted like a theater. The plush seat almost swallowed me whole as I sank my weight into it. Silas plopped beside me while Finn remained standing. "If the humans are so busy looking for Atlantis somewhere in the middle of the ocean, they'll be too busy to find us here, won't they?"

I have to admit it was a good point. Having not received a snarky response Silas leaned away, an arrogant grin on his face.

"You know I'll literally go mad if you keep me underground?" I muttered and shifted away from him in my seat.

Silas nodded, "It's a good thing we aren't underground then." I furrowed my eyebrows confused.

"But you just said—"

"In the human world, yes, we're underground. But we have left the mortal side of the veil." Silas stood and dramatically outstretched his arms gesturing to the space, "Welcome to Purgatory, home of the supernatural." I deadpanned.

"You all live in a cave."

The platform jerked to a stop and Silas sighed, looking toward Finn exasperated.

"She really has no sense of joy, does she?" A thin smile was playing on Finn's lips, but he said nothing as he strode towards the exit.

Passengers were complaining as we approached, and I realized it was because the platform had stopped a couple yards below the actual level. It was just a step up for the larger creatures, but smaller ones needed to jump or get assistance from others to be able to exit. When it was our turn I frowned, realizing I was the latter of the

two groups as the level began at my chest
height.

Silas swung himself up no problem
and continued on his way. Finn hoisted
himself out next, turning to me and
offering a hand. I could use my vines to
pull myself up easily, but people were
watching. I didn't know what parts of my
magic here would be considered normal,
or which would put a target on my back,
so it seemed I was left with only one
irritating option.

Slowly, I reached up and clasped
Finn's hand in mine. His grip was strong,
but he didn't yank me out. I ended up
gripping his other forearm with my free
hand to get out of the way faster.

When my feet touched the ground
again, we were chest to chest, and I felt
my breath hitch. According to our track
record, he had kidnapped me, and before
that had tried to kiss me. My mind was
fried at this point. Thankfully he released
me and started after his brother, again
leaving me to decide for myself if I would
follow.

On this floor the roads were quieter
and darker. Torches lined the walls
shining with white and blue flames,
making shadows bounce around the edges
of expertly carved stone doors and
windows in the cave wall. We walked for

about five minutes before Silas produced a second key from his pocket. The door we stopped outside of could have been made of pearl, and I found myself resisting the urge to reach out and touch it. There was a soft click, and the door swung open with the soft grind.

"And here we are," Silas said. "Home sweet home."

The room was carved from black marble, and two crystal chandeliers drooped from the ceiling. Twin curved staircases curled up to frame a large, picturesque window which made up the entire outer wall of the home I realized. Stunning didn't begin to cover the view.

This side of the veil's resemblance to the mortal realm was remarkable, however, the colors were off. Rather than green, trees stood in vibrant hues of turquoise and violet. The grass was various shades of citrus, and the sky was a hazy magenta. I saw a shimmering golden brook crossing the border of the horizon and the sigh that left me was nothing short of pleasure.

"You'll have your own room." Finn's voice echoed off the marble floor. I turned and realized Silas had already gone, leaving the two of us there alone.

"Show me." He nodded, headed for the left staircase and I followed, marveling at the pure silver banisters. "I thought vampires were sensitive to silver." I wondered aloud and he nodded.

"As long as it doesn't penetrate our skin, we're fine." Interesting.

We continued down a darkened hallway, almost the same shade of burgundy as the vampire's eyes, and I wondered if they did that on purpose. I wouldn't be able to step outside my room without feeling them watching me.

The room in question was (thankfully) on the same side of the window wall, but I was disappointed to find my windows were sealed shut.

"Believe me, it's more to make sure nothing gets in rather than you getting out." Finn commented before I could brat about it.

"And what if I want fresh air?" I asked and he gave me a slightly humored but mostly confused glance,

"Well, I guess you will just have to go outside then?" He held my gaze and I understood: I wasn't locked in here. Again, it was my choice to stay or go.

I coaxed my gaze from the view to take in the room. A large four-poster bed took up most of the space, carved from some type of wood that was red like cherries. A matching writing desk and bureau sat against the adjacent wall. Of course, I had my own chandelier poised above one of those ornate, gothic lounge chairs that was higher on one end than the other. The crystals in this chandelier matched the red of the furniture though, and the silk on the seat was black as night.

"We've told her to stay out of your way, but Rebecca does live here." I stiffened but ignored the comment.

"You'll have to see her eventually," Finn added. I could hear the smile on his lips. I continued to ignore him and poked my head into the connected, blessedly private, bathroom.

White candlelight flickered against the wall. The sink, shower and what I assumed was a tub were carved from the same black marble as the rest of the house. I gaped at the waterfall shower that in and of itself was as big as the bathroom at home. The wade-in soaking tub in the corner was even more extravagant.

"I would rather have proof of all your claims than a five-star hotel room," I said flatly. "If you have nothing but more glamor to shower me with, leave me alone now." I turned to swing the door shut, planning on putting that pool to good use, but Finn slammed his foot in the gap keeping it open.

"What?" I snapped, glaring up at him. He smiled widely, making his fangs glint in the dull shine of the room. "...What?" I asked again, softer, and stepped away from the door, putting some much-needed space between us.

He pushed the door open lazily and swept his golden locks off his forehead. Running his hand over the back of his head to rest on his neck he leaned forward, raking his eyes up and down my body before resuming eye contact.

"I do genuinely want you to join me, but I've already been so patient with you. I don't want you forgetting what I really am, Angel." He pushed himself off the wall and started closing the extra space I had created.

"Don't get me wrong I very much enjoy your company and the chase, however. My brother is right to a degree. I do wish to catch a glimpse of that golden blood of yours. And the amount of time I've put in with you, holding myself back in your presence, warrants a taste. Wouldn't you say so?"

Goosebumps peppered my skin, and I felt my heart jolt in my chest, adrenaline snaking out through my vertebrae and through my veins. Ready to fight. Or run.

Finn picked up on that rush of energy, and it only made his eyes gleam brighter, nearly crimson by the time he had me backed into the shower. He tilted his head, gaze locked on my throat but made no move to take another step forward. I tore my eyes from his face and looked away, fists clenched at my sides.

"Just get it over with already," I breathed out, hearing my voice breaking slightly. "This feels so pathetic, just get it over with and leave me alone." I repeated, leaning back against the wall and shut my eyes.

"The only reason you feel pathetic now is because you don't know how. No one bothered to teach you." I could feel him step forward, and his scent wafted over me.

We had been in close quarters before yes, but in the woods covered in dirt and sweat. I never had gotten a good scent of *him*. Beneath the metallic tang of vampire, he was a musk of honey and clove, raspberries and smoke, tulips and charcoal, soft and dark all at once and I leaned straight into it wanting more.

His breath washed over my face, and I felt his lips against my jaw, the shell of my ear, my neck. My heart was assaulting my ribcage so violently I was sure a bone was about to snap but I remained still. I could shadow jump away at any moment and with that insurance, I allowed my curiosity to get the better of me.

I was expecting the same piercing bite I had received from Silas, but a shocked gasp ripped from my lips, feeling Finn slowly drag his tongue up from my collarbone to the soft space beneath my ear.

"What are you–"

"I'm teaching you." Finn's voice rumbled through his chest into mine. I hadn't even realized he had plastered the two of us together. His lips passed over my jaw again, "Anything in particular you wish to be taught, Angel?"

"Bag it," I huffed out and he chuckled against my skin.

"Very well." His voice dropped, becoming serious, "Now hold still."

And there was the pain. Two sparks shot through my neck like electricity, and I jerked back into the wall. Finn slammed his hands down onto my hips forcing me still, and he bit down into me deeper once I had.

I was panting now, fists digging into the back of his shirt, trying to keep ahold of anything besides the pain that was beginning to slowly ebb away. Something pooled in the pit of my stomach and instinctively my thighs pressed themselves together.

"Your body reacts to me marvelously," Finn mumbled against my skin. He lapped at the blood spilling over my collarbone, grazing his fangs along the arch to my shoulder. He lifted a hand and expertly worked my sleeve down my arms, freeing up more skin for himself to pepper kisses across as he explored the new space. "Now if only your brain would comply as nicely." I groaned and began to shove him away, my hands pushing against his chest, so he shifted, pressing his pelvis into me instead and we both stilled.

He was thick and stiff, pulsing lightly against my abdomen, and was now breathing just as hard as I was. Desperate, I lifted my hips off the wall slightly, pushing him away but he hissed, drilling me back into the marble so quickly all the breath left my lungs. Then he pulled himself away, backing up several paces while blinking rapidly as if in shock. My legs felt numb and slowly, I slid to the floor while raising a hand to my neck to press against the bite.

I didn't look at him as he turned and slowly left the room. He even shut the door behind him giving me a solid barrier between us that I desperately needed. Once he was gone, I sucked in a gulp of air and released a frustrated groan. I smacked the floor, leaving a smeared golden handprint in its wake.

CHAPTER 11

I was bitter when I learned Rebecca had stocked my room with everything a female might need. The bathroom was filled with beauty products, sanitary products, even creams for sore muscles I could use after training. My bedroom closet was even filled with my preferred taste in clothes: ripped jeans, leggings, t-shirts, sweaters. I even found a pair of fishnets tucked in between the sneakers and boots. The only thing I despised was the multitude of evening gowns that were now among my possessions. I can't imagine ever needing those.

However, the bitterness didn't fade no matter how close she got my style to a T. She almost got my brothers and I killed. A few free outfits wouldn't erase that.

"So, is she ever gonna show face or keep hiding like a coward?" I grumble to Silas across the dining table. I'd been here about a week and spent most of my time wandering around Purgatory finding hidden spaces to practice my powers.

Elemental Manipulation, the vampires called it.

In just this short time, vines sprouting from my skin no longer caused me to ache or bleed. I didn't need to cry to cause any rainfall, and likewise could summon the brightest of fire when I was completely calm.

During one of my more rageful disputes with Silas, who had followed me without my knowing, we discovered I could even make the Earth rumble beneath us. As for shadow jumping, I stuck to drifting in and out of different spaces in the house.

Rebecca wasn't the only one I hadn't seen since arriving, Finn had also remained scarce. Our encounter in the bathroom hadn't exactly left me shaken, but I was even more confused than before. His lack of explanation didn't help any.

I found myself growing more irritable with each passing day when I was only in the company of Silas' arrogance and mischief. We didn't often speak with one another, but he was always hovering.

In the evenings I denied both training and Silas' constant presence and would disappear into Purgatory to explore. The animals were just like the wilderness, similar to the human realm but so different at the same time. A large peach colored creature, like a deer, drifted through the brush on ashy clouds at its feet. The waters were filled with shimmering golds and harsh blacks of darting fish– some with wings which allowed them to fly between bodies of water.

But the true gem I found was a cascading waterfall the same shade of red as wine. I almost missed it as it was shielded by long, navy willow branches, glittering with what resembled stardust. In a way, it reminded me of the clearing I met the Hounds in. Ethereal, and safe. After particularly harsh days, from both the humidity and my practice, I bathed there under the rising moon which was the only familiar thing: a shimmering cylinder of silver bobbing in a black sky.

I'll admit, now I felt more giddiness than fear. More feral than mad. I was enjoying this freedom and growth. The ability to have my own back was refreshing. To make my own decisions was even more so.

Still, every night a small part of me hoped that as I drifted to sleep my brothers would find me and drag me from this place. Not because I needed rescuing, but because part of me feared that they didn't care where I ended up based on my recent behavior. We couldn't have left things in a worse place than we did, all being in a fight. It made me sick to think about it.

"Well, you have threatened to kill her." Silas' voice clanged through my skull, bringing me back to the dinner table we were seated at. He smirked at me over his glass of wine. I always assumed it was wine, I didn't want to assume it was anything else. After a pause he added, "I prefer her alive." I raised a brow.

"Protective of your girlfriend? And just when I thought there was nothing chivalrous about you."

"Hah! Don't give him any compliments, they go right to his head." Rebecca's voice trickled down the stairs and immediately I froze. Silas cursed and set his glass down, both of us turning to glare up at her in synch.

She was draped against the banister of the stairs opposite mine. an amused smile curling its way onto her lips as she looked me over. Her eyes settled on my fork which I hadn't realized I had clenched in a white knuckled grip.

"Boo, Raven. I thought we were friends by now." She called down to me, feet tapping on the stairs as she descended to the dinner table and slid into the chair beside Silas. I couldn't look at her without wanting to punch her, so instead I studied him.

He raised his glass again, downing its contents in one gulp. Smacking it down on the table it splintered at the base, but he paid no mind as he continued to busy his hands by yanking his tie off. Though he wasn't directly looking at Rebecca or myself, his whole body was rigid with anticipation. He was nervous.

Akashi's words clanged in my head, and slowly I unwound my fingers from my fork. Control your temper, I reminded myself, leaning back in my seat. Calmly, I folded my hands in my lap and looked her over.

"Friends don't usually try to lure one another into an alley to die," I responded, words hot. Her answering smirk radiated cold, yet those fierce blue eyes scalded me.

"As if your guard dogs would give anyone the chance to kill you." Her smile was all teeth as she added, "Though it seems like they let their pet off her leash for once. How's life fending for yourself?" To hell with remaining calm. I let my words drag,

"So, if you're not a piece of ass like I originally guessed, what are you? A hunter? Lackey? Or just his bitch?" I settled on that, grinning despite knowing I was just being cruel. I knew they were a couple, but for some reason that just pissed me off more so I snickered and added, "I wouldn't have expected any supposed sister of mine to be so embarrassingly manipulated like this."

Silas was in my face then, teeth bared in a defensive manner, but I expected that. What I didn't expect was for Rebecca to break the table in two, pick up one of the larger splinters and hurl it towards me like a javelin.

I leaped back from the table, somersaulting into a shadow at the base of the stairs behind me and reappeared at the top of the ones she had just come down.

"What? You don't have the stomach for petty insults?" I laughed and assumed the same position she had moments earlier, leaning against the banister smirking down at them.

Silas' fangs were still bared, but the relief in his eyes that I retreated was unmistakable. Relief that the danger went away. A jolt went through me, something negative and in pain but I ignored it, shifting my eyes back to Rebecca.

"So, what are you?" I pressed, eyeing the spikes of ice growing from the floor. That must have been what caused the table to explode.

I should have been more specific. I should have asked what she was to him, kept the focus on their relationship. Or that magic, what was it exactly? But instead, I gave her a millimeter of wiggle room to bring me into it, which she gladly took advantage of.

With a wicked feline smile, she strode past Silas and made her way up the stairs. Confident and coy and all but sweet as she whispered right into my face,

"You don't remember me at all, do you big sis?"

I think I shocked them both when I fled the house. When would a person like me, a war weapon or whatever they said I was to the rest of the world, choose not to fight?

I took advantage of their shock, slamming the door behind me as I left, shadow jumping before they even began to pursue me. I sprint through the dark, the veil between realms thinner now that I've been allowed to practice. A blurry scene of Purgatory sped alongside me, wriggling and unfocused like an image underwater. I wonder if there will be a time when I can run through this world and have both realms, Human and Purgatory, side by side next to me.

A current of black shot past me. Rebecca? No, she would appear in this realm as whole as I did since she could travel in it. Someone was teleporting, just on the outskirts of this realm. One of the vampires, of course. They had my scent, just as the Hounds did. Two sets of brothers who could eventually find me no matter where I ran. Terrific.

I broke to the left, slipping further into the shadow of the Earth and began climbing my way up the levels to the busier night district on platform 3. In addition to my pursuer, a low thumping reverberated through the veil. Music. A party must be going on somewhere.

I slid out of the shadows underneath a makeshift deck of some kind. There was definitely a party going on in the building above me, thumping and hollering and music echoing from inside. It reminded me of the club in New York, but the scents...I could practically taste the cherry lipstick, the ashes, the sweat. This must have been how overwhelming it was for my brothers. Peeking through a crack in the

floorboards I caught glimpses of
partygoers.

From what I could tell, my dirty
leggings and cotton tank top would not
blend in. Above me was a disarray of neon
and glitter, metal and skin. I think many
partygoers wore masks or headpieces,
however a few of the feathers and antlers
could be naturally occurring I realized. A
pit began to throb in my stomach.

I wanted to go in. I wish I had
clothes that matched. Mentally I cursed
Rebecca– she had put clothes in my closet
which would have been perfect for this.

I dug my fingers into the dirt
beneath me in frustration, and to my
surprise a pale glow began radiating from
my clutch. Tendrils of smoke wafted up
towards me and I bucked backwards.
Wait, it wasn't smoke, it was steam. My
clothes were evaporating from my body.
The space under the deck suddenly felt
like it was caving in on me. Not only was
I a stranger in a foreign place I was about
to be a naked stranger surrounded by
drunks.

Just as panic began to set in, the
steam around me grew thicker. It twisted
and pulled at my now slime-like clothes,
molding and reorganizing the fabric onto
my body in new shapes, colors and
patterns. I realized the more I steadied

my breathing the more solid the new
outfit was becoming.

A few more moments passed until
the dull light fully subsided, and when
there was a brief moment of quiet on the
street outside the building, I quickly
pushed my way out from under the deck.

My crummy athletic clothes from
before had been completely replaced by a
shimmering body suit. Black silk clung to
my body, occasionally broken up by sheer
cuts of lace showing off glimpses of my
skin. I traced the fabric lightly with my
fingers, utterly confused about its
appearance and slowly more insecure of
its design.

The high halter neckline was
secure below my hairline, but did nothing
to hide the bodice seams which were
pressing my tits together. The lace cut
along my abdomen, curling down towards
my pelvis before dipping away over my
hips to curve around my ass. I swore,
slowly turning in the lamplight, realizing
my only source of comfort was the boots
still on my feet. Before I could inspect
myself further Silas' voice popped up from
behind me.

"Well, I can't say I expected this."
Mortified, I turned around already
fumbling for an excuse, but was surprised
to find a proud smile on his face.

"What's happening to me?" I asked, sounding a little breathless.

"Elemental manipulation." Finn materialized beside his brother and I'm pretty sure I stopped breathing altogether. If he sensed my embarrassment, he didn't care. He let his gaze travel down my body, taking in all the details of my manifested outfit with the same type of pride in his eyes as his brother.

I could feel myself blushing, but from a different type of embarrassment now. Just a few seconds ago I was freaking out, but now I felt calm, even a bit proud. The vampires were looking at me as if I had achieved something and wanted to celebrate.

Bitterly, I realized no one had ever looked at me that way before. If this situation had come about at home, it surely would have been met with concern, if not rejection.

"Care to elaborate?" I grit my teeth, refocusing on the present. I had just created clothes out of thin air. I needed answers, now. Finally, Finn snapped out of it and met my eyes.

"Elemental manipulation," he repeats, "is just the surface of what you're capable of. To put it simply, what is cloth made from?"

"Cotton," I said, sarcasm leaking into my voice. "Though if you're looking for specifics it could also be silk or wool or satin or leather." He eyed me with a half-smile.

"And where do all of those things come from, Angel?" I scowled at him for calling me that in front of his brother as I answered.

"Well, I would assume animals and plants..." I paused, realization dawning on me.

Before being processed, dyed, and made into clothes or objects, most things came from something natural of the Earth. So, I guess by a stretch, it could be an extension of my magic.

If this idea were true, then what I thought I was capable of before just multiplied by a thousand. It's one thing manipulating plants and wind, I could almost feel normal doing that now. But willing things into being simply because they exist in the right format? That's a ball game I'm not sure I'm prepared for.

I was processing too many thoughts and emotions to reply to either of them right now so instead I turned and marched up the stairs of the porch I had just crawled out from under.

"It's a masquerade Raven," Silas drawled from behind me, "and you don't have a mask."

I paused on the top step. The door was just a few feet in front of me. Just a few feet, and I could forget about Rebecca, and vampires, and magic, and my brothers. I could just forget I existed for a few hours dancing, or in the arms of someone, I didn't care at this point.

"He might be an asshole but he's not a liar. You seriously won't get in without a mask, house rules."

I whipped around at the sound of Rebecca's voice. She was already climbing the stairs, her face hidden by an icy blue mask which matched her eyes. In fact, everything about her outfit gave the illusion of ice from the pointed shoulder pieces to the dripping net of diamonds around her legs which I guess she counted as a skirt. She came straight up next to me despite the foul grimace I'm sure was on my face.

"Believe me, the owner is a stickler. Luckily for you, you can just make one. Unluckily for me since I already spent a fortune on your wardrobe. Wouldn't have done that if I'd known you had that particular talent."

"You weren't asked to, so don't complain." My words had an underlying bite, which earned an immediate dark smile from her. Her blue eyes were laughing at me as she said,

"Admit it: you're grateful. And you hate me for it."

"You got one thing right," I muttered pushing past her. That strange glow radiated from my hand again, and slowly a plain black mask with a single feather drooping down the side materialized into being. "I do hate you."

CHAPTER 12

Silas and Finn didn't come in with us, but my mind was transfixed on other things. First of all, this building. It looked like a rickety little shack from the street, but inside it was a three-story silver and gold club. The space was split into three levels: bar, lounge, and a dance floor far below. And the creatures...I didn't even know where to start processing all the colors, teeth and scales. Rebecca's tinkling laughter reached my ears, undoubtedly about the shocked expressions passing along my face.

I shifted my weight forward over the balcony to get a better look at the full dance floor. Half of it was some type of hot spring where beings with tails lazily reclined or swam. Others participated in, well, lewder activities. In fact, most of the people down below were participating in what seemed to be—

"It's called a pleasure den." Rebecca whispered into my ear, making me jump. I turned my back against the railing, blocking out the scenes below.

"Am I supposed to understand what that means?" I managed to choke out, pressing my palms to the eye sockets of my mask. She grins.

"It's not so different from an actual club. We call it a pleasure den because unlike when we go out in the human realm, we don't need to hold back against what feels good here. No one is going to judge the slip of a hand or sexual contact, unless of course it's non-consensual. Then that person is practically beaten from the crowd."

"You seem to know a lot about it despite having a boyfriend," I accuse, sending her a weak glare. She shrugs, eyes glittering.

"I don't know why you think everyone is as controlling and possessive as that wolf of yours," she said with a roll of her eyes. "Believe it or not, most supernatural's have multiple partners. Sometimes at the same time, sometimes individually. We live so long it just makes sense." I dropped my hands and sighed.

"He's not my wolf. He's just my brother." I corrected, grabbing a drink from a passing tray. I don't care what it is, I just need it. The amber liquid is cold, and tastes so sweet of strawberry I pucker my lips.

"Stepbrother," Rebecca muses. "Yea, so what's the real deal with that? We never got to finish our convo." She pokes her fingers into my hip, pushing me toward a staircase leading to the lounge below. I don't want her company or this conversation, but she's made it clear she's going to follow me, so I don't see any way of ending it.

"It's not up for discussion," I mutter stepping towards the stairs. I collapse on a stark white couch right at the base of the stairs refusing to go any further. Rebecca snorted and plopped down beside me.

"So, when should I expect to be dragged in front of Lucifer?" I ask. She releases a shocked laugh.

"You won't be. What made you think that?"

"You clearly remember me, so I just figured." I look away, taking another swig of my drink.

"I just pretended to so I could get under your skin." I frown. So, her memories were wiped too. Then that still leaves the possibility that we aren't sisters after all. I release an exasperated sigh.

"At this point your existence does that."

"Somehow, I don't believe you, otherwise you wouldn't be talking to me right now. In fact, I dare say you're more curious about who I am and what I know, rather than holding onto a petty grudge from New York." She smirked at me, and I fumed, following Silas' earlier example and finishing my drink in one gulp. I slam my now empty glass down on the table beside us and stand with a single clap of my hands.

"Just do whatever it is you do here. I can handle myself thank you," I say and march away. She laughs, and again falls into step beside me as I make a beeline for the next staircase and begin going down to the dance floor level.

"If I leave you alone, you'll get eaten alive," she says with a sigh. "Essentially, I'm stuck here until you decide to come home. Unless you truly came here to work up a sweat?" She wiggled her eyebrows, and I immediately felt myself blushing.

"Don't even. I didn't even know what this place was, how could I expect this?" As I said it, a woman with fairy wings and dusty blue skin flitted up the stairs towards us and leaned her petite frame into my side.

"Expect what deary? Pleasure perhaps?" Her tiny hands circled my waist, and I jerked out of her grip. Rebecca grinned and just waved the fairy woman off.

"You are so uptight," she commented with a laugh. "I can practically hear your blood pressure rising."

"Shut. Up." I spat and she shook her head.

"I'm saying it genuinely. You need to chill out. All that rage is gonna explode one day and you won't even realize it."

"I'm NOT mad!" I nearly shrieked, attracting the attention of some dancers closest to the bottom of the stairs. I quickly lowered my voice, realizing my behavior and words were contradicting each other.

"I'm not mad," I repeat more civilly. "I'm stressed out. And you keep fucking following me which isn't helping."

"Oh, yes, very clear." She rolled her eyes, "So why do you only hate me again? I didn't kidnap you."

"Because you tried to feed me to your boyfriend."

"So shouldn't you hate him too then?"

"I do! Okay?" This was too exhausting to deal with right now, so I waved her off, "Just... go participate in whatever the fuck this is. And leave me alone." I repeated, jumping down the last three stairs and into the edge of the crowd.

If another fairy or some other thing came along, I just might let it stay. With luck it would knock me out and I could forget everything for a while.

"It's because I'm his daughter too, isn't it?" Rebecca's hand caught my wrist loosely. The know-it-all grins and mocking eyes she's been giving all night are suddenly gone. Under the mask she looks downright grim, but that doesn't prevent the venom from lacing my voice.

"You don't get to speak to me about–"

"In fact, I do." She cut me off. Her icy eyes challenged me silently, "I'm not a Hound. Not an adopted sibling you can bully into silence. He's my father too, so I can speak of Lucifer if I wish. You have no right to tell me otherwise." My stomach churned.

"How are you so sure we're related when we don't even have half our memories?"

"Want a blood test?" She asked sarcastically.

"Yea, lean over and give me a taste," I growled but stopped short, stunned by my words. Rebecca looked equally shocked before a humored smile graced her lips.

"So, that's another thing we have in common. The demon halves of us at least." I was still too stunned to speak, so she turned and waved to someone over her shoulder.

Seconds later another fairy had made their way over to us, this one appearing to be male with golden skin the same shade as the sun. His eyes were all black, but I could tell he was inebriated by the way he clung to Rebecca's arms as she pulled him in between us.

"We aren't vampires, we can survive without this." She traced her finger down the column of the boy's throat, seemingly transfixed, "But I've found restraining myself, for the sake of my pride, did more damage in the long run. After all, I only gained the strength to shadow jump, which is our Fathers specialty by the way, after indulging in other habits of his."

As she spoke two pointed canines appeared, pressing against her lips. She purred against the boy's throat, eyes glossing over, and bit him.

I was expecting it to be more dramatic or sensual, but it was just...simple. Rebecca had bitten a stranger and started sucking their blood right next to me.

She released him after a few seconds and when she pulled away with a gleaming red smile, I felt a familiar tug in my gut. One I experienced after successfully pinning one of my brothers under me during a training session. In the school over top that female vampire. In the bathroom with Finn as well I realized. I was salivating, and the fairy was offering his neck to me as well.

I don't know if I would have bitten him or not, I didn't get the opportunity to think that far ahead. Because behind him coming down the staircase, I noticed two masked men. One with hair the color of night, and the other the color of day. One pale and one bronze. One in a dark suit covered in glitter, and the other in gold trousers, his pale and unbuttoned top showing off the muscles I knew he had but hadn't gotten a peek of since training in the woods. Silas and Finn casually strutted down the stairs, and I never felt so feverish in my life.

"One last thing," Rebecca said. My eyes shot back to her, watching as she wiped the blood from her mouth and sent the fey boy on his way. Her eyes were locked on Silas, a small smile playing on her lips, "You can try to fool yourself into hating everyone and everything sis.

Believe me, it doesn't work. Now, enjoy the rave, Rave."

She snickered, spinning away from me before I could protest against the stupid nickname and slid into Silas' outstretched arms. Immediately his nose dipped to the curve of her neck, giving her affectionate little nips and bites before she pulled him further into the dancing crowd, the two of them disappearing.

Finn stood at the bottom of the stairs. With his eyes deadlocked on me, he casually popped open one of the few buttons he bothered to clasp. His tanned skin looked warm and inviting and with that thought I knew the mystery drink I'd chugged had hit. I turned away from him marching straight into the crowd of swaying bodies.

Welcoming arms and legs gently grazed against me, but Rebecca's words thrummed in my head above the music. Choose indulgence over pride? I felt my brow furrowing beneath the mask.

Shadow jumping was the only dark thing I allowed myself to indulge on this far in my life. If she hadn't even been able to before drinking blood, then how the hell was I? I felt sick to my stomach, wondering just how much I might have inherited from my Father. The shadows, the smoke, the bloodlust.

I wanted to drink blood. And I shouldn't. But I can.

"You are an infuriating student to teach, you realize that yes?" Finn's voice broke through my cloudy thoughts at the same time his hands broke through the cage of bodies around me, pulling me to him. I twisted against him, and he didn't bother suppressing a pleased groan as I accidentally grinded against him. For the second time I felt that long length of heat between us, this time throbbing against my spine as I nearly wiggled free.

"I dare say the opportunity to dance with you here intrigues me more than rewatching your performance in New York." He snickered, palm finding the back of my neck. His grip was tight, holding me in place, but not painful. As always if I really wanted to get out, I would be able to. His thumb traced up the side of my neck.

"You sick fuck. Tell me there's not a copy of the tape?" I gasped as a hand passed between my legs. Not Finns, I think it belonged to a woman in the crowd beside us. His breath cascaded over my neck as he chuckled.

"Don't you worry. I made sure to delete the evidence, for the small price of keeping one camera angle in particular for myself." His hips rocked back and forth slowly, coaxing me into rhythm with the music pounding around us. His hand left my neck, lightly sliding down the front of my body before pressing into my lower abdomen forcing us to be flush against each other.

Suddenly, the image of Akashi dancing against the woman in New York flashed in my brain and another wave of sickness hit me. What the hell was wrong with me? I had a perfectly good-looking man, annoying as he was, right behind me. I frowned, forcing the image from my mind. These boys were getting under my skin at all times of day, and I was getting sick of it. Unable to deal with one, unable to get back at the other. Or could I?

I felt my back arch of its own accord, hips rolling with the movement, trying to let the dance ease me into sweet numbness. Finn's body was strong against mine. And hot. That overwhelming temperature that scorched me from even the smallest of touches was now plastered to my whole spine making my head dizzy. I raised my arms above my head, my hands dropping to his shoulders above me. But then he had to go and cup my boob in his free hand snapping me back to reality.

Finn was secure in the idea that I knew nothing about these types of activities, and that I was usually too embarrassed to try anything on my own. He was confident that he would be the one to teach me everything about pleasure, so I knew just how to tick him off: let someone else teach me.

I grit my teeth, but purposefully grinded as much pressure towards his hips as I dared, needing him to get so caught up in feeling me that he didn't realize what I was planning to do. His body answered, hips bucking forward into me rougher than before.

I broke free using the force of his own thrust against him, slipping from his grip and drifted out of reach. Both the security and the pleasure slipped from his face as I slowly stepped backwards into the arms of two male goblins who materialized on either side of me.

I was in over my head within seconds. One buried their face into the nape of my neck, tongue and teeth making me gasp from pure shock. The other had dropped to his knees, hands exploring the gap between my legs, assaulting the heartbeat pulsing at the apex of my thighs with his knobby fingers. I was seeing stars in my vision as my body was twisted back and forth between the two, the hand between my legs causing me to cry out louder for a whole new reason.

And then suddenly, both were gone. The whole room was gone actually, disappearing down a column of black as a now enraged Finn teleported me out of the center of the show.

"You really have no idea what you get yourself into, you just stubbornly forge ahead and to damn with the consequences!" He chastised as we landed at our destination. Blurry eyed and disoriented I realized we were on a balcony overlooking the outskirts of Purgatory.

"Are we home? The house has balconies?" I asked, trying to get my bearings. Finn, I realized, had gone still and silent, looking at me as if in a daze.

"What's your problem?" I asked, warily taking a step away not wanting to repeat a bite scene while my body was already overwhelmed with new sensations.

"You just called this place home," he mumbled. I groaned and pressed my hands against my temple.

"Please, I'm begging you, no sentimental bullshit right now. I've been through enough tonight."

"You did that to yourself."

"Enthusiastically."

"It seemed more desperate than enthusiastic, Angel." He gave me a long look before taking his leave, disappearing inside the house.

The quiet closed in on me. I was alone again. Just like I wanted to be.

Right?

CHAPTER 13

Desperation is exactly what I experienced the rest of the night. Before passing out, I caved to my curiosity. I tried passing my hand between my legs the same way the woman and goblin had, switching angles until I left myself gasping for breath. Then once asleep my dreams plagued me.

I was back at the New York club, but instead of two goblins I had Akashi and Finn on either side of me. At first, Finn's words of encouragement drifted up from between my legs, against my ribs, my collarbone. His tongue and fangs shamelessly experimented on sensitive areas of my body. Then Akashi yanked me to the floor, green eyes boring into mine from above. His bangs tickled my forehead, one hand pinning my wrists above my head, the other sliding between my legs. His mouth drifted closer and closer to mine, then suddenly jerked lower to hover just inches above my exposed–

I bolted upright, waking in a cold sweat and blinking against the harsh rays of sunlight streaming in through my open window. I was naked I realized, noticing my bodysuit abandoned on the floor. There was no sign of anyone with me though. I had simply passed out before grabbing my pajamas. I could live with that.

I skipped breakfast that morning and exited the house as fast as I could. There were too many things happening all at once so to clear my head I set out for the waterfall. Usually, I reserved my visits for twilight hours, but I really needed space to think. And breath.

The willow branches seemed heavier in the day than they had at night, the drifting boughs groaning as my touch pushed them to the side so I could climb over their maze of roots. The water was rose red under the sun, almost blinding me as I stepped out from the shelter of the trees.

I was surprised to see the array of creatures here. A group of Fuanrir, the peachy deer-like creatures, were wading in the shallow depths slurping up fish and tadpole-like creatures. Phoenixes were perched against the water's edge, steam rising from their feathers where the water lapped as they feasted on the vegetation. The tiniest of fey zipped around between animals and trees, vivid green bullets shooting through this kaleidoscope of color. Three of them were in my hair I realized, and gently I brushed them away. They looked like human babies but the size and color of hummingbirds.

"Play play play!" One sang out circling my head.

"The Raven Raven singing song!" A second one trilled. I tilted my head,

"What's the Raven song?" I ask curiously.

"They mean your heartbeat." Rebecca's voice echoed in my ears. I released a groan of annoyance not seeing her on the shore, so lifted my head to search the trees for her and immediately blanched.

Instead of seeing Rebecca I was looking up into the face of a leopard, or maybe a Saber-tooth tiger, lazing in a coiled bed of branches. It was the same impressive size as the Hounds, with a thick tail covered in dark spikes and jet-black fur that put even the darkest of nights to shame. Large silver claws glint in the sunlight as it stretched, yawning to reveal identical silver teeth. The only tell-tale sign this creature was Rebecca was the icy blue eyes studying me.

"Rose Bud blooming!" The little fey sang and abandoned me to go hitch a ride as the cat leapt from the tree.

"And that's my song, Rose Bud."
The cat's maw didn't move as she spoke.
Just like the Hounds, I could hear her in
my head, "They'll think of something
creative for you. Will-o'-the-wisps always
do."

"I thought those were blue?" I ask
drily, eyeing up the vivid greens of their
wings and skin. The cat snorted.

"Yea and Sphinxes have wings, but
you don't see any on me do ya?" She
shook out her fur sending the Willow
Wisps on their way.

So, a Sphinx, that's what she was.
Up to this point I genuinely believed that
humans cooked up the story of them, as
they had with many supernatural
creatures once learning we existed. Luna
hadn't mentioned anything about them
either. Then again, Luna didn't mention a
lot.

When I didn't speak, the Sphinx
snorted once more and drifted around to
the back of the tree. After a brief flash of
light and some shuffling around, Rebecca
appeared in her human form pulling a
slipknot t-shirt over her head, giving me
a wicked grin.

"Were you hoping to see me
naked?"

"That's disgusting."

"Why? I thought you had a thing for gawking at your siblings?" I groaned and turned my back to her, making her laugh. She was always laughing at me and all I wanted to do was drill her head into a rock.

"You're so uptight I bet if I shove a lump of coal in your ass it'll make a diamond."

"If you call me uptight one more time, I'm gonna lose it," I growled.

"Sorry, sorry, how'd you call yourself? Stressed? That better?" She grinned as if we were sharing a joke.

"Well at least I'm not slumming it with vampires. Getting girls killed," I muttered. I could feel her gaze narrow on me even though I wasn't looking.

"They get killed when, like you, they fight it. If they rip themselves away and tear an artery they're done for. If they hold still, they are left conscious enough to walk themselves back into the club. We don't kill."

"Then why was my family sent to New York for a vampire problem if you weren't killing anyone?" I turned on her.

Instead of being met with the look of guilt I was hoping for, a flash of genuine fear passed through her eyes before being replaced by her usual empty stare. I tsked, shaking my head. So, there is a vampire problem in New York. They just don't know who, or what, it is and failed to keep it under wraps. When she finally spoke the edge in her voice returned.

"You expect me to be very forthcoming but offer nothing up yourself," she pointed out.

She had me there. I sighed, lying flat on the ground and shut my eyes. The sun beating into my skin felt wonderful, but I didn't let myself drift off.

Half of me wanted to continue to fight the trio who brought me here, thinking it would make me feel better in some way if I was always coming out on top. But the other half recognized I was creating the fights. They kidnapped me, yes, but usually that sort of thing results in selling and torture and slavery. I was living a life of luxury, with more freedom than I ever had before.

Now the question was, why? If it wasn't some sort of huge manipulative tactic in order to pass me or information to my father, then what was really going on here?

Rebecca had remained standing beside me, silent and motionless. She had made the offer to share some information, so long as I also shared. That was another thing we had in common, I realized silently to myself. Being open and vulnerable meant we demanded a price from the others involved, some type of physical or emotional insurance to protect ourselves. I felt the pit in my stomach ebb away a bit and for the first time with her, I relented.

"Fine. Ask me anything."

"You get the orders from Heaven?" The question blew through me like a shockwave. She frowned when I stayed silent. "You don't know where you get the orders from." It was a fact, not a question. I shook my head.

"New York was the first time I was let in on anything," I admitted, hoping I wouldn't regret giving the information. "Our Alpha, Luna, receives the orders, usually from human organizations such as churches or the CIA. They don't know what we are, and don't ask question so long as they get their desired result. But yes. All requests are filtered through Heaven first. By whom, that I don't know."

Rebecca released a frustrated sigh and plopped down next to me. I don't know why but I wanted to keep talking to her, at least about this. Rebecca, however, seemed done with it as she dropped down and copied my position, stretching out beside me under the sun.

"I take it back. You're not uptight. Definitely sheltered, it's obvious they taught you nothing–"

"They taught me how to fight." I interjected and she laughed, blue eyes reopening and looking at me with pity.

"They taught you how to suppress your instincts. You know how to punch a person and manipulate them for sure. But what you're practicing here? That's what they should have been helping you with all along. Instead, they tried to bury it."

"It was to protect me."

"It was to suppress you," she snapped. "To keep you at a level they could control. You think that Silas can control me?" She propped herself up on her elbows, "You're so dependent on those Hounds it sickens me. And why? Were you taught about magic or supernatural creatures? Womanhood? Reformation? Or did you just box in your basement all day and eat sugar cookies for dinner?"

I was on her before I even realized I'd begun to move. No vines, no shadows, just a good old-fashioned tackle. Well as good as a tackle can be when two people are already laying down.

And she was laughing. That high trilling, mocking laughter that I was beginning to hate as much as my Father. I cursed in her face and pushed myself off, getting up and stalking away back towards the house through the trees.

Screw this place, screw the vampires and screw her. I was going home.

I really should have gone home. A bar is not where one should go when they're pissed off, depressed, or vulnerable, which pretty much summed up my current state.

I don't know how much alcohol I drank. All I know is that eventually I was dancing, but this time as me. Jeans and a tank top, no partner, no show to put on. No hidden agenda of having to best a vampire. And no rules to follow under the watchful eyes of Hounds.

I was utterly free, and maybe that's why I did what I did. Maybe that's why I followed the cute young fauna who was wobbling his own way home. His goat legs were click clacking their hooves across the cobblestones which made him easy to track. Conversation was easy, he was so inebriated he probably would have started talking to the cave walls if I hadn't come along.

I honestly don't even remember biting him, but once his blood was gushing down the inside of my throat I couldn't stop.

Bleary eyed and hiccupping I fell through the front door of the house. I giggled, crawling across the floor on all fours. His blood was on my shirt and teeth, and I knew the three of them had materialized, like moths drawn to flame, as soon as the scent of it flooded the house.

I dragged myself to the window and pressed my forehead to the glass, gazing at the moon drenched landscape below.

Maybe this would get them to back off now. Or maybe this would just get me kicked out and sent on my way to do whatever I wanted. I didn't care. All I knew was that I had crossed a bridge that I couldn't uncross.

"Y'know that thing ya told me, about you guys not killing people?" I hiccupped, feeling Rebecca's icy gaze on the back of my head and let out a drunken laugh.

"Well, it turns out I do.

CHAPTER 14

Akashi hadn't slept in weeks. Or showered. None of them had.

Luna had cut off all contact with outsiders, her energy purely focused on finding her beloved daughter. They began their search where she disappeared, crossing every square inch of North America before moving on. Her blue hell fire orbs thrashed around her, racing through the trees, just as they had the night they first found Raven. They tore through valleys and across desert sands, searching wintry forests and damp caves, but came up empty handed.

Then they crossed the sea to search Europe, the birthplace of vampires. The island countries were covered in less than a week, and in that time the search turned to an argument: should they change track and head south, or continue east as they originally planned?

Akashi stood above the tempered ocean, eyes in narrow slits facing the horizon. His adrenaline was beginning to wear off, being replaced by a raw, gutting sense of fear. The only condolence the pack had was knowing Lucifer hadn't gotten his hands on her. If he had, he would have already acted. This much time wouldn't have passed in silence from both sides of the war. If anything, as nerve-racking as it was, it might be a good thing that Raven was missing. Neither side seemed to know where she was.

"She's not on this damned rock. Tomorrow, I say we start in Spain." Kumas voice was hoarse. "Make our way in country by country."

"No." Hikari interjected, "We'll be detected too easily by humans. Germany would be best and has always been a favored place for those devils. They helped cause two damned world wars."

"But it seems too obvious." Anzen protested, "It's been radio silent, so they took her somewhere with guaranteed privacy."

Akashi swallowed, throat feeling raw. He didn't want to imagine what privacy with vampires could mean. He turned from the horizon, motioning for the jug of water at Kuma's feet. As he drank his heavy eyes drifted around looking for his mother.

Luna had been in her Hound form since they set out on their search. Currently, she paced the cliff's edge, her orbs duller than Akashi had ever seen them. She was using too much energy, the spell sapping the life right out of her.

"You need to rest," he said flatly, giving her a wide berth as he approached and sat on the cliff's edge. His legs swayed freely, one inch too far and he'd go over. Luna continued to pace.

"She'll definitely be dead if you overuse your gift and can't find her." He dared to point out. A growl ripped from her throat, and she snapped her teeth in frustration. He turned to look at her fully, "You can't search everywhere at once so will you please let yourself rest—"

"I will not stop trying!" Her voice thundered through his skull. She sounded like she was in agony. Bile rose in his throat, and he doubled over, heaving up the tiny bit of water he just drank. Coughing, he sat back.

"I know you feel like we failed her." Luna froze, ears twitching towards him as he spoke, "We all do. I know the goal was to protect her. But honestly mom, we never prepared her for anything. Perhaps some of her anger was warranted, because look at where we are.

"She's been taken, with no control or awareness of what she can do on her own. She depends on us for strength and protection, and we aren't there. So, if someone breaks her rage... she'll have nothing." Akashi stood and turned towards Luna. He looked broken, guilty and desperate all at once.

"She was only careless because I always made her feel useless. Or stupid. I beat her down hoping to keep her small and under me so that she would let me protect her. She would always beat back at me, wanting to fend for herself, and instead of helping her I let my own ego get in the way, and now she's gone!"

Akashi was yelling now, fist slamming into his chest repeatedly, "At least the last conversation you had with her was somewhat productive. You know what the last thing I said to her was? I should have just called her a monster, reminding her of my scar like that! I refused to even look at her!"

"Calm. Yourself. Down." Luna's growl was so deep it caused loose rocks to skitter down the edge of the cliff behind her.

By now his brothers had gathered around them, wary of Luna's claws ripping up the earth beneath her. Kumas mouth was set in a thin line and Anzen was shaking, but it was Hikari who met Akashi's eyes. With a subtle shake of his head, it was clear: he was having a pity party, and it was helping no one. Least of all Raven.

Akashi snarled and turned his back on all of them, copying his mother and paced at the edge of the cliff. He ignored his brother's useless ideas, ignored Luna's jaws nipping at his heels. His eyes were wild and set on the skies above. A lethal sound left his lips, and he picked up a rock, chucking it towards the darkening clouds.

"I don't care if I have to set the whole goddamn planet on fire!" He bellowed, "I'm going to find her! Do you hear me!? And I'll burn down every single one of your God's precious kingdoms to do it!"

In a burst of light and smoke he transformed, tearing into the ground in a fury, all of his muscles on fire as he bit and barked and howled in his rage up towards the Heavens, a promise he would destroy everything God had created in order to find her.

"If you're quite done child." Growls sounded up on every side of him. His family had transformed and surrounded him without him even being aware. Akashi whipped his head towards the new voice with a snarl and spotted a figure standing a few yards away. No, hovering rather, because they were idling over the open sea.

"Gabriel. Leave us." Luna growled from Akashi's side. Akashi was barely able to mask his surprise. So, this was Gabriel?

The Angel didn't appear as anything other than mundane. Tanned skin, black hair, white eyes. His robes were unflattering shades of gray and cream and his face was void of any expression. However, when he spoke his voice was laced with contempt.

"All due respect Luna, but you receive your orders from us, not the other way around."

"If you even think of laying a finger on my son—"

"Unless you plan on killing an Angel today, just let him get it over with." Akashi cut her off, his rage subsiding enough to recognize the gravity of his threats. Luna bared her teeth but slowly backed away from her son, his brothers following her lead. Gabriel flashed a smug smile, approaching Akashi's side nonchalantly.

"At least one of you still knows how to submit to a master. Perhaps he should be in charge of Heaven's little task force from now on." With a raised brow he shifted his gaze to Luna, "How about it? Time for retirement?"

"Just to be clear, if kicking your ass wouldn't waste more of my time from finding Raven, you would be so dead right now," Akashi muttered. Gabriel chuckled and raised his palms.

"Relax. Just making small talk about the future." His tone grew serious, "To ease your rage I can assure you we have the same goal. It is not wise to leave the half angel unchecked, given her company, so I'll help you find your heart's desire." Akashi bared his teeth, hackles raising. Gabriel just raised his eyebrows further, while releasing a humored laugh, "Oh, I see that's still a touchy subject."

"If you know where she is you're toying with me—"

"Only the Almighty himself knows, and he hasn't offered up that information." Gabriel cut off what was sure to be another death threat. "Alas, there are other ways I can help you." He edged close enough to place his hands on either side of Akashi's skull, a crackle of electricity popping at the contact. Gabriel's grin was dark, "Now be a good pup, and yield." He commanded.

There was a burst of white-hot pain behind Akashi's eyes, but he swallowed his howl and remained still. The pain steadily grew, so much Akashi was forced to the ground and panting by the time Gabriel finally dropped his hands. He felt like his head was in a fishbowl, hearing the shouts of his mother but couldn't make out the words. Gabriel offered no words before he shot towards the sky, leaving the Hounds there as Akashi finally submitted to his agony.

"What do we do!?" Kuma's voice. Akashi was surrounded by a hazy white glow that was burning his eyes and making his fur steam. He could hear Luna barking and growling, snapping at the light but unable to penetrate whatever shield had been encased around him. His heart was beating like a beast, and for a moment he thought his ribcage would burst open from its impacts. And as abruptly as it appeared, the light retreated.

"Akashi!" The anger from Luna's voice had all but vanished, replaced with a frantic terror which made his head snap up despite the aching in his body. She had transformed, her tiny human hands cradling his head.

Drool was dripping from his muzzle, and he panted heavily, eyes drooping against the remaining sparks of pain in his skull.

"I will find her." His voice echoed in his family's heads, tired, but determined.

All of them, including Luna, were frozen in shock as he stood.

His green eyes were fixated on the horizon again. A fiery pulse was within them, matching the flickering green light snaking from his body down the cliff. They darted across the sea and to the land beyond it. "I will find her." He repeated, and then dove off the cliff, leaving his family to follow.

"What the fuck!?" Kuma shouted.

Anzen had already followed, the auburn-haired Hound diving off the cliff after his brother with no hesitation.

"Is he soul-searching?" Hikari was frantic in his confusion and searched Luna's face for answers, but she was staring at the sky in a daze. Slowly she stood just as Kuma disappeared over the edge as well.

"Mother!?" Hikari snapped, harsher than he intended. Luna's eyes drifted to her eldest son.

"Let's go. We best not waste the gift your brother received."

CHAPTER 15

There was shouting when I woke. Something was thrown against the wall, the pieces scattering across the floor looked blurry, so I rubbed my eyes. Rebecca was standing over me, but her back was to me. Her finger was pointed at something across the room, and she shouted again. More glass smashed above me and again she shielded my body as it rained down slicing at her skin. I shoved her off, bracing my arms against the wall trying to stand.

"What's happening?" My head was throbbing like I had gotten kicked in the skull. She ignored me, still arguing with whoever was across the room. I turned and looked over my shoulder, finally realizing what the problem was.

The fauna was standing in the main hall, chucking pots and glasses and other miscellaneous objects the crowd forming at our door were tossing to him.

"Shit," I hissed, ducking in time to miss someone's shoe flying at my head. I could make out Finn's broad shoulders against the crowd, his golden hair flying as he kept shoving people back outside.

"Murderer!" The fauna leveled a finger at me, pure hatred burning in his eyes as he readied himself to chuck someone's walking stick.

"You would have to be dead for that to be accurate," I grumbled. Rebecca smacked me on the back of the head, and I saw stars. I sank back to the floor, just beneath the frenzied flight of the walking stick as it soared for my head.

"Shut up Rave! You tried to kill the guy! Do you know what this place does to awakening vampires who can't keep their bloodlust in check?"

"Awakening vampires?" I met her eyes confused. Her steel gaze relented just for a moment and that moment was all I needed to get the picture.

It was a cover story for my unprovoked attack. An explanation for why I was living here and my foul temper. Rebecca averted her gaze and began yelling back at the fauna and crowd once more. She rained a mixture of explanations and threats down on them until most of their rage began to dissipate.

Briefly, I wondered if it was also her cover story. Surely, she was hiding who our Father was as well? And it would explain why she openly drank blood in public and no one bats an eye. But why was she defending me so fervently?

Suddenly, Silas was worming his way out of the crowd, popping out from under Finn's shoulder to march across the threshold towards the fauna. Dramatically he dropped the black burlap bag he was carrying at his feet, kicking it with his boot to spill gold coins across the floor that skittered against the man's hooves.

"I just went to the bank. This should be more than enough to compensate for your medical bills and mental health." He said while dusting his hands off on his coat.

"Ooh you keep your blood money," the fauna kicked at the coins like they were pests, launching a few out the door to the spectators who moments before were aiding him but now ate up the free money. He squared his shoulders, getting in Silas' face, "I don't want anything from you devil born beasts."

Goosebumps littered my skin as my heart rate suddenly jumped into my throat. How dare he speak like that; he doesn't know the half of it. I lunged forwards but Rebecca caught my arm and knocked us to the floor.

"Oh, Rave come now, you're too ill to stand." I flashed a glare at her, but she answered with one that had more venom in it than I could handle at the moment. Silently I nodded and played along.

Silas hadn't reacted other than the gleam in his eye brightening slightly. He took a half step forward, crowding the fauna, and when he spoke his voice was lower than normal.

"I am a blood born devil as you say, so perhaps don't forsake my kindness." The fauna took a step back, suddenly realizing his position. Silas pressed on, "Who is anyone here to know why you were in an alleyway, half naked with a woman you don't know? Clearly a woman who is going through a great deal to top it off."

The crowd at the door wavered and for a moment, I felt bad. These people were just trying to defend themselves, and not from a perceived threat. I had tried to kill. But living in an underground city with vampires, willingly being there and not running the vampires out? Their reaction seemed incomprehensible to the trio currently defending me.

"This was not a matter of intention, but one of circumstance." Finn spoke up, "You are all aware of newborn vampires' tendencies. So, try to be more aware of yourselves, rather than attacking this young woman for her behavior. By doing so, you're acting no better than a human."

There was a collective groan of disdain and remorse before the crowd began filtering out of sight. The fauna, swallowing his pride, bent to claim the bag on the floor before disappearing along with them. Once the door clicked shut blocking out the street, the united front turned on me.

"What were you thinking, exactly?" Finn forced out between grit teeth.

"She doesn't think! She just does whatever she wants because she's never had to deal with the repercussions before." Silas materialized in front of me, slamming his boot into the wall beside my head. Behind him Rebecca stared down at me with dead eyes.

"Let's get one thing straight you little bitch," he snarled in my face. "I will not save you from yourself again. We are not your dogs, and you are not our master."

The tile beside my head cracked as he pushed himself backwards. Rebecca reached out to him, but he ignored her, stalking upstairs and out of sight. She winced as we heard the echo of his door slamming shut.

I swallowed; my tongue felt like leather in my mouth. I didn't know what

to say. Rebecca turned and also left,
disappearing through the door
underneath the stairs, leaving Finn and I
alone.

He looked disappointed. I felt sick.

The door under the stairs reopened
and Rebecca emerged with a glass of
water. Crossing to me she forced it into
my hands before climbing the stairs. I
heard her knock on Silas' door. Knock
again. A third time. I released a breath I
hadn't known I was holding when I heard
the door finally open allowing her inside.
Then and only then did I raise the glass
to my lips, appreciating her small but
kind gesture, and drank.

"Why did you try to kill that fauna,
Angel?" Finn asked. The question hung in
the air between us like a ticking bomb. I
stalled and took another long drink of
water. But I was exhausted, so I
answered honestly.

"I thought it would make you guys
want me to leave." The silence between us
was deafening. I could see Finn's jaw
working as he developed a response.
Again, I tried to stand, slowly pushing
myself up against the wall. "What
happened to my head?"

"First time with someone else's
blood in your body. Eventually it doesn't
happen, unless you drink someone's blood

who's been poisoned." His response was monotone, so I acknowledged it with a simple nod before shuffling towards the stairs to my room. Dear lord, the stairs.

"I didn't dismiss you."

"Dismiss me? What am I now, YOUR puppy?" I couldn't help the snarl that ripped from my mouth. "You know, you and your brother might talk a better game, but you're the same as my brothers. The only difference between you is that you don't forbid me from finding out what's natural. But none of you help. All of you fear or think the worst of me. So, if it's all the same to you, I would like to not be wanted so leaving doesn't hurt anybody."

"It would hurt you."

"Well, I'm hurt anyway!" I screamed as I reached the banister, slapping my hands down on the rail to keep myself up. "I'm hurt, confused, scared, and punished for not knowing how to handle anything flawlessly, especially myself. As far as I'm concerned you all can rot in hell!"

Finn had his hands under my arms then, holding me up as I began pulling myself up the staircase. I ignored him being there, I had to. I couldn't cry in front of other people. Couldn't be weak because I'd be a target. Couldn't fight back because I was dangerous. People could hurt me, yes. But I could kill somebody without even knowing how I did it.

So, step after step I dragged myself up, tears falling at my feet soundlessly. Finn kept me upright all the way down the hall and into my room before I shoved him away slamming the door in his face.

I collapsed in my bed, shrieking into my pillows. I was in agony, absolute agony. My thoughts raced, bringing with them punishing images. Akashi's scar. My mother's body in a pool of golden blood. The shadowy hand of my father reaching out towards me. Rebecca's snarky laughter beat against the clang of my mother's sword, and I felt like my skull would explode.

I couldn't breathe so I pulled the pillows off my face, openly wailing into my room. Was this grief? Frustration? Fear? My heart pounded in my skull so viciously I felt like I would faint. But through that painful haze, there was a gentle caress.

Cool fingers parted my hair. My back was pressed into a solid, unwavering chest behind me. I could feel Finn's calm steady breath, the polar opposite of the ragged gasps my lungs desperately sucked in. His hand slid over my eyes, pulling me with him to lay down. I twisted, pathetically trying to slip from his grip but his arm snaked around my waist keeping me in place.

I focused on regulating my breaths. Sleep started to mull my mind, so I was confused as my cheek rubbed against the silk of Finn's shirt rather than the soft fur of Akashi's bulk. Immediately I felt the tears coming again.

When did he stop comforting me? When did I suddenly become a burden to him? When did we drift apart, pretending like we were never vulnerable with each other, like we didn't care that we once were? The last thing I remembered was the soft thuds of Finn's heart, spaced so far apart, before sinking into nothingness.

CHAPTER 16

"Silas?" When I woke Finn was asleep under me, golden hair again splayed out around him like a halo. His grip was relaxed, so it was easy to pry his arm off and slip into a shadow at the base of the bed. I materialized in the kitchen, waiting there for a breath to make sure I didn't wake him before creeping up the stairs to Silas' room. I paused outside, not wanting to knock and risk it waking Finn. I didn't know how good his hearing was, but at the very least I knew Silas could hear me through the door. If not smell me. I tapped my foot impatiently. "Silas open up. Or I'm coming in." I whispered through grit teeth.

"Jeez, you're so pushy." The door swung open and immediately I took a step back. Blood was dripping down his chin onto his bare chest. His hair was a ruffled mass of black, making his ruby eyes seem to practically glow in the dark. For a moment, I thought he would rip my throat out right there. That was before I noticed a flash of movement over his shoulder. Illuminated in the moonlight, Rebecca sat on the balcony rail, her bare back to me. I could see a trickle of blood rolling from the back of her neck to disappear over the front of her shoulder. Silas eased the door shut keeping her just out of view. "Thank you for interrupting what was sure to be a marvelous evening for me."

"My apologies." I tried sounding sarcastic, but it just came out flat. I tapped my bottom lip, "You have something right here." I muttered. Silas grunted, turning to wipe the blood off his mouth, eyes catching on something behind him before turning back to me.

"If you can muster a little bit of patience, let's go for a walk. Let me find a shirt first." The door swooshed shut, so I stepped back and waited against the railing above the stairs.

When he reopened the door, I was taken aback by his insanely mundane t-shirt and jeans, so unlike his typical gothic garb I did a double take. Rebecca wasn't with him. Apparently if there was a goodbye between the pair, it was brief. His words to me were clipped.

"Now, we will walk. But in all fairness my patience with you is completely spent, so," I stifled a yelp when he grabbed me by the wrist, yanking me with him as he began to teleport.

We emerged somewhere outside, and instead of just releasing me he shoved me backwards. I landed with a splash, and realized we were at the lake. The waterfall seemed to roar louder now, and the red pool appeared more purple in the pitch black. I bit back an immediate complaint, thinking back to one of the last conversations Luna and I had. My temper would be the death of me. She didn't say so directly but given my present situation I knew to choose my words carefully if I wanted to achieve anything here.

"I know I deserved that," I muttered, hoisting myself to my feet and wringing my hair out.

"You deserve much worse," Silas drawled, casually leaning against the trunk of a willow while pretending to inspect his nails. I frowned.

"You don't truly mean that." His gaze snapped to mine, and those red eyes flickered,

"Unless mind reading has emerged as one of your powers, you can truly never know how any of us feel about you."

"I know for some reason you care the most." My comment seemed to stun him. That arrogant posture and know-it-all smirk wavering. "Finn always keeps a level head, then tries to seduce me.

Rebecca acts unbothered, while pressing me for answers. Out of the three of you, you're the one who keeps letting your emotions get the best of you." I knew this because I as well, when I cared, let my own emotions rule my reactions. I wade out of the water, moving to stand beside him.

"At first, I thought it was just out of some feeling to protect Rebecca, but the fauna had nothing to do with her. She wasn't in any danger, and yet you still reacted more vividly than anyone in the room. More than myself even. Why?"

Silas frowned at me. I could tell he was arguing with himself about what information was worth giving up, so I did the kindest thing I could. Brushing past him I weaved my way out of the drooping willow branches and began to walk across the darkened terrain. When I heard him start to follow after me, I released a breath of relief. We walked silently for a few minutes, which I didn't mind because I hadn't gotten to see what this place looked like in the dark yet.

Stars flickered like tiny orange flames against the black night sky. A half-moon reflecting purple light flickered between the tree branches. Petite golden fae zapped about in the dark like fireflies at supersonic speeds, leaving a fading

trail of golden dust in their wake. The
breeze was thick with the scent of
peaches and rosemary, an interesting but
pleasant combination. Upon further
inspection I realized it was the scent of
black flowers blooming in thick clusters
at the end of a few branches dangling
over us. I took mental note of that, hoping
to maybe come back and forage a few to
make a perfume out of.

Something itched at my spine with
that thought. I never bothered with
anything girly like perfume before, why
should I bother with it now? An annoyed
sigh came from behind me, and I stopped,
realizing Silas had gone still a few paces
behind me.

"You're irritatingly perceptive," he
grumbled, and I bit back a smile. "I don't
know how familiar you were with
vampires before meeting us–"

"You were the first one I met." He
frowned at the interruption.

"How unfortunate for me," He
drawled and shook his head. "Finn and I
do not live our lives as most other
vampires. There's the common trope,
living in the human realm and sucking
them dry for food and sometimes
pleasure. Then there's the vegans, who
somehow believe they are less monstrous
than everyone else because they drain

less intelligent beings," he emphasized with air quotes, "which is just every other warm-blooded creature that's not humanoid. They can't communicate with them like we can human or fey or others like them, so they feel less guilty. Then there's us, the rarest–"

"Of course, because you're dramatic like that." I interrupt again and earn another glare from him. "What? Are you Shakespeare presenting a monologue or are we walking and talking?" He snorted, slightly humored before continuing,

"Finn and I only drink from humans when it's necessary, to stay healthy. Then we wipe their minds of the event. Believe what you want but we get no satisfaction from the torture of it all. That makes us unique, like your family." His words grew heavy, and he released a sad chuckle, "Evil creatures not enjoying the inherent evil natures they possess? What to do with them? Perhaps utilize them for good instead?"

I couldn't tell if his questions were rhetorical or not, so I didn't answer. He let out a disappointed groan, "That thing about you being perceptive apparently doesn't carry over to reading between the lines, does it?"

"Well, you're beginning to speak in riddles so how am I supposed to–"

"Bad creatures used for good errands, Raven." He leveled his gaze at me, "Don't tell me that phrase doesn't fit your family's work."

It clicked into place now. My family, Hellhounds, designed by the Devil to destroy everything in their path at his command, didn't like their job. Didn't like their lives, so they left and got a new one. I hadn't met any other vampires living in Atlantis, and Finn and Silas were living with Rebecca instead of their own kind who usually stayed together in covens of at least twelve. They must have left some type of life they felt miserable in too.

"So, what does your freakishly good nature have to do with me and Rebecca then? I can't believe you wound up with both the Devil's daughters by mere coincidence." I push slightly further. I'm not trying to trample on the details that Silas clearly felt vulnerable sharing, but I needed more.

I took a step towards him, "Please Silas. I know you know something about me that I don't. Someone in my life needs to stop trying to protect me or teach me, someone needs to tell me something."

I was begging now. I knew it, he knew it, but it didn't feel weak to do it. It felt necessary.

Something in his eyes shifted, something almost like pain, and he opened his mouth. But before he could say anything a roar broke through the night, and I could smell blood.

CHAPTER 17

"What the hell is that thing?" I screamed over the avalanche of noise behind us. Silas and I were sprinting now, cutting between the trees like bolts of lightning.

"Think of it as your equivalent to a bear!" He shouted back, zig zagging out of the way of a flying boulder. A whole tree branch whizzed past my head like it had been shot as an arrow. "A very angry viking bear!" He added lunging to the left to knock us both out of the way of the rest of the tree that branch belonged to.

"So then why the fuck are we running? Can't we teleport?"

"It can teleport!" He responded and swore.

"Shadow jump?"

"I can't do that," we dodged another flying log, raising our arms to shield our faces from the spray of dirt and pebbles it sent up, "and you, my dear girl, are not talented enough to drag me through that veil with you yet."

"So, then what can we do?"

"They don't like water."
Incredulously, I whipped my head towards him,

"Then why are we running AWAY from a literal body of water?!" I shrieked, lighting flames on my forearms to burn through a patch of brush ahead of us to make our path clearer. I glanced at Silas again and his face was blank. I raised my eyebrows, "You got so wrapped up in our conversation you forgot you threw me in a lake?"

"Pond."

"Whatever!" I let it drop though because we had switched course, running back up the hill towards the willow trees. My heart throbbed thinking of the beast behind us tearing through their thickly woven trunks and drooping branches, I didn't want them destroyed. I reached out a hand towards them, whispering out a desperate command, *"Reformidant."* The trees disappeared before our eyes, getting sucked back down into the Earth to hide and wait this out.

"Enough games, now get in there!" Silas hissed, shoving me ahead of him. I launched myself into the water, swimming to the far side of the pool towards the waterfall.

Another loud roar sounded behind us and I sucked in a breath, ducking my head under the water, passing under the fall. When I broke the surface I immediately turned and yanked Silas into the tiny crevice in the rock from centuries of water running over the stones. Despite trying to pull him in, Silas' shoulder still broke through the current of water, so he was still very much visible.

"Shit! It's gonna see you! It doesn't like water, but will it tolerate it to attack us?"

"Zip it!" Silas spun us around, pressing his broad frame into the crack as far as it could go and pinned my back to his chest. I protested, turning my face to the side and out of the rushing water.

"Listen to me!" He hissed, "You have about ten seconds. Manipulate the water to fall around us enough to hide us, and make it look natural." He leveled his gaze at me, appearing completely calm. "This is part of your power Raven, now's not the time to hold it back. Do it!"

There was a heart wrenching yowl from behind us which drowned out any possible doubts or hesitations. Ten seconds. I took a single breath, then let myself explode.

Well, expand, really. It wasn't a forceful burst of power; this was something more delicately woven. My palms lay flat against the water and slowly, almost too slowly, it grew into a thick cocoon around us.

"Get my foot on the ground." I whispered and Silas obliged, guiding my leg back to rest my foot on a small outcropping between his own feet. I pressed my heel into the stone, forcing the earth backwards, making the gap behind us grow deeper as the water in front of us grew heavier. At this point I was only still upright because of the grip he had on my waist.

Just as I became fully hidden by the curtain of water in front of us the creature crested the hill. I would have shrieked in horror if not for Silas slapping one of his hands over my mouth.

Its head was a bare skull, with flaps of dried, dead tissue hanging from its empty eye sockets and maw. Its gray body did indeed resemble a bear except it walked on its two hind legs. All four limbs were just sharp exposed bones dripping with blood, flesh and shredded entrails of beings that I didn't want to think about. Silas and I stayed frozen like that as the creature paced at the water's edge, barely twenty feet from where we hid.

My hands were starting to go numb from the excursion of holding the same intensity of power for this long. I never realized how little endurance I had until now and this was NOT the time to run out of energy. The 'bear' continued to pace but started working its way further down the bank clearly having no interest in approaching the waterfall at all. Until the spell began to ripple differently.

I was silently panting now, and Silas could feel it. I felt his grip on my waist tighten, a warning sign to not let up now or we'd have to run again to have a chance. Suddenly, the hand he had firmly pressed against my mouth surged forward, and his wrist was pressing against my lips.

"Bite me." His voice was a breath above a whisper, "Now. For energy." I shivered but did as he said.

I don't know if my normal teeth simply retract and are replaced by fangs, or if they lengthen and sharpen. However, it happens much too naturally for my comfort level.

I sank my teeth in, surprised at the difference in taste. While the fauna's blood was tart like citrus, Silas' was sweeter like the old-fashioned hard candies Luna used to bring home from the city. He bent his hand away, not enough to rip my teeth out himself but enough to ask me to let go. Greedily I sucked in one more gulp before complying.

The water around us wasn't rippling anymore but the bear still stared our hiding place down. Momentarily I panicked thinking it would catch a whiff of blood on my lips, but it didn't. After what felt like an eternity, it gave one last roar of annoyance before disappearing back down the hill.

I didn't let up on the water right away, I kept that shield up as long as I could until it finally wavered once more before completely dropping around us. The Earth behind us lurched forward back into its normal formation knocking us both off balance and back into the water. This time it was Silas who reached for me and pulled me along to the opposite shore from the one the creature disappeared from.

I heaved myself out of the water and rolled onto my back on the bank. Silas did the same beside me. When I finally caught my breath I raised my hands to my face, rubbing my palms into my eye sockets trying to ease the headache I could feel coming on.

"I'm only gonna ask you this one time, and I'm not above trying to kick your ass right now if I think you're lying," I mutter, feeling Silas sit up beside me.

"There was no way we could get away from that thing. We had to hide, and I had to use my power. Right?"

"There was another way to get away." He didn't even hesitate, and I felt my anger flare. Dropping my hands, I glared up at him, but he quickly went to add, "If I didn't think you were capable, I would have teleported us to the house. Yes, the thing can teleport, I didn't lie about that. But we have wards put up. The only ones who can teleport in and out are me and Finn."

"And Rebecca." I add, but he releases a laugh.

"No, she shadow jumps. Like you." He ran a hand through his dripping air, "Unfortunately for us we don't know how to block that, so I guess you can also pop in and out whenever you want."

"Well, how convenient," I mutter sarcastically, feeling the ache in my arms as I push myself off the ground. Silas reaches up catching my wrist.

"About your earlier question," I pause, not ripping my hand away since I want him to continue. "I was trying to allude to a fact without saying out loud… because I've never said it out loud."

There was a shadow of guilt on his face I had never seen before. The muscles in his arms were tense. Whatever he was about to tell me was causing him physical stress and pain even now. His voice was strained when he said, "The only reason why the Hounds needed to save you was because I failed." I felt a pit of confusion and fear drop in my stomach,

"What?"

"They don't know." Silas' eyes met mine. They were so clear, so giving, "I swear to you, they had no idea about me or my brother until you came to our club. In fact, I don't think they even knew about your sister because we successfully got her." I felt my knees buckle and Silas cursed, shifting his body to break my fall.

"That doesn't make any sense," I breathe out, mind spinning.

"Yea well, Angels never make sense. And never want to get their hands dirty. We are valuable chess pieces for them to play, considering our abilities. Same with your family." I could hear my heartbeat pounding in my ears, like a freight train getting faster about to mow me down as he continued rambling explanations, "The Hounds saved you, but if I didn't screw up, we would have gotten to you before what happened in that church–"

"Enough!" Finn was standing over us. He pulled me to my feet while snarling at his brother, "We agreed no manipulation. No history. None of it. She's supposed to have a fresh slate."

"Even though she's asking for the opposite?" Silas leaped to his feet as graceful as a cat, retreating a few yards away from his brother.

"I didn't hear her asking anything about how we are connected to Angels."

"She wanted to know how we were connected to her, and last time I checked she is an Angel."

"You know what I mean—"

"Were you there when my mother died?" My voice wavered but both of them fell silent. I lifted my chin, adamant, "What aren't you telling me?"

"We weren't there when Mary died." Finn said, easing some of the bite out of his voice. Though his features were hard, and his eyes trained on his brother, I could feel the guilt sweeping off him in waves. Off both of them.

"You're leaving something out," I pushed, feeling anger begin to flare in my body once more. Finn must have sensed it because he took a step away, as if remembering being impaled by thorns the size of traffic cones.

"We were with Rebecca, after her mother Kitty died." Silas said, exchanging another glare with his brother. "We were too late getting to you. You were already

gone. And Mary was already ash."
Abruptly, I started laughing.

"Kitty? The name of an ancient
mythical creature, the Sphinx, ruled and
revered, was Kitty?" I doubled over, tears
dripping down my cheeks. I was laughing
so hard my stomach felt like it was
flipping.

"It was a nickname," Silas
muttered.

"Angel, I think it's best if you
return home now." Finn said, hand
cupping my cheek. "You've had an
emotional day and ingesting blood for the
first time does unkind things to the body."

"And ingesting *my* blood on top of
it will definitely throw you for a loop, if
not make you high as a kite." Silas added
cheerfully.

Perhaps I was high, my head was
definitely feeling like a balloon now, the
pace of the freight trains pounding
retreating into peaceful waves. Finn's
demeanor shifted to that of absolute
death.

"You drank his blood?" He asked
slowly.

"Pinned against me behind a
waterfall no less. I might have been the
screw up between the two of us, but—
geez!" Silas cut himself off, jumping
backwards as Finn lunged for him. I

sobered myself enough to put myself between them, shoving into Finn's chest and feeling us skid a few inches.

"Stop it. I was running out of energy manipulating water. To hide us from that…thing. It gave me more energy. I'm running out of energy." I repeated, now feeling somewhat dazed. I circled the conversation back to the topic at hand, twisting my face to Silas while keeping my palms pressed to Finn's chest.

"What do you mean you screwed up?" He visibly winced and looked away.

"We were supposed to take you and Rebecca together. It was all set up between your moms and the Angels. However, we were… I was lazy." Silas corrected after another lunge from Finn which I somehow managed to hold back. "I didn't watch our trail and led Lucifer straight to you all. We got Rebecca out. Mary fled with you. Kitty… didn't make it. And once we failed to get you, we weren't given another chance. The Angels had the Hounds step in, a backup plan we weren't even aware of at the time, and that was that."

My pulse was beating like a drum against my skull as I backed away from them. All this information— all of these facts about my life which I finally had access to. I should be demanding more answers, getting the rest of the puzzle put back together here and now, but there were two facts that I didn't expect, and it was throwing me off.

I had known Rebecca as a child. We were supposed to be saved together. So why don't I remember anything about her at all?

CHAPTER 18

"If it's any condolence I don't remember you either," Becca muttered. I made it a point to shorten her name, as she seemed content with calling me Rave until the end of time. If she had any argument while I shouted for her in the club, she didn't voice it while shoving me into the seat across from her.

Her lips puckered, taking a long swig from the bottle in her hand before grunting, "And on the flip side if you feel insulted, I AM the youngest out of the two of us, so if anyone should be remembering anything, it should be you big sis."

I grimaced, looking away over the balcony which was a mistake. Just like last time the… events a few floors below us were already in full swing.

I was beginning to learn how to track my half-sister. Just follow the music and the lights, and if I came up empty handed on that path then switch to searching outside in the wilds of Purgatory. Unfortunately, that's usually by tracking her Sphinx form, following the trail of bloody pawprints she left in her wake while she hunted.

We sought out the same environments, but I could tell on her part it was in an attempt to disappear. In a crowd or in the woods, it has the same effect. However, I craved those scenarios to be around people, or find myself. I guess after a lifetime of having limited access to society, it made me want any type of company. Even if it happened to be in places with such, revealing, activities.

I could hear her snickering at the look on my face and quickly dragged my eyes back to her. Again, it was required to wear masks to get in. Her icy blue eyes laughed at me from beneath the blood red rubies crowning her forehead and nose, stitched into a shimmering obsidian cloth which she had tied neatly below a simple braided ponytail. Since she seemed to be hanging out on the bar level tonight, she was in normal clothes, jeans and a black t-shirt.

I grimaced at the memory of my entrance. I had made a fool of myself by entering in a latex catsuit, this one black and gray like the shadows in the street. After her laughter attracted the attention of nearly everyone on this level, I quickly morphed the costume into a gray sweat outfit before seating myself. As if reading my mind, she released a dramatic sigh.

"Even though I was making fun of
the outfit you originally wore in here
doesn't mean that it was bad. It certainly
did more for you than this," she said,
plucking at one of my loose pant legs. My
mask was also simple, a plain rectangular
strip of black cotton with two holes cut
out for eyes.

"I only created that thing because I
thought it was a part of the dress code." I
groaned, again averting my eyes. While I
now appeared to just have rolled out of
bed, Becca still looked immaculate in the
simplest of attire. It was irritating.

She leaned forward a bit and
dropped her voice, "If you stop
threatening to kill me left and right, I
might have some pointers on how to dress
yourself."

"I know how to dress myself," I
shot back and she snorted, eyeing me
from head to toe. At this rate I was going
to need my own bottle to chug. She leaned
back and began counting off on her
fingers.

"Leather jacket, jeans, jean shorts,
combat boots, t-shirts, on a single
occasion fishnet stockings— tch. It's all
you wear! And now a sweatshirt." She
threw up her hands, annoyed, "You know
you have a whole closet full of clothes,
right?"

"Oh, you mean the one you filled with literally only those items? Plus, the ridiculous number of gowns that I'll never wear."

"Why not?" She was staring at me deadpan, the question completely serious. Uncomfortably I shrugged.

"No occasion other than training in my life. No skirts necessary."

"Is that why your hair is also only ever styled in a ponytail? And that you seem to believe mascara and ChapStick equals makeup?"

"I haven't worn mascara since the night you tried to kill me ya know?" At that she blanched.

"No fucking way you liar. You're wearing fake lashes at the very least!"

"What are those?" I saw her mentally about to pounce and I held up my hands, "Can you please stop butchering my appearance? I grew up with guys in the woods. And no offense to Luna, but an older lady who taught me nothing except how to survive." And how to care about other things besides my rage. Becca groaned.

"All I'm saying is if you can literally make clothes out of thin air why not have fun with it? I would."

I didn't have a response to that, and luckily, she didn't persist any further. I should let it go, it's not like it's one of my more useful abilities. Or dangerous ones. But...did I truly appear that plain and ugly?

I thought of my brother's reactions to me that day at the club. They really were thrown off by the outfit. I thought it was just because they never saw me in something like that before, but was it deeper than that? And Finn... he never really complimented me. Just my blood.

I could already feel this itching at me, so I waved my hand to get the attention of a female goblin working as a waitress and ordered my own bottle of whatever my sister currently had. Before I could ask about payment the Goblin nodded her head and said it would be added to the households tab. Well at least I was getting free alcohol in exchange for being kidnapped. Shamelessly, I ordered a second bottle.

We sat in silence for a while, but I could feel those blue eyes watching me, working out some unshared calculations about me. Just as I was about to tell her to cut it out she said, "I'm surprised, actually. With your lack of confidence. It's not something we were expecting." It was my turn to scoff this time,

"Yea well, try living your whole life being told everything about your abilities is bad and dangerous. Only to find out that you've been suppressing something that feels more natural than anything you've ever done. On top of being isolated from the outside world. I know your mom died too," She bristled but said nothing as I finished, "but at least you got to live to some degree. I don't know what to call what I've been doing."

It dawned on me then that perhaps I was a little mad at my family. There must have been many other ways to safely handle my situation, Becca was proof of that. But instead, I pretty much got locked up.

Luckily, the waitress returned before I could say anything else to make myself sound like more of a whiny bitch than I already felt. I grabbed the first of the two bottles and without hesitation started to chug before abruptly ripping it from my mouth with a gasp, "What the fuc–" Becca whistled and clapped her hands.

"Second time drinking blood within a day. Damn you're gonna be a mess." She said and started laughing.

"Third, actually." I managed to choke out, staring at the bottle in my hand. Blood in a beer bottle. At this rate nothing about this place should surprise me. Becca's eyes widened.

"Damnit Rave, who else did you bite?"

I hesitated a moment, remembering how viciously Finn reacted to it, before deciding to be honest and quietly whisper, "Silas." Immediately her eyes narrowed.

"Explain." I did quickly, describing why we went for a walk in the first place, encountering the creature (a Monexblier she said), what happened behind the waterfall and how all that led to me searching her out here with sudden questions about our childhood memories.

I could see her visibly relax once understanding the nature of the bite, so I asked, "What does it mean? Drinking a vampire's blood?" I had a clear basic understanding of what it was for them to bite us, but the other way around I was unsure. "I mean I get that it's probably some type of intimate since Finn nearly took his own brother's head off over it."

"Men." She rolled her eyes, snagging my second bottle and helping herself to it before I could protest. "It's not overly complicated," she finally said, "Think of it as something you would do with a boyfriend. Or a girlfriend, I don't know how you swing yet. You wouldn't kiss anyone besides them on purpose unless you were in a situation which demanded it would you?" I nodded, understanding now. "What I don't get is why Finn was freaking out." She suddenly added, "It's not like you two are a thing." At my silence her mouth dropped open in shock, "No fucking way. Spill, now."

"There's nothing to spill. Silas bragged about getting a taste of my Angel blood– that was your fault by the way. So, Finn decided he wanted a taste for himself. That's literally it."

"Boo, that's boring." Becca slumped back in her chair disappointed. I kept a thin, slightly apologetic smile plastered on my face. She didn't need to know the extent of our interactions, whatever they were. To me it felt like flirting, sometimes, his incessant need for teaching me this or that. But he was a vampire. Surely all of this was just in his nature, right?

There was a knock on my door, so soft at first I barely heard it. Becca and I had returned to the house a few hours ago after we, dare I say, had a good evening out together. She muttered something about meeting her in the morning for a training session on the way up the stairs. At the look on my face, she rolled her eyes, insisting it would be a one-of-a-kind experience designed for her and I, unless I preferred boring boxing. I shot a small column of flame her way, just enough to make her cover herself in a thin sheen of ice before she disappeared down the hall, her laughter echoing behind her. I was beginning to not be so annoyed by the sound of it now.

I had a sarcastic remark geared toward her already coming out of my mouth as I opened the door, but cut it short when I realized it wasn't my sister paying me a visit. Finn was propped in the doorway, leisurely leaning against the frame. He flashed me a charming smile.

"I was wondering if you'd be up for a nightcap?"

"I'll pass. I have something to do in the morning." I shut the door halfway, blocking my pajamas (a faded Blink-182 tee and literal boy's boxers) from sight. I cringed on the inside briefly, feeling self-conscious and then disgusted for feeling self-conscious. As if sensing my unease Finn straightened himself, sliding his hands in his pockets.

"Genuinely just a quick conversation then?" He asked. I met his eyes, catching the hopeful and curious winks as his gaze shifted from my face to over my head into my room. He was wondering if I was hiding something. Disgruntled, I turn and walk to my bed grabbing a blanket to wrap around myself. Finn took that as his cue to come in, leaving the door ajar behind him. Somehow that action was comforting.

He doesn't hide the fact he's expecting to find something as he marches straight past me and into the bathroom. I sigh and look at the clock. 1:15. I need to go to bed.

"If you just ask, I'll let you know if I have a hostage that I'm sucking dry. Or where to find the weapons I've conjured and hidden." I hear him emerge from the bathroom but keep my eyes on the clock feeling myself smirk, "If you ask nicely, I might even be inclined to let you know which drawer my nice underwear is in." Real, real smooth you sick and twisted–

"The pair you have on now suits you just fine," he says and immediately I feel myself frowning. "They leave much up to the imagination," he continues, "and mine likes to run rather wild at times."

His breath hits my neck, and I don't need to turn to know he's seated himself beside me on the edge of the bed. Under the blanket all my muscles tensed.

"If you don't mind getting to the point, I'd appreciate it," I mumble, hugging my knees to my chest and propping my chin on top of them.

"I was just searching for any signs of your Reformation," he says, his tone downright cheerful. I side eye him.

"My what now?" His smile falters.

"Your Reformation. Every supernatural being goes through one when they physically mature." He says slowly. At my blank expression he stands up looking minorly concerned. "It manifests once your abilities strengthen. Did the Hounds never discuss it with you?" I wince and look away.

"There was a lot that was never discussed, apparently. I'm sure they truly believe it was for my own benefit." My stomach started to ache, the guilty and angry pains sweeping back in again.

"Well now that you've ingested blood there is no doubt Reformation is upon you. You're going to experience some changes."

"Is this going to be like a period talk? Because I don't need to go through that with a male again," I say holding up my hand to get him to stop.

Luna was horrified when I bled for the first time three years ago. The Hounds had believed up to that point with my mixed blood I wouldn't experience a menstrual cycle like my mother had during her humanity. Unluckily for me that bit seemed to have carried over, albeit a little late. Damn genetics.

I was with Hikari when it happened, and it was he who explained it all to me and got me tampons and my first heating pad. Every six months or so I dragged that heating pad out and buried myself in my room for a week. Up until New York, my blood had always run red. I shivered, not wanting to think about a golden period.

My thoughts snapped to Luna. It was the only time in my life I could remember her not being the strong-willed force she is. The shame of not preparing me still hung over her to this day, so I know if she was aware of this Reformation thing, she would have mentioned something to me.

"You... get a period?" Finn sounded half confused and half shocked. I groan, dragging my hands through my hair and feeling my face heat up.

"Never mind, I'm going to bed. Have a wonderful night, Finn." I stand, keeping the blanket firmly wrapped around my shoulders and cross the room to the open door. I look back at him expectantly and find him watching me with curious, and disturbingly hungry eyes. I slap the doorframe, snapping him out of whatever perverted vampire thoughts ran through his head.

"It's not going to be like that experience." He immediately reverts to the topic at hand, "Physical yes. But more so one-time visual changes, which will remain relatively the same then for, well, eternity." I harden my gaze on him and finally he jerks forward towards the door. Before I could slam it behind him, he slides a foot in the gap, "I'm sorry if I made you uncomfortable. I just wanted you to be made aware. So that if something happens you don't lock yourself in your room terrified–"

"I wouldn't do that."

"Or run away." He finishes softly. Reflexively my fist squeezes the blanket tighter.

"What could I expect to happen?" I ask softly. His red eyes flash– with sympathy not desire.

"I'm not worried about you being unable to take the physical strain. Some Reformations cause broken bones, others shedding, or development of new limbs." I picture it in my head, my body contorted in pain on the floor. Passing out probably. He continues, "I'm worried about the mental part for you. Lots of times the knowledge of forever dawning on someone is too much to bear. That and there's another thing as well."

"What other thing?" I snap, so sick and tired of information being kept from me until the last minute.

"When a person's memories have been lost or erased, they usually all come rushing back during Reformation. Rebecca's memories of you did not come back, because those were lost again after her Reformation six years ago." Six *years?* Damn I was behind.

"What are you saying?" I ask, voice quivering. There is true pain in Finn's eyes now as he says,

"Someone is purposely trying to guarantee you and your sister can not regain your memories of one another."

CHAPTER 19

Luna had not spoken since Akashi's powers were gifted to him. Akashi in turn had begun giving orders, which after only one moment of hesitation from Hikari, had been followed flawlessly by each Hound for the remainder of their search. It was an odd mix of pride and displacement Luna was experiencing. She had always hoped, known in her gut, that Akashi would take over for her one day. Though she never believed her alpha duties would be passed on to her son this soon.

Under his orders she had remained out of her Hound form, giving her body and spirit a chance to recover from being overworked. A chance to feed and bathe. To sleep.

Kuma had offered to be her carrier, so for the past few weeks she rode atop his back as they searched. She didn't protest this arrangement, though she was itching to be useful rather than succumb to the frantic thoughts tapping at her mind's door. She was able to remain composed, because unlike her haphazard

and frantic search Akashi was focused
and eerily calm.

Luna marveled at the difference of
Akashi's spell from hers. When she would
soul search, her misty blue orbs would
scatter with the winds, searching for their
target as a Hound would scent on the
breeze. Akashi's forged into the earth,
lighting up routes and avenues either
taken by the soul or in the direction of it.

She wondered briefly, if his spell
was so direct in its search because of his
relationship with Raven. It was most
definitely not an anonymous search.

They had swum across the short
channel between the United Kingdom
and France and remained on a strict
south-eastern course through Europe.
Akashi led them through the countryside
avoiding cities, traveling through
afternoons and nights only stopping to
rest when the sun began to rise until it
crested at noon. Finally, they banked
south into Italy and their pace slowed
down.

Wherever Raven was, it was within
this ocean-ringed country. The glowing
green spell pulsing in the ground leading
from Akashi's feet was a guarantee of it,
and the Hounds finally felt a glimmer of
hope. That was until the trail
disappeared beneath gentle waves

breaking on the beaches of the Mediterranean Sea before them.

"No, no, no!" Akashi was in a full sprint, plowing into the waves in a fury. In the dark, the faint glow of green drifted up from the seabed, continuing to the south-east before disappearing into the depths. Luna dismounted from Kuma who, with the rest of the Hounds, stopped on the shore.

She waded into the shallows up to her waist, disregarding her soaked clothing and Akashi's temper flaring beside her. Slowly she spread her palms against the surface of the water, a thin outline of blue glowing around her outstretched fingers. Not hearing a protest from their new Alpha, who despite his rage was paying full attention to his mother's actions, she let her powers drift out for the first time this month. Her light blue orbs appeared ahead of them, bobbing on the surface and following the fading pulse of Akashi's green beneath the sea.

"I believe our next destination will be Greece," she offered, voice thick and grating like sandpaper against her vocal cords. She realized she hadn't spoken since they threw themselves off the cliffs into the sea. "We can't swim that far. It will leave us useless once we reach the coast."

"We could rent a boat?" Anzen spoke up, his nervous gaze set on Akashi who had finally stopped pacing in the waves.

"We don't have their currency on us," Kuma muttered with an annoyed grunt.

"We don't need it," Akashi growled, eyeing a pier about a quarter mile down the beach. Luna frowned and shook her head.

"I am as desperate as you, but we do not steal Akashi. That won't bring any good fortune."

"I don't need good fortune." Akashi transformed, stalking down the beach on two stiff human legs, "I need to get across this damn oversized saltwater lake."

"It's a sea," Hikari said with a sigh, before surprisingly falling into step beside him. "There's only a few more hours of darkness. Let's go everyone— Akashi put some clothes on." The Hound shook the packs he carried off his back before also transforming. He tossed a black backpack to Akashi before he could protest, then grabbed his own to pull on jeans and sneakers.

Kuma and Anzen both hesitated before following their lead. Once dressed,

Kuma reached back for Luna, offering her his hand before they set out down the beach towards the pier.

Analyzing it as they grew closer, they realized it wasn't a tourist stop but seemed to be a docking and unloading pier for local fishermen. Other than the locked gate and single security camera, there was no security. Silently, Luna coaxed one of her orbs to float up from the sea to hover in front of the camera, blocking them from view as Kuma ripped the fence out of the ground. They weren't picky with their boat choice, climbing on to the first vessel to their left covered in crab traps.

"How do we start this thing without a key?" Anzen asked, brows creased in worried lines.

"There's probably a spare somewhere. Check the compartments," Hikari suggested. After a few minutes of searching, they did indeed find a spare, tucked away in a tackle box inside a storage bin. Anzen came up from below deck, announcing he found several refrigerated meals in a small cooler. With a single nod from Akashi, Anzen, Kuma and Luna retreated to below deck to eat. Hikari held his brother's gaze until he relented, allowing him to stay.

"Does this thing steer like a car?"
Akashi muttered while inserting the key
into the ignition. Hikari shrugged.

"I am not a sailor. But relax, we'll
figure it out." He clapped a hand down on
Akashi's shoulder and gave it a squeeze.
Together they cut the lines tying the boat
to the dock, and once the engine roared to
life Akashi slowly steered it out into open
water. A few turns later and it was on
course to follow Luna's bobbing blue orbs.

After several moments of silence
Akashi shifted his gaze to his brother and
asked, "How's Mom?" Hikari sighed,
running a hand through his hair.

"I think she's in shock. To be fair,
we all are. Raven being kidnapped, and
then thinking you were going to be killed
right in front of us. Not to mention we are
all trying to adjust to you being Alpha."
Akashi swallowed hard, his grip on the
wheel tightening. "Relax brother," Hikari
said, immediately noticing the subtle
changes, "none of us have a problem with
it. You won't be challenged for it. It was
just...out of the blue. I honestly didn't
think you would be Alpha until Luna was
no longer alive."

"Neither did I," Akashi admitted. It
was strange to suddenly be giving orders
to her. Even if he didn't outright
command her, it still felt odd. Unnatural.

"I'll admit I'm having a hard time addressing her. No offense to you guys, but I've always bossed you around. This doesn't make much of a difference. Except now I won't be told off by her when I'm about to screw up."

Hikari barked out a short laugh, "Well luckily most of the crap you come up with works. I'll be in your ear when I think you're about to go over the top. Respectfully." He added in at the end. Akashi leveled his gaze on his brother.

"Don't do that."

"Do what?"

"Make it weird." They felt the boat rock under their feet as they entered deeper waters, and Akashi accelerated the speed to make better time than they currently were. "I'm going to make it clear to everyone in the morning that nothing changed except Luna and I swapping positions. You're still Beta, if you wanna be. And no one needs to change their behavior. We don't need to revert to what we were taught as kids."

"Alphas are supposed to be revered and respected, not friends," Hikari recited with a roll of his eyes.

"We're family," Akashi said with a nod. "I want to be treated as such."

"And so you will be." Hikari agreed.

They spent the rest of the night in silence, Hikari eventually retiring downstairs to eat. Akashi spent the whole night up, deciding he would eat something quickly in the morning. This was his duty now. He needed to push himself as his mother had. They needed to be able to rely on him as they relied on her.

At daybreak Hikari returned above deck, relieving Akashi with a gentle proposition to go eat and rest. He would alert him when land was spotted. It didn't take much for Akashi to stumble downstairs, helping himself to the food they had saved for him before passing out for a few hours.

He awoke when he heard the engine cut off. Moments later the boat dragged onto the sand, creaking as it rolled back and forth with soft waves breaking against it. He met Hikari halfway up the stairs who immediately reported his soul-searching spell was laid out up the hills of Greece before them. They hiked for several hours along the coast and by sunset finally spotted some type of ruins outlined against the skyline before them. Exhausted as they were, they ran.

"Raven?" Luna called out immediately as they descended upon the ruins. The ground was more lit up here, flecks of green in the shapes of footprints, and highlighting areas of spilt liquid. Blood. Akashi snarled, catching Raven's scent over one of the smaller patches of blood. Several yards beyond that, it appeared as though someone else had bled out. Anzen was peering over a small crumbling wall just beyond that pool of dried blood and seemed frozen.

"Anzen?" Akashi barked and his brother flinched like he had been struck. He turned to him wide eyed.

"Raven was definitely here."

All of the Hounds rushed to Anzens side and peered over the small drop, and they understood why he seemed terrified. Thorns the size of small missiles littered the ground and were covered with dried blood. Akashi gulped and looked at Luna.

"I don't remember her ever making thorns that large."

"She has probably created far worse since being taken. Hopefully."

"Hopefully?" He repeated and Luna dropped her head.

"I was so scared of her powers drawing attention to her that she never learned how to properly use them. Just maintain them." Tears pricked her eyes, but she stood firm, "I hope she listened to her instincts, and created enough to protect herself. Come. Admiring what she's made here will not help us find her."

They refocused on the lines of green, the most prominent one leading up a crumbling staircase to their left. Climbing in single file with Akashi at the lead they rounded a sharp corner at the top and were faced with a solid black marble wall.

"Interesting," Kuma mumbled, "How likely is it that in the center of a thousand-year-old ruin, there is a single wall left in pristine condition."

"While being tucked away out of sight," Hikari added. Akashi was already working his hands around the crevices looking for a lever or switch of some kind. Suddenly there was a resounding crack, and the wall before them lowered into the earth transforming into a set of stairs leading down into the dark.

"Well, that was lucky," Anzen said from behind them. They turned to see him pushing a piece of marble the same shade of black as the wall into a hole in the ground at his feet. "I figured it might have something to do with it as it was the same material." He said with a shrug.

"Good job," Akashi said. Anzen smiled at the praise.

He took a few steps down into the earth, inhaling the scent of the darkness.

He paused, blood running cold. "Luna. Do you smell that?" His mother's mouth was set in a thin line. Every single one of them bristled as they took a deep breath and recognized the familiar scent of Purgatory, one of the realms of the underworld.

No wonder Luna's spell hadn't worked, this entrance was sealed off from the human realm. The last place she could have gotten them was the scene at the bottom of the staircase because, unlike Akashi's gifted ability, Luna's search couldn't travel between realms. Bitterly, Akashi realized he would have to thank Gabriel at some point.

Akashi straightened himself. Now was not the time to let his mind drift. They couldn't be distracted by the thoughts of the last time they were in this realm. Nor was this the time to hypothesize as to why the vampires brought her here. The only thing he focused on was the only fact they had: she was close. Armed with that reassurance he began to descend into the dark, his family following at his heels.

"We're coming, Little Bird." He whispered as the entrance above them closed, locking them in as they began to cross the veil between realms.

CHAPTER 20

I didn't get a wink of sleep. My mind was buzzing with the thoughts of locked away memories I didn't have access to, while my eyes were glued to the mirror in my room. I didn't particularly like or dislike anything about myself, but the thought of abruptly looking different put me off.

I ran my palms over my muscular stomach, turning to the right trying to accentuate any type of curves I currently had. My hair was longer than where I usually chopped it at the shoulders, but it was just flat and brown. Plain. I turned to the left trying to find something to pick out, something flawed or immaculate, but came up with nothing. In fact, the only thing I learned about myself from my intense search was that I liked my eyes. Like a body of moving water, they shifted from a deep blue at the edges to light green in the middle. There were even flecks of gold here and there, like sunlight reflecting on the surface.

Suddenly, thoughts of the gargoyle child shoot into my brain, about their comment of how my eyes went black in the school when summoning my father's power. I pray they don't change and stay like that.

By the time dawn rolled around I was buzzing with anticipation of the whole ordeal. I was so distracted by the thoughts of when it would happen, where, if my brothers would be there, that I had completely forgotten Becca and I were training. A quick left hook to my temple had me seeing stars and flying back into the present.

"You're now losing twelve to four. Are you even trying?" My sister cocked her head to the side, lightly bouncing on her feet as she danced away from the kick I sent towards her skull. We had exited the house a while ago, sparring in the morning light far beneath the outer windows of the house. I was surprised when she insisted on starting with hand-to-hand combat, but the familiarity helped shake off some of last night's anxieties. Some.

"I'm a bit distracted," I admitted while (finally) effectively blocking my face from her next attack. "Finn stopped by after we parted ways." I shook my head as her brows shot up in curiosity. "He only wanted to inform me of Reformation."

"Oh that?" Becca ducked as I spun, the heel of my boot narrowly missing her head. "I couldn't tell if you'd been through it yet. I figured not but I didn't want to be rude."

"Because I'm flat as a board?" I caught her fist in front of my face, twisting her wrist and sending her over my shoulder to slam against the dirt on her back. "Twelve to five." I mutter, hoisting her to her feet. She let out a grunt.

"Among other things." We began to circle each other again, "You're older than me, but visually I appear older than you. That's a bit off putting."

"I'm only in my immortal twenties, so don't get comfortable calling me old." I swing an elbow towards her neck. She deflects, and still manages to block my foot from cracking her ribcage.

"That's my point," she rolls, swiping my legs from under me and slams her palm into my chest, pinning me down. I growl and send her flying over my head again to land in the dirt behind me. "You're in your twenties and look like a teenager," we parried strikes to the face, "I AM a teenager and look like I'm in my twenties. Because I used my abilities." She sends me down with the same palm strike to the chest again. I try to hop back on my feet but slip on the sheet of ice she spread under me and land on my ass.

"Cheater."

"I think you mean winner. I reached thirteen first." She helps me up with a smug smile.

"What abilities caused your Reformation?" I ask, studying the ice under us as it steadily melts into nothing. She shrugs.

"I don't remember much about it before our moms, but I know that I've been able to use all my powers since I've lived here. So, I'm guessing she taught me about them all, and the strongest most likely caused my change. What about you?"

I study my hands. What powers do I possess? Do I have more than I'm aware of?

"No one really taught me about them. We don't know everything I'm capable of." I say, turning my hands over to study the backs of them as if there will be any tells of the missing information there. "When I disappear in the evenings, I usually come out here, trying to figure out how to work what I have. It's the most I've ever used them."

Becca stands there for a few minutes, contemplating what I've said. Finally, she turns and holds up a finger.

I'm confused until I see the mist appearing at her feet, not so unlike my brothers, as she transforms into her Sphinx form. The large black cat stretches out, opening its maw in a wide yawn. Those silver teeth glint near blinding in the sunlight.

"So, here's my idea," her voice enters my head. "Obviously you have a phobia of killing anyone let alone hurting them, regardless of what your angry outbursts claim." I frown but she continues, "I'm much harder to harm in this form. My bones are made of solid silver, and I can freeze my blood where I'm cut. So, let me see what you've got so far."

The cat sits and stares at me expectantly. When I don't move, she heaves a long sigh, "Raven you're wasting precious daylight."

"Aren't we too close to the house?" I ask, nervously glancing over my head. The rock face of the mountain can't be more than twenty yards away, putting the windows within range. The distorted landscape reflecting in the glass is the only sign of our home nestled in the stone, save for the few balconies protruding from our private rooms. Becca's cat form rolls its eyes.

"Face the other way. Dimwit."

I find myself turning, facing the open lands of Purgatory in front of us. I can feel the heat of flames thrumming in my fingertips, but I don't let any sparks pop just yet.

"What is the purpose of this?" I ask, not turning around to look at her. Does she want to confirm how dangerous I am? I've been comfortable here, but it's still possible they're plotting against me and this whole experience is a charade. I can be used as a weapon— are they planning to sell me out?

I feel Becca's bulk move to my side, and I grow rigid. She's completely relaxed and calm, laying out to sunbathe beside me waiting to see what I'll do.

"I think somewhere along the line, someone neglected to remind you that these powers are an extension of you." Becca's voice came up lazily from the ground where the Sphinx was sprawled out, "Not Dad. Not your mother. Not someone else's tool. They're yours. And if you don't want to use them at all today, I don't care. I just think it's important for you to know what you can do and be able to decide how to use them yourself."

Something inside me shattered at that. Smoke and flames billowed out into the woodlands, scattering all types of wild creatures but I didn't care. Controlling it didn't matter right now. Not when I was growing a rose garden beneath the columns of flame in the air. Not when those flames twisted and warped, dulling from their vicious orange to vibrant violet. Not when a world of shadows burst around me, the night taking shape as a shield around my body. Clouds swirled in the amber sky overhead, and I realized Rebecca was right.

These powers were *mine*. If they weren't they'd be representing the elements of this place, but the clouds overhead swirled in vicious blacks and blues. The lightning strikes were white and blinding like at home. I could feel my canines lengthening against the pouring rain and this time I didn't shy from it.

I could only imagine what I looked like standing there, the sun shining high overtop my own little world of perfectly balanced chaos.

I don't know how long I spent exploring my powers, pushing my stamina to its limit, but I knew when I had spent myself. I was on my knees, body shaking as I tried to reel it all back in. It was surprisingly easy to stop, I noted. I should make amends with Luna when I see her, because it turns out she was right. When my emotions weren't out of check, it was easy to summon my powers to turn on and off as she predicted.

With the last of my energy, I perfected the rose garden. Solidifying the vines, strengthening the roots, and searing the petals so hot they turned to glass and would never wilt.

Panting I dropped my hands to the ground, gratefully meeting a thin bed of ice spread under me. I lay flat on my belly, steam rising off every inch of me as my body temperature slowly cooled down and my heart slowed to a more normal rate.

Becca said nothing as I gathered myself, in fact she had said nothing since I let myself loose. I turned my head, surprised to find both Silas and Finn had joined the two of us outside. I blinked to make sure I wasn't seeing things.

"What time is it?" I finally asked, voice raw and averted my gaze from their three blank stares.

"Dusk." Finn's voice. "You kept that up all day." All day? It had barely felt like minutes to me. I shut my eyes, resting my forehead on the ice, feeling it crack slightly under the heat.

"Is this the part where you kill me?" It took me a moment to realize I asked out loud. I took their silence as confirmation and pulled myself to my knees.

To my surprise I wasn't met with a blade to my throat or mocking smirks. Becca was trying to appear nonchalant, but by the way her widened eyes gawked at the space before us I knew she was speechless from the power I displayed. Silas had his arm around her shoulders, eyes flitting between the glass roses and myself, a mixture of pride and relief on his face. Finn was the only one who seemed to have heard or decided to react to my question, concern masking the pride that was there moments ago.

"Whatever would we do that for?" He asked as he bent, capturing me in his arms and lifting me onto my shaking legs. I didn't know how to answer so I just shrugged. I didn't know what to expect any more from living my life backwards.

Just as I part my lips to explain myself my vision goes sideways. I hear Finn's voice but it's murky. Becca sounds far away. I rub at my eyes, feeling blinded as a white light grows and grows completely absorbing my field of vision.

My brothers always told me to never go towards the light as a kid. They never told me what to do if said light was erupting from my chest.

CHAPTER 21

It's a strange thing really, being asleep but being aware. They say that's what a coma feels like.

"She's pulsing." Silas.

"It's the Reformation, most likely." Finn.

"What if it's not?" Rebecca. She had to be carrying me, I felt fur against my cheek. Unless—

"Akashi?" Blindly I reached out. Who was I with? I remember who I saw last, but that could have been hours ago.

Disoriented.

I feel a strong hand grip mine. I don't feel fur on my face anymore. The scent of honey and cloves invades my nose. I flail my arms pushing the thick musk of it away.

He smelled wrong. His scent is damper, fresher. This is overbearingly sweet. And I'm burning up so much I fear I'll melt whatever it is so it's best to push it away. I feel like I'm floating in this heat, in the freezing ice covering my skin.

"I want Akashi." I moan again, curling in against myself on my side.

"You're going to be fine, Angel."

I nearly weep when I don't hear *Little Bird*, since when did I start missing that? I clamp my hands around my ears not wanting to hear the wrong thing again.

And then the pain hits me so fast I black out before I even get a chance to scream.

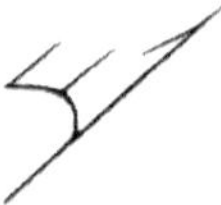

I expected to awaken one of two ways: in agony, bleeding and screaming, or like a goddess rising from a restoring slumber. Reality is a disappointment as I woke up like I took a normal nap.

Bleary eyed I sat up, causing my head to spin faster than any hangover. A quick pat down of my body confirmed that even though (thankfully) no new limbs sprouted, I did indeed change in my sleep.

Someone had changed me into one of my t-shirts and boy shorts pajama combos. My gut twisted hoping it was Becca and not Finn. I felt slightly off balance as I stood, making me wonder if I grew a couple more inches.

I surveyed the room. My bedroom door was open, but I was alone. I wanted to get a look at myself first before anyone else. Figure out what to do about anything I didn't like. Figure out my emotions if there was some giant change like a third eyeball or something.

I braced myself against the wall and slowly made my way into the bathroom. The light was an assault on my eyes, but after dunking my face in the sink the pins and needles ebbed away as I pat myself dry with a cloth. I braced myself, before finally looking up into the mirror.

The first thing I noticed was my hair. Before it was brown and had just brushed my collarbones. Now it cascaded down my back and over my shoulders in black waves with iridescent, golden highlights. My skin was clear of acne and freckles, and a bit paler than before. I hope it will tan and not stay this light.

I exhaled a sigh of relief after studying my eyes. No pitch-black darkness like I feared. In fact, the blues, greens and golds of them just stood out more against the contrast of my darker hair and thicker lashes.

The rest of me was remarkably unchanged. Apart from the slight swelling of my breasts (not much but at this point I'd have taken anything) everything else seemed normal. I twisted, raising my arms over my head but abruptly hissed and turned back to a neutral pose. So much for no new limbs, it certainly felt like I had a rock or two in my back. I held my breath as I repeated the motion, slower this time, and gently pulled my shirt up along my spine to get a clear view of what I was dealing with.

A sob-like noise of both shock and fear ripped from my throat. It looked like I had gills cut into my back. Two pairs of wriggling flaps of skin rested in a diagonal cut between my shoulder blades and spine. I held my breath until I almost passed out, but they kept up their movements on their own. Not gills then, since I wasn't breathing through them.

I dropped my shirt and turned away from the mirror not wanting to see them anymore. After a moment of focus I was relieved to find that I wasn't aware of them moving unless I could see them.

I exited the bathroom, marched through my door and down the hall no longer caring that I was in pajamas. True, they hugged me closer than before, but it was only pajamas not something scandalous.

"Becca?" I called out first, not wanting to draw the attention of the vampires just yet. I didn't have my brothers with me and the more aware of that fact I was the more I started freaking out. "Becca?" My voice pitched higher, and my breath stopped coming so easily. Suddenly, she popped through my own shadow at my feet and knocked me off balance.

"Christ, why are you up? Sit down immediately!" I plopped at the top of the stairs, beginning to shiver once more.

"Shit." I grit my teeth as she knelt beside me, a hot towel finding its way to my forehead and a blanket being weaved around my shoulders. "I thought it was over because I woke up. Does it usually do this? What's happening?"

"Slow down, breathe and drink this." A hot mug was nudged into my hands. It smelled of rosemary and lavender, but I was starving for what was beneath it. My senses flared and I practically threw the cup into my face, gulping down the tea holding fresh blood within it.

"Everything is heightened for you right now." Becca spoke calmly to me as I drank, "Taste, sight, touch, smell, and sound. They're all at full force right now. Your body needs a few hours to adjust to the intensity. If you keep being an idiot wandering around, you'll end up in a fever induced sleep."

I nodded in understanding, nearly dropping the mug when it was empty. When I moved to stand Becca shoved me

down by the shoulders again, muttering
about holding still for a few minutes for
my temperature to regulate before getting
back into bed. She held up a hand when I
began to protest, before turning her back
on me and walking down the stairs.

Defiantly, I shifted my body to at
least have a better view than staring at
the wall in front of me. I intended to look
out the window at the view of Purgatory,
but my breath caught at the sight of the
main hall itself.

Everything was crystallized in
either black, purple or silver. Pots of
lilacs, cornflowers and white roses lined
the room. The original chandeliers were
replaced by one massive one, made from
dripping black diamonds and amethyst
clusters. It was set aglow with the light of
hundreds of flame burning candles. Two
long, glass tables stretched through the
center of the room. Bowels of white
peaches, plums and cherries were placed
tastefully between cheese platters, seared
meats and decorated cakes dotting the
long silver runners down their centers.
Towering silver candlesticks stood in the
center of the room, designed to look like a
bird's outstretched talons.

"What is all this?" I breathed out. I
was expecting Rebecca to reply but it was

Finn's thick voice sounding from the bottom of the stairs.

"This is a tradition of ours in this community, for those who recently reformed." I turn, finding his gaze already boring into me. Even with the blanket thrown over me, it's like he's looking me over from head to toe all at once. The look on his face is one of absolute admiration and, dare I say, wanting.

"This will be your banquet to honor you, Angel. In finally finding the strength to take your rightful place." I furrow my brows.

"My rightful place?" I say, feeling my defenses, as well as my fever, spike. Finn's charming sunshine smile washes over me and his eyes dance with mischief.

"This is your world, Raven. You need not hide from embracing it any longer."

I slipped back into a fever induced sleep halfway to my room. Distantly, I felt Finn scoop me into his arms. Becca's chittering voice funneled into my clogged ears, and I giggled, feeling lighter than I had in years.

I swan dived down onto the bed, sinking into the silken comforter. And then I was alone.

Music swirled through my head. Something high and melodic; a choir singing. A faceless choir in a sea of silver and white. I did a pirouette, my hair spinning about me.

I spun faster, keeping pace with the chorus. Though, the faster I went, the less beautiful the sound was. What started off as woeful crescendos was quickly morphing into panicked shrieking.

I couldn't see. Everything around me was a blur of black and white, gold and silver, smoke and flame. Something sharp dug into my shoulder and I cried out, kicking my feet into the air as I fell.

My own shriek loosed from my throat as I tried to claw away from the grey wolf standing over me. Their eyes were black pits, maw dripping gold.

"Raven!"

The wolf disappeared, taking all the light that blinded me with it.

"I need you to run for me. Run and never stop!"

I gasped, eyes flying open. My hand was thrown out in front of me, outstretched fingers glowing the dimmest of golds in the otherwise black room.

My mind ran in circles. Was that just a dream or a memory? What did it have to do with my Mothers last words to me?

Falling back to the pillows, I was troubled to find my mind circling one particular thought. A thought that made no sense. A thought that had no merit or evidence to give me the right to imagine.

A warning bell rang in my head, a tether of my past snapping into place as instinct took over. I wasn't running away from my Father in that church.

It was the Angels she told me to flee from.

CHAPTER 22

"I will absolutely not wear the blue one," I snap, yanking the gown from its hanger and throwing it over Becca's head to subdue her persistence. Ice coats the floor beneath my feet, but with a single tap of my toe heat emanates from the soles of my shoes melting it completely. With my fever gone and my strength restored, I have more control over my powers than ever before. The precision of it makes me feel downright giddy. Becca yanks the fabric off her head.

"Well, you're not wearing any of the black ones like you're attending a damn funeral!"

"I want to feel comfortable in the first gown I ever wear." I huff and she rolls her eyes at me.

"They're not meant to feel comfortable in. Now try the turquoise one, it will make your eyes pop."

Half of me feels like the tradition of this banquet is asinine. Parade myself about in public to announce, 'Hey this is what I'm gonna look like until I'm dead!' sounds like utter hell. But at the same time, this is the only thing they have asked of me. They stole me away here, sure, but every second of my time spent here they've proven it was in fact for my benefit and not for some underlying scheme they had. In fact, the only negative thing I have left to say about being here is the fact that I'm not with my family. That and Becca's unforgiving persistence.

I mumbled something about bullying as she forced me into a figure-hugging turquoise gown, donned with hideous pink diamonds across the neckline. I shake my head. I wouldn't be caught dead in this. However, there is a foreign type of pleasure in trying on dresses with my younger sister. It felt familiar somehow, and despite her deadpan looks and sarcastic remarks I could tell that she was enjoying herself too.

As always, she was stunning, almost violently so in her outfit. She had on a satin ballgown, which hugged the curves of her upper body before cascading in bloodred waves for the skirt. There was a long slit from her hip to her toe giving a generous visual of the fishnet stockings she wore underneath. The sweetheart neckline was outlined in the same black lace as her gloves and belt and riddled with shimmering ruby studs. She wore a simple pair of black hoop earrings to draw attention to her most outrageous accessory, her necklace.

The clusters and dribbles of scarlet rubies mimicked the idea of blood dripping down one's neck from a vampire's bite. An appropriate touch I thought. Her hair was swept over her shoulders, fresh curls bouncing each time she took a step. All of that glamor and all I had managed to do was brush my hair.

"Seriously you need to stop bickering and just pick one. We open the doors to guests in twenty minutes. So, if you have any sense of self-preservation–"

"Alright I get it," I huffed and turned back to the closet. With a smirk I pull out a long, fitted black dress despite the grumbling protests resounding from behind me. "Will you relax?" I quip over my shoulder, "You said no ALL black. Give me a chance to edit before you condemn it."

"That rhymed," she pointed out and I rolled my eyes. Together we wiggled the gown over my head and down my body. Becca began cinching me into the corset back, much to her glee I'm sure as I was bent over wheezing by the time it was tied off. I tried not to complain though as she was gracious enough not to mention the slits in my back and made sure that they were covered comfortably.

I motioned for her to drag the large standing mirror over. She had Silas bring over the gothic piece of furniture from his room, as it was much more helpful than the small one mounted on my wall. I turned slowly, studying my reflection from every angle. Becca perched on the edge of my bed as wisps of shadows danced to life at my feet and I began my work.

I chose this dress because it was plain, save for the back, which immediately I began to accentuate. I adorned the punctured holes of the corset with microscopic diamonds, which glittered with the tiniest of movement. This overlapped the edges where the ties pulled at elegant pleats in the fabric. A pattern of roses and thorns began weaving their way into the bodice, the silver thread climbing the front and back of the dress from head to toe. I outlined the design with tastefully placed clusters of diamonds, both black and white, and amethysts much like the ones in the main hall. The sweetheart neckline morphed slightly, curling into little devil horns below the apex of my shoulder and collarbone. To finish, I conjured lace gloves for myself, long ones that came to rest above my elbow.

Satisfied, I turned on my heel and gestured down at my piece of art, "Well? Does it pass?" Becca seemed dazed but nodded.

"Yes. Even though it's still black." She rose from the bed slowly. Cautiously. I frowned, realizing the room had grown quite dark and turned to look at myself in the mirror again.

A woman shrouded in shadows and black stared back at me. Beyond her, Becca's reflection stared back at us as well. Her blood red outfit appeared more vicious in the gloom. With a snap of my fingers the smoke evaporated into nothingness, and the light flooding the room seemed to put both of us at ease.

"Isn't it kind of weird to be dressed like this just for dinner?" I asked, desperate to fill the silence.

"This is more like a gala or a ball than a dinner." Silas' voice sounded from the doorway and Becca and I both turned an equal scowl in his direction.

He matched her perfectly, diamonds studding his wine-red shirt and black silk pants. He had on some type of half-cape thing dangling from his left arm which matched his pants, and he swung it out towards her playfully, "You look absolutely delicious by the way."

"You should have knocked," she muttered striding towards him. "What if we happened to be naked?"

"Then it would have been our lucky day." Silas answered without missing a beat, eyes glinting as he took my sister in from head to toe. Before I could ask who 'our' meant, Finn appeared leaning in the door behind him, his humored smirk evaporating the second his eyes landed on me.

Becca was chittering something else at Silas, but I didn't hear her. I allowed myself the grace to slowly look Finn over myself, as he had done to me many times before— and God did he look *good.*

I was expecting him to be in his typical light aesthetic, however he seemed to take a page out of his brother's book and wore head to toe black. The dark silk made his golden locks, curly I realized since they were finally free of a tie or gel, stand out all the more. I didn't miss the glint of purple he had on his belt— amethyst studs, much like the ones on my dress. It had to be a coincidence. His ruby eyes were practically glowing as they raked over my body, but the sound of my name snapped me back to reality.

"Huh?"

"Your earlier question," Silas clarified. "In case you haven't realized by now, there are greater pleasures in life than training and fighting."

"What my brother means to say," Finn interjected, stepping forward and pulling a small box from his pocket, "is that despite your heritage and upbringing, a beautiful woman such as yourself should be pampered once in a while." It stung, the unintentional jab at my upbringing like it was wrong and horrible, but the sting faded from the shock of being presented with the gift inside the box.

"Are those...?" I couldn't finish the question, the memory of the item in front of me blurry and vague, but luckily I didn't have to.

"Yes." Finn gave me a smile that could melt the sun, "I know that a lot has happened since we brought you here. And unlike my brother, I don't have to watch my words or actions as closely when it comes to you–"

"You're right he does, and before this gets weirder, we're leaving. Come on." Becca snagged Silas by the ear, shooting me a wide-eyed look which promised I'd be hounded for details later as the pair disappeared out the door. Finn continued without so much as glancing in their direction.

"And because I have that freedom, I intend to use every tool at my disposal to win whatever pieces of you that you wish to give. After we failed to save you, I wanted to save at least one thing that I knew you'd accept, should we ever find you again. So please, do me the honor of wearing these tonight? You deserve them."

Finn didn't remove the ear cuffs from the box, he just held it aloft waiting for me to decide if I would or would not wear them as he requested.

Frankly, I was just proud of myself for not drowning the house in a typhoon, or at least my own tears as I stared down at my mother's golden ear cuffs. They weren't spectacular items, the solid gold bands may have been half an inch in length, but to me these were the most precious items on the planet.

"I would ask how you managed this, but I really don't want to know the details." I finally said, snatching the box like it was the last food on the planet, and I was starving.

His laugh was genuine, but his eyes still held the remnants of that night. The flames. My mom. Him having the only pieces of jewelry she ever wore was proof enough that they had been there, that they did indeed try to save me as they said they did. I shook my head, sending the memories on their way. Not tonight. I didn't need to drown myself tonight.

With that mindset I approached my mirror, fastening a cuff securely to each ear. Once satisfied I turned back to Finn.

"I don't have the words for this." I said apologetically. He simply shrugged.

"I don't need any." In a few steps he was before me, fingers dipping under my chin to raise my eyes to meet his. "I'm glad your eyes didn't change." He said softly after a few minutes of examining me up close, "Though I am curious. Have you sprouted any new appendages?"

My brain snapped to the slits in my back, but before I could mention anything Finn dipped his face to the crook of my neck. My breath caught in my throat, the scent of honey and cloves clogging my brain cells as I felt him trace his tongue along the exposed skin above my collarbone. I felt him chuckle into my skin, "And I'm pleased that your body hasn't stopped reacting to me this way Angel."

"Bag it," I mumbled. He chuckled, his only acknowledgment to the retort before his mouth closed around my neck. Instead of biting me he just sucked at my skin, releasing me with a soft pop.

I pushed my palms into his chest, and to my relief he relented, giving me a few inches of space to breathe. "W-we need to get downstairs. Becca will have my head if I'm late and I still need to find shoes."

"Tell me." Ignoring me, Finn cupped my face with both hands. His eyes bore into mine as his fingers drifted into my hair, "Is your heart beating so rapidly out of anxiety right now?" I grit my teeth. Of course, he could hear it, my stupid body was betraying me.

"No," I said, drawing out the word carefully. His mouth quirked into a small smile.

"Out of rage perhaps?"

"No," I repeated. His smile widened, pleased.

"Perhaps," his voice was a whisper against my skin, "you want me more than you're willing to admit?" His lips brushed mine gently, hot and soft, before pulling away. This wasn't like the tree, where he sat against me to see what I would do. No, here he broke me open. Laid out the pathway. But still...

"No," I repeated, taking a step away. I felt his hands slip from my hair

as he dropped them back to his sides. "I
don't know what this is. And I don't have
the energy to find out right now." He
nodded slowly, as if stunned.

"Well. I'll get out of your hair then
so you may finish getting ready."

"Thank you," I said, catching his
wrist before he could disappear. "For not
pushing me. And for my mother's—"

"You don't need to thank me for not
forcing myself on you." His words were
clipped, and I winced. He noticed,
softening his voice, "And you also don't
need to thank me for simply returning
something that I'm sure would have
belonged to you. I'll see you downstairs
Angel." He raised my hand, kissing my
knuckles before disappearing down a
column of black.

Curse Becca and her jokes. I was
met by a butler (I didn't even know we
had those) in the hallway outside my
room, presenting me with a mask as they
were mandatory for tonight's party. A
Masquerade for the Woken, turned out to
be the theme for tonight. I assured him I
could make my own but apparently all
attendees were wearing this mask in

particular for 'uniform tradition', whatever that meant.

I secured it in a loose knot, tucking the strings away under my hair which I decided to leave down for once, before making my way down the staircase and into the throng of people.

I wouldn't be surprised if every resident of the city was here tonight. Pixies, mages, centaurs, fauna, hobgoblins, regular goblins, and all sorts of other glowing, feathered or scaled creatures littered the main hall.

There was music filling the hall from somewhere, waiters bustling about with trays and so much food on the table I half believed it would snap under the weight. I wasn't sure if people knew they were here for me or if they just came for a party with free food.

Shamelessly I grabbed a plate, helping myself to an assortment of cheeses, a few caramel cubes, a small pile of raspberries and some blue mixture that resembled whipped cream to top them. I then sought out the quietest corner of the hall to enjoy my snacks, tucking myself in a nook behind a grand piano that had been set up outside the kitchen doors. No one was playing it yet, so it was a perfect obstacle to keep between me and everyone else as I adjusted to the environment.

As I settled in studying the crowd, I felt my mind drifting. How wonderful would it be if my brothers were here? I could imagine them all cleaned up, escorting Luna who definitely deserved a night out on the town. Since the night was for me, perhaps I could even convince Akashi to dance with me, under the pretense of protective older brother of course.

It was too easy to imagine swaying against him, all dressed up in this gown, in his arms, pretending things were different for once. I could already feel the guilt creeping into me knowing Finn would love to be in the position I just imagined. I hadn't seen him since he disappeared from my room, and I hoped he was okay.

Abruptly the music cut off and I could hear the crowd murmuring to itself and literally watched it turn in sync to face the picture window at the end of the hall. Silas hopped up on a small black stage, tapping at a microphone to make sure it was on before addressing the crowd.

"Hello, good evening, everyone. As some of you may know, we have a newly awakened vampire in our city." A few chuckles rose from the crowd, as well as comments about my attack on the fauna a few days ago. I felt my face heat up in embarrassment. Never again would I let my rage get that bad.

Silas' voice boomed through the chatter, "She has been such a trooper through the process. We know that vampires in that current state are the most wicked, so please enjoy yourselves tonight to the fullest as we express our thanks and gratitude for you bearing with our unique family during this time. Tonight is one of celebration. As the immortal world has gained another soul, we must remind one another to remain allies for all eternity."

"For all eternity." The crowd echoed, raising glasses to the toast.

"Raven dear, would you grace the crowd with your presence? Perhaps an apology for recent outbursts?"

The room flooded with laughter once more, but before I could feel shame, I saw the smiles. No one was mad. With that simple reassurance I began maneuvering my way around the piano, the crowd parting in front of me as they finally noted my appearance.

"You're really making me get on stage?" I grumbled, stopping at the base of the short steps beneath Silas and he shrugged.

"Can't have you hiding in the shadows all night, can we?" I rolled my eyes, but took his extended hand and hoisted myself up on the platform beside him. Suddenly shy and awkward, I kept my eyes trained on the chandelier overhead before a female voice called from the crowd.

"What's your power?" The crowd chittered excitedly and looked at me expectantly. I looked at Silas who nodded his head.

"All vampires get a single gift besides immortality. I can puppet you once I have your name. Finn can paralyze in the same fashion. Rebecca can teleport between realms." So that's why no one bats an eye to her shadow jumping, and why she spends a lot of time as a Sphinx in the wilds of Purgatory to remain unseen. Silas continues, "We have agreed to share our gifts with the residents of this city, so that we may live to trust one another. It's your turn to share, Raven."

He was being formal for the sake of the crowd, but I understood his words. I could choose one and only one of my powers to show the city. I would have the freedom to exercise it in front of everyone.

But I must keep the rest of mine hidden. I was playing a vampire after all.

I hesitated for a moment, wanting to choose one powerful enough to give me some security, but not so powerful that they would doubt our cover story. My eyes snagged on one of the vases of flowers, a burst of color in the otherwise black and silver room. Suddenly the purple decorations and the amethysts on Finn's belt made perfect sense.

I motioned for Silas to back up, before holding my palms outward towards the crowd. There were gasps, and then applause as brilliant violet flames licked to life along my skin. Nervous I made a bad choice I looked to Silas again, who offered a small reassuring smile before I dropped my hands, the flames disappearing. The music started once more, and I gladly took that as my cue to get off that stage.

I made my way through the crowd, receiving praise and admiration for my gift. I politely smiled and shook hands but kept making my way towards the stairs in need of some quiet. I've never been surrounded by so many people in my entire life.

Twice I needed to divert my path and take a longer route because I saw the flash of Becca's red dress and did not need to get caught and peppered with questions about Finn that I didn't know how to answer, but finally I made it. My hand gripped the banister as I greeted and thanked one more Fey at the base of the stairs, a male with sprouting twigs for hair. Then I snagged a drink from a passing tray and climbed to overlook the party from above.

I took a sip of the viridian liquid and was rewarded with a cool minty taste on my tongue as I leaned against the banister looking down trying to spot Finn. I hadn't seen him since I left my room, and although he remained cool and collected, I knew my reaction upset him.

Sensing movement behind me, I turned to address whichever partygoer followed me to politely ask for a moment alone. I was caged in against the balcony before I could even set my drink down.

Their front was pressed to my back, arms dipping underneath mine to place their hands on the banister on either side of my hips. I couldn't catch a scent which was odd but given the suit sleeves I assumed it was a male. Plus, the chest against my back had no softness about it.

Purple flames flickered to life on my fingertips, but the relieved sigh against my neck extinguished them immediately.

"I told you I would find you Little Bird."

CHAPTER 23

"Akashi stop!" I hissed at his back. He had immediately ripped me from the balcony and dragged me down the hallway behind us, away from the eyes and ears of the crowd. My heart was beating frantically against my ribcage, my brain working overtime as I tried to keep pace with what was happening.

He came for me. Tears were prickling at the corners of my eyes, and I wanted to throw my arms around his neck and never let go. I probably would have done exactly that or something even more stupid if he wasn't dragging me down the hall as forcefully as he was.

He had ignored my every question and protest, yanking me by the wrist after him in search of a separate exit. I was smart enough to not start yelling, but surprised that the vampires nor Becca weren't already chasing us down.

"I have been tracking you for months," he snarled, gripping my wrist even tighter. "I'm not about to stop when I've finally found you."

"You're not listening to me!" I jerk my wrist, but he doesn't release his grip or stop walking, "Let me explain!" No change. "AKASHI!" I finally yelled, ripping my hand from his forcefully.

I grabbed him by the collar and swung him into the wall, the two of us spilling through a shadow and into my bedroom. Once our feet were back on the floor, I released him.

He skidded across the floor, finally coming to a halt at the foot of my bed. The abrupt location change, or perhaps shadow jumping itself, seemed to snap him out of whatever strict trance he was in. His green eyes snap to mine, filled with concern beneath the party mask.

I was finally able to get a good look at him, now that I wasn't being dragged behind him. Though the outfit was simpler than Silas or Finn's, he was also formally dressed up. He had on all black, suit jacket, dress shirt and slacks, but somehow was stealing my breath more than Finn's overwhelming presence ever had. Damn him.

My heart was slamming in my chest, but I focused, crossed the room to him and pulled the gloves from my arms, letting him study the unmarred skin.

"I'm sorry about throwing you in here. But you wouldn't stop. You wouldn't let me explain that I was okay."

"Okay?" He repeated, the word sounding foreign on his tongue.

"Yes." I quickly explained the details of what happened, what living here was like, how I was treated, how I've been training and learning about Rebecca. I left out some things like the rated R dance club and bites to and from the vampires, but enough for him to get the gist of what went on down here.

"I know the last thing you saw was me being dragged into a black hole, but I really am okay. I haven't been brainwashed. I'm not being used as a puppet by Silas. In fact, the only time he took control of my body was to get me to stop hurting myself and Finn. They've done nothing to harm me and haven't tried making me harm others. And they've had Becca this entire time since she and I were separated—"

"Separated?" Akashi cut me off then, eyes wide. "You knew her?" I averted my gaze.

"I did. Now that I've gone through the Reformation, I suppose those lost memories will start coming back. That's what should happen anyways." I release a strained laugh, "Though I haven't even been like this a whole day yet, so I'm afraid the only information about our past together is what I already told you."

"From Silas and Finn, your new best friends?" I winced as he laughed in my face. "Jesus, you're being manipulated right now! I'm disappointed you've believed a word they told you." I grit my teeth,

"Well, how is it any different than me believing in you guys? I didn't have any of my memories when I met you either." He stopped laughing, and I put some distance between us, "You put me in a bottle marked dangerous and weak and I stayed that way. Until now. Either get with the new program or leave me here."

The silence between us was so thick I was half tempted to see if I could cut it with a knife. Suddenly the bedroom door cracked open, startling us both. Akashi rushed to my side, throwing me behind him before we realized it was only Kuma poking his head in the door.

"Ya'll are getting too noisy and dramatic, and mom wants to come in now."

"Luna?" My voice broke and she was there. Her arms went around my shoulders as I started to sob, hands drifting down to rub my back. I held my breath as her fingers narrowly missed the newly formed slits in my skin, realizing that area was quite sensitive now.

"You really are the most troublesome of my children," she muttered into my hair, but I could feel her shaking against me too. When we parted, she removed my mask and took my face in her hands, studying me at this angle and that as the rest of my brothers filed into the room.

I noticed all of them were trying not to stare at me, the changes, the dress. When she determined I was not harmed in any way she made me take a seat at the foot of my bed beside Akashi, before seating herself in the large armchair across from us. My brothers removed their masks by now too, and I could see how exhausted they all were. That familiar wave of guilt washed through me, knowing they wouldn't have suffered if I just left this place and went home.

"Now it's not my place," her eyes momentarily flit to Akashi before looking back to me, "but I think we owe your sister the time to fully explain, and the trust to decide for herself."

He bristled beside me, and I felt everyone looking our way. I furrowed my brows, glancing at the rest of my brothers in turn. All of them had their attention trained on Akashi as if waiting for his permission.

I had fully expected to be questioned by Luna and withheld from my brothers until she was done. But instead, I found myself being piloted by my brother, explaining myself and giving information to him that the rest of them still didn't have. Kuma even asked for permission to enter, and for Luna herself to enter. A quiet gasp left me, and I turned to face Akashi fully.

"Don't tell me you're the Alpha now?" I breathed. His eyes slid to meet mine.

"Would that be such a bad thing?"

"We'd be doomed." I laughed before I could think better of it. His gaze hardened and I frowned. Just what kind of an asshole was he being with his new privileges? "Relax brother," I let the words drag out, "I'm not disrespecting you. However, I'd like to bring your attention back to the immediate issue at hand. Get with the new program or leave me here." I repeated. His teeth bared slightly at the order, and I could feel the rest of my family holding their breaths.

"I said I'm not leaving you, now that I finally found you," he said quietly. He sighed, running a hand through his hair. "I'm sorry guys... it's been a very stressful five months."

"Five months?" I blurted out, stunned.

I knew time moved differently down here but I didn't imagine that much of it had passed. I hesitated, debating on pulling him into a hug. I didn't, knowing what little resolve I had in the midst of this confusion would break and I'd bury myself in his scent. Pine and rain and smoke. Home. I sighed.

"Alright dumbass, I forgive you for being such a dick before I left." I felt the rigidness in his body start to leave as I combed my fingers through his hair, mimicking how I would with his fur. It was several inches longer than it had been since I last saw him, proof of the time passing, "And I'm sorry for making you worry. Truthfully, I could have left. But it isn't all that horrible here. In fact, if you chill out, you might even like it."

"Oh, that I doubt." Growls sounded from around me as Finn's voice piped up from the doorway. I jerked myself away from Akashi and Finn smirked, "He wouldn't be able to stand the sight of his precious little Angel getting cozy with a vampire." Shit. I stood, scowling at Finn.

"I just got done telling him what good guys you and your brother are, don't turn me into a liar." I say, and his smile turns sickeningly sweet.

"Did you ever break her skin when sparring?" Finn presses, eyes not leaving my brother, "I highly suspect you pulled your punches. Otherwise, you'd know her blood runs golden, rivaling honey in both appearance and taste."

"You won't have her," Akashi said from behind me, aggression coming off him in waves. Suddenly I'm yanked backwards and perched in his lap. Heat floods my face, and I move to stand but he wraps an arm around my waist, pinning me there. I try to ignore his hand, resting on my ribs just below my breast.

Sure, I've had my own brief daydreams about him growing up, and sure I've been on top of him before in the sparring ring. But the possessiveness in his voice and that immediate reaction sent a lick of heat crawling down my spine I've never experienced before. Finn lets out a laugh and narrows his eyes at my brother.

"She is not a Hound young Akashi, so unfortunately you can't continue to dictate her as you have in the past. I set her free."

Just as I feel Akashi readying to shift, a bored sigh sounds from the opposite end of my room.

"Oh cool, males fighting for dominance," Becca drawls, playing with her hair absentmindedly. "Totally macho and stuff, but in case your dicks clogged your brain cells there's a party happening downstairs that's kinda for her. Now if you'll excuse us." She grins, cockily weaving her way between Kuma and Hikari who had placed themselves between us before pointedly staring at Akashi's unwavering grip on me. Her crystal blue eyes glitter.

"You can get back to playing house after I'm done enjoying a night out with my sister. Rave, if you wouldn't mind calling off your puppy so I don't get bit?" I groan. This isn't going to work.

"Silas, I know you're in here," I mutter, ignoring everyone participating in this stupid battle for my time.

"Wherever Rebecca goes I'm not far behind." He confirms, stepping out of my bathroom door and flashes a grin at my family to only show off his fangs. I give him a deadpan stare until he stops with a dramatic sigh, "Oh fine. What?"

"Tell the guests I've excused myself for the evening, order all the alcohol up here that you can, and for God's sake someone get me out of this dress." I harden the edge on my next words, "We won't be leaving this room until we are all on the same page, or I'll do the exact thing none of you want: disappear." The threat hits home immediately, and Akashi lets go of me so I can stand.

I feel two heated sets of eyes on me but pointedly ignore them as I grab one of Becca's hands and one of Luna's, marching them into the bathroom with me before slamming the door shut.

Much to my pleasant surprise, Luna and Becca got on remarkably well after the first few minutes of awkwardness. As ordered, in the bathroom I had each of them transform one by one, so they could take the other in and not recognize them as a threat. Becca seemed quite pleased by the compliments Luna gave about the strength of her Sphinx form and didn't let another 'dog' comment slip. I was hoping to put an end to that bullshit today.

As they chatted with each other I transformed my clothes, seriously being done with the gown on my body restricting my movements. Once replaced with more comfortable attire, black leggings and a tank top, I motioned the two of them over to me. Wordlessly I lifted my shirt over my shoulders, facing my back to them. Rebecca silently removed the gauze cushions we had been placing against the slits in my spine, giving Luna a full view of my hidden transformation.

If the three of us had a general consensus on anything it was these two things.

One, those slits were more than likely for wings to appear should I have them.

And two, it was nice to have our numbers rise, the three of us having been outnumbered by the men outside for decades. I think it was that thought in and of itself, which had Luna and Becca transform once more before we exited the bathroom.

The boys, if they had been bickering in our absence, were deathly silent as we entered the room together. Anzen, Hikari and Kuma all flanked Akashi who was leaning against the wall by the bathroom door. Silas and Finn stood opposite them, a rolling cart of the alcohol I requested behind them by the door.

Luna's pale fur bristled, and a soft blue glow illuminated the ground at her feet. Rebecca stretched, her silver claws remaining unsheathed. Both had their eyes pinned to each group of men in the room, somewhat daring them to challenge us as we took full authority of the space.

I don't know what came over me as I maneuvered the three of us between the groups. Maybe it was the years of holding myself back. It could simply be the fact that two very powerful men were about to rip each other's heads off over me. Whatever it was, I let it fuel me, and stopped suppressing the aura of my power. It reached every corner of the room, thudding through the space like a silent heartbeat.

Flanked on either side by a Hound or a Sphinx, I seated myself in the empty armchair. Small wisps of purple flames coated my arms, shadows completely obscured my feet and there was a golden light dancing across my skin that I'm quite certain had never been there before. Despite my lack of transformative skill or size, and sitting here in gym clothes, it was undeniable I was the most powerful person in the room.

"I'm going to keep it simple," I said, fighting the urge to fidget in my seat. "When I'm done, drink however much you need to cope. Or fist fight it out of your systems I don't care. But everyone in this room has the same goal, so stop looking at each other like you're enemies."

“And what goal would that be?” Akashi’s words were clipped, the burn in his green eyes rivaling my fire. I sat back, giving him a smile.

“Defeating the Devil, of course.”

CHAPTER 24

They all listened intently as I spoke. It was no shock to my brothers that I wanted my father dead, and Becca seemed quite keen with the idea as well. I felt as if I had gotten a little lost in the time I spent here for my very unplanned family reunion, but having my sister's presence and support for this goal of mine just made it feel even more possible than before. In fact, by the time I finished speaking, every single one of them seemed prepared to leap into action now, but then they were utterly at a loss when I told them we would all be staying together until that time came.

Everyone was a valuable asset and important to me. More than that, they had been important enough to be chosen by the Angels who seemed to be dictating everything on the sidelines. So, I decided we all play nice for the time being and stay in the vampire's residence. It's not like there weren't any rooms to spare.

There were protests from the boys of course, but I told them to take it up with each other, pointing out that I wasn't the one who had a problem with anyone. They needed to work out their petty shit and get their heads straight, otherwise saving my sister and I all those years ago would have meant nothing. That got them to quiet down.

Hikari made an effort first as I knew he would and was now speaking with Silas over glasses of wine in the corner. I could pick out pieces of Silas recounting the story of how the vampires were assigned to get both me and Becca, Hikari listening on with polite nods and some questions.

Anzen and Becca seemed quite interested in studying each other's transformed strengths and weaknesses, discussing abilities of their nature, and battles they had been in. Kuma watched on from a few feet away, wary of my sister's long silver teeth as she circled our youngest brother but participated in the conversation with short comments here and there.

My eyes shifted to Finn and Akashi. The two of them hadn't stopped glaring daggers at each other for the past twenty minutes. I glanced at my mom, still in her Hound form, and she met my eyes with a knowing look.

She rose from her place on the floor, stretching and shaking out her fur, before approaching Finn and began peppering him with questions about the years he spent raising Rebecca in Atlantis. The bulk of her body cut off any visual he had of my brother, so I took that opportunity to loop my arm through Akashi's and pull him with me into a shadow. He didn't hesitate, gliding in after me with ease and we stepped out in the quiet dark of the glass rose garden below the house.

"I didn't say it before, but I know the vampires aren't lying. I have proof," I said as soon as our feet touched the ground. I tucked my hair behind my ears, allowing Akashi to see my mother's gold cuffs. His eyes sparked with recognition, and he looked away.

"She had those on in the church."

"She never took them off. And we only ended up at the church because Finn and Silas didn't get to me in time."

"I should have just trusted you when you said it. I'm sorry," he said. I dropped my hair, thoughts beginning to drift before he added, "I actually have something from that night as well."

My eyes widened as Akashi reached into his suit jacket, pulling the black and silver blade of a dagger from its inside pocket. "I've hung onto it ever since you decided to take a swipe at me with it. Figured it would become useful for you one day, preferably a day you're not pissed off at me."

He held it out to me, and I took it slowly, turning the blade in my hand watching the moonlight glint off its smooth edges. Uncomfortable having it out so close to him I quickly conjured a sheath for it around my waist, securing it on my hip opposite of him.

"Why can't I catch any of your scents?" I breathed out, needing my attention to be anywhere else than the memories currently whizzing through my brain. I turned my attention to the roses, giving them a real once over for the first time. Frankly, I can't even imagine how I managed to create them. They were the matching shades of white and red like back home, but the blooms were of shimmering blown glass. I traced my finger down the cool, smooth edge of a petal, mesmerized.

"That's seriously what you want to talk about? Not smelling me?" Akashi forced out a rough laugh.

"Well to be honest it's throwing me off. I was genuinely getting ready to toss you over that railing earlier because I didn't know it was you," I said, side eyeing him. He shrugged.

"I found a mage who would mask our scents as soon as we entered the city.

Didn't need those bloodsuckers," I leveled a glare at him, and he quickly amended, "the vampires, to catch our scent and drag you off again." I rolled my eyes.

"They wouldn't have done that."

"Well, how was I supposed to know that? The last thing I saw was them abducting you. So of course, I assumed the worst, can ya blame me?" I shook my head. He was right. I would have reacted the same exact way if our roles had been reversed.

He sighed, shuffling forward towards the roses I was admiring and reached around me, slicing his thumb open against a razor-sharp thorn. The smell of rain, smoke and pine washed over me as soon as a small line of his blood spread over his skin. Subconsciously, I leaned back towards him, inhaling him deeper, but then I froze as the scent of his blood reached my nose as well.

I never really understood why the vampires described the smell of blood as delicious or intoxicating, until this moment. I turned, my brain fuzzy as I stalked a few yards away from him with a hand pressed firmly over my nose.

"I smell that bad huh?" He laughed over my shoulder, "I guess it has been a while since I took a proper shower."

Despite the pounding in my ears, I could hear the slight click to his teeth when he clenched his jaw. Heard him shuffle out of his suit jacket and toss it to the side. The soft cracks of his spine as he stretched his arms over his head. The steady pulse of his blood in his veins.

My senses were flaring up like they had in those moments right after my reformation. His shoes dragged on the dirt coming closer to me, "Hey, are you okay?"

"I'm fine," I choke out. "Just thinking. I'm fine." I repeat. I needed to get it together. He can't see me like this. Already I can feel my fangs pressed to the inside of my lips. He strutted a few lazy steps towards me.

"I can tell when you're lying Little Bird."

"I said I'm fine!" I snapped. Whirling on him, I automatically bared my teeth.

He stiffened, eyes flitting to my mouth and locking on my fangs. I waited for the chastising. For the reminder to not be like my Father. For the reprimands of how out of control I have become since living here. None of them came though.

Akashi slowly raised his eyes back to mine and held my gaze as he crossed the rest of the space between us. I held my breath as he lifted his hand, running his cut thumb along my bottom lip.

Damn him. My lips parted in shock, but I refused to move. Refused to allow my tongue to run over the smear of blood he left. He needed to see I could control myself. More so, I didn't deserve a taste.

My eyes were now locked onto the scar running across his eye, and absently I reached up, one of my own fingers tracing the thin white line from top to bottom.

"I can't hurt you again," I breathed out. My breath came in and out in jagged puffs, the dagger on my hip mentally weighing me down.

His gaze never wavered as he reached for the buttons of his dress shirt. He undid them to the third, then the fourth, before stretching the collar over his shoulder and baring himself to me.

"It's okay, Raven." I shuddered hearing my name on his lips. I wanted to hear it again and again. I wanted him to never stop saying it.

His hand found the back of my head, nudging me towards his neck gently, "I never want you to feel like you have to hold yourself back with me ever again." His sentence ended in a hiss as my fangs punctured his neck.

It was startling, how good he tasted. The fauna had tasted of tart fruit, Silas like candy, the bloody drinks I'd been sipping on a mixture of berries, but this? Akashi was *definitely* my taste.

His blood was like all good things wrapped into one place. Oozing melty chocolate, crisp fresh apple, thick, sweet wine. I couldn't get enough. I felt his chuckle reverberate through my chest, and realized I had plastered myself against him as I drank.

Immediately I retracted my fangs from him, greedily sucking against the last bit of his blood spilling from the bite mark before pulling away, panting lightly.

"I'm sorry, I shouldn't have, I should have stopped." I cut myself off seeing the look on his face and cocked my head concerned. "What's your problem? Are you about to pass out? Akashi–"

"Will you for once just *shut up*?" He groaned, hands sliding their way up my neck and yanking me forward into a sudden kiss.

This felt nothing like the way Finn had kissed me. Back then, it had felt like a steady assault of a thousand suns threatening to make me combust. This felt like we both already had.

I could feel Akashi shaking as his arms circled me, hands searching my body for whatever place he could get a grip. His kiss was urgent, desperate. Hungry.

He forced me backwards, arm bracing against the stone wall of the cliff suddenly at my back as his kisses grew more rampant. His teeth bit my lower lip simultaneously as his hands went under my legs, lifting me off the ground and wrapping me around him.

I gasped at the sudden contact, face flushing, the bundle of nerves between my legs immediately recognizing the hot column he was pressing against them. I shivered, in both pleasure and shame.

Just a few weeks ago we functioned as nothing but siblings. There was nothing beyond heated gazes and quick remarks, nothing I should have wanted anyway. But strangely, I didn't have any urge to push him away. And the bastard took that moment to slide his tongue into my mouth.

Years of curiosities and buried urges exploded from me. I parted my lips, slanting my mouth against his and he groaned, satisfied by my response. The sound sent a skittering pulse of electricity through my whole body.

I raked my fingers through his hair with soft tugs and clenched my legs around his waist. Cautiously, I spread my hands along his back, small vines gently swirling against his vertebrae and into his clothes, allowing me to touch even more of him than I already was. Another shiver rocked his body, and he responded by shifting his mouth to my neck.

A moan ripped from my throat when he immediately found weak spots I didn't even know I had. His lips suckled above my collarbone while his fingers circled the soft space below my ear, nails dragging as his teeth bit into me. His free hand slid under me again and two of his fingers roughly traced the slit between my legs dragging yet another moan from me. He paused only for a moment to tease, "You can make that sound all day," before resuming toying with my body.

He was hurtling us towards the edge, but alarm bells started ringing in my head. What would our brothers say? And Luna? She had already tried to warn me, and I failed to heed her words.

Despite my body's obvious want for him I dropped my hands to his shoulders, pushing gently.

"Akashi..."

"Don't!" He growled, face reappearing in front of mine, mouth catching me in another hungry kiss which stole all my breath.

Finally, his hands released my thighs. Slowly, I slid my feet back to the ground, body screaming in protest as the heat and friction were replaced by nothing but empty, cold air. He didn't fully release me though, catching me under him by tilting forward to gently press our foreheads together.

"I'm sorry if I crossed a line. It's just these past few months... I didn't know if you were alive or dead." His voice was raw, exhausted and a wave of guilt crashed through me. He peeled his body away from mine, running a hand through his mussed-up hair, "I know you view me as just a brother, and I didn't even ask before I... just don't hate me. I'll never touch you again if you promise not to hate me," he finished in a whisper.

My vines were still in his clothes, like strings connecting us, straining to not tear them off and continue down whatever rabbit hole we both very clearly had been dodging until now. But we couldn't.

I cursed under my breath, calling my vines back to me, giving up my hold on him. He couldn't know how much I wanted this. He couldn't know that Finn only made me feel a fraction of what he just sent coursing through my body right now.

"I'm sorry," I said, voice catching in my throat. "With everything going on right now I don't think it would be smart for the two of us to… entertain this." He nodded, turning away with a mixture of relief and regret on his face.

I took a breath, "I just want to be smart. And safe. All of us. Nothing matters more to me than everyone staying safe."

"Nothing matters more to me," his eyes snapped back to mine, "than *you.*"

I don't know what I would have responded with if I got the chance to. We both jumped as a pure, blinding white light shot down from the sky, slamming into the side of the cliff.

The windows above us burst and Akashi dove forward, his body shielding mine as glass rained down. I sent up a funnel of wind above us, scattering the shards away from us so he wouldn't be cut. They hadn't even hit the ground yet when I heard Silas start screaming.

"Rebecca!" My heart dropped into my gut, his terror echoing down to us. "They took Rebecca! She's gone!"

CHAPTER 25

The house was in a frenzy. I dragged Akashi back into the shadows to re-emerge in the living room seconds after the light had faded but it was already too late. The chandeliers were shattered into pieces on the floor. The stage was split in two. The banquet tables had been blasted into the wall. Every surface was covered with food or debris. If any guests had remained after we retreated upstairs their escape route was marked by the gaping hole in the wall where the door used to be.

Every one of the Hounds had transformed and Silas' enraged screaming threatened to shatter what few windows remained. Finn was a silent, emotionless wall between my brothers and his. And there was blood on the floor, so much blood reeking of Becca's scent that it nearly made me pass out.

But a glint of metal in the center of the red pool caught my eye. My hands were shaking with rage as I bent to lift a small, silver cross.

"I'm going." Fire was licking across my skin as I said it, twisted red flames of rage crackling to life. My feet were moving for the stairs, but Luna threw herself in front of me.

"Raven don't let your emotions cause reckless actions." With a sweep of my hand, I sent her skidding away on a blast of wind. I was sick and tired of hearing that.

Kuma launched himself over the railing, snapping his teeth at me but I just opened a shadow at his feet and deposited him behind me in the room. I pinned Anzen and Hikari together in a web of vines when they came at me two on one. By the time I reached the top of the staircase Akashi was launching himself up after me, but he wasn't the one who caught me first. Finn materialized, a flash on my winds, blocking my path.

"And how exactly do you plan to get through the pearly gates with that devilish blood of yours?" His voice was as cold as his eyes. If not for my rage I probably would have been taken aback by his demeanor, but I just pushed past him before responding.

"Haven't you been the one calling me Angel all this time? I'm sure my blood will figure it out."

Akashi launches himself at Finn and I leave the two men there to fight, or bicker, I don't care. To ensure they don't actually kill each other though I do release Hikari and Anzen from where they are bound before tuning the scene out completely and walking down the hall to my room.

I walk straight to my closet and throw the doors open. All the clothes Becca stocked away for me stared back in mocking silence as if telling me I should have been more grateful. Furiously I start to strip, uncaring if anyone wanders in the door and yank random items towards me to put on.

I have to get to Heaven. I know that's where she is. I can't believe my Father would fake an attack from the Angels, only to take her when he's after me. Especially since I was the easier target being outside and... distracted. Plus, he wouldn't have waited for my Reformation. He would have killed me when I was still weak and taken out Rebecca as well. Two birds with one stone.

That thought makes me pause as I entertain a narrative I hadn't thought of before. The vampires and Hounds were both connected to Heaven, and under its orders saved Becca and I. We were placed under predetermined care, with two families that could track us if we ever disappeared. Heaven also employed my family which was how we ended up in the club in New York even though it was a vampire refuge. A refuge that Silas and Finn seemed closely connected to since they defended it against us.

That meeting place for my sister and I which got this whole ball rolling could had been predetermined.

Shell shocked, I slowly buttoned up a pair of jeans I can't believe Becca put in my closet and didn't swipe for herself, trying to focus my thoughts on what the Angels might want with powers like ours. Definitely ours now since they took her, probably as a ploy for me to follow.

My whole life everyone had feared my powers and what would happen if they attracted the attention of my Father. With our indirect relationship with Heaven, it never crossed my mind that perhaps my family was stalling my Reformation because of the Angels. Did the Hounds have the same suspicions as my mother and believe it would be the Angels who would drag me into the war?

"Raven..." Akashi's voice sounded from the door behind me.

"I'm going." My throat felt paper dry as I forced myself to turn towards him.

His eyes were wide, shifting from my back to my face. I didn't have a shirt on yet I realized, and my bra had done nothing to hide the flaring slits of skin between my shoulder blades. Oddly enough, him seeing where my wings could come through made me feel more vulnerable than him getting the view of my breasts right now. I yanked a shirt over my head, followed by my leather jacket for good measure.

"You can't talk me out of it or prolong it anymore." My words were clipped, "If I don't go, they'll come back."

There was a momentary flash of fear in his eyes before he looked away. It was so subtle I thought I made it up, but it was enough to confirm my racing thoughts.

The Angels were not an ally. They should be considered the same type of threat as I considered my Father to be.

I grabbed a pair of boots and laced them up. Then I replaced the dagger and sheath on my waist before striding for my now glassless window.

"How are you going to get there?" He asked. Just like Finn. The two of them were driving me nuts with their doubts. I released an annoyed huff.

"Well, my mother *was* the full-blooded Angel of Mary, so perhaps I can use that half of me right now to get where I need to go." I paused. Lowering my voice to a whisper I added a fact that chilled my blood, "And before he fell, Lucifer was an Angel too."

I didn't give Akashi a chance to say anything else. I didn't let my mind drift to wonder why he wasn't trying to stop me. I didn't avert my eyes to Luna who burst into my room behind him. I didn't flinch hearing Silas wail out in anguish once more.

I just leaned back and fell out the busted window. Brushing my fingers against my mother's ear cuffs, I willed my shadows to give way to light, and prayed.

CHAPTER 26

I don't quite understand how I did it, but I never want to do it again. When I hit the ground below the house I disappeared into a pool of shadows. Racing through the dark, I had sought out any sources of light.

Frustrated, I wasted time popping in and out of shadowy crevices, before finally ricocheting myself into a beam of light. After that, my movements were a blur and barely controlled. I bounced off reflections of glass, through flaring strobe lights and even hazy sunbeams filtering between the leaves. I was darting between those bright spaces like I was a streak of light myself, the pace getting faster and faster.

And it *burned*.

The longer I stayed in this fractured world of light, the longer I was exposed to its relentless heat. I could practically feel myself tanning even through my layers of clothes. Rivulets of sweat trickled down my body and I wished for nothing more than Becca's ice to cool down this blasted heat.

That just pushed me on faster to find an entryway to Heaven in this blinding world. And boy did I find it.

I was shooting myself through the glinting sunshine off a bell in a steeple tower when the damn thing swung out from under me and started ringing. The collision of that Holy sound with the world of light I was traveling through yanked me like a bungee cord, dragging me like a fish on a hook to crash land behind the pearly gates.

With a pained groan I wiped at the blood trickling out of my ears. When the bell rang, I felt like my head was going to explode, so this was probably some effect of my Father being banned from this place. My blood glittered on my hands, the gold dazzling against the near silver hue of this place.

The emptiness of this place was startling. The way humans described Heaven was like a city made of clouds and light, but I was kneeling in a flat empty landscape in about two inches of ashen water. The air was thick and moist but freezing. It made my lungs scream as I stood, sucking in breaths between clenched teeth.

I'm honestly glad I crashed in this lonely space rather than interrupting someone's peaceful afterlife. Perhaps that's why it appeared empty for me: I was alive in this plane, where one's soul was supposed to travel after they died.

Whatever reason for it appearing barren I knew I wasn't alone here. In fact, if Kuma were here, I'd bet him a whole month of gym cleaning duty that someone was already on the lookout for my arrival. Whether they would come out and say hi or drag me to whatever cage they had Rebecca in I was unsure.

I started to walk, the water lapping at my feet soundlessly with each of my steps. The silver coloring to this place was thanks to a thick mist I noted settled over the water, seamlessly fading into the milky sky above. Occasionally I heard voices filter through the mist. They were muted, not directed towards me, so respectfully I passed by those souls leaving them to their affairs.

Finally, I noticed a break against the horizon. Appearing as a crack against the skyline, a cave rose in the chalk white hillside before me. My hand automatically rested against the hilt of my dagger as I approached. Thinking better of it, I flipped the sheath upside down, tucking the blade between my rib cage and arm. If I had any hopes of avoiding violence in this place, I didn't want them to see the Devil's daughter approaching with a weapon.

Once inside, instead of the light growing dimmer it somehow shone brighter than before. Pillars of clear quartz and pearl arched over my head towards the roof of the cave. The ceiling was a shattered kaleidoscope of whites, silvers, bronzes and golds. Silver stalactites reached down from above, dripping into wade pools of glittering water emerging from the crevices of the rock. It was one long room that just kept going with no doors or stairs. If all Angels traveled by using their wings, or whatever type of light travel I just did, I guess those things wouldn't be necessary.

"You arrived faster than anticipated. If we had known, we would have met you at the gates." I turned towards the voice, a mistake as this Angel was in its true form and I was staring directly into the blaze of Holy Light. I slapped my hands over my eyes, the pain throbbing like I had been seared by a branding iron.

Two sets of hands grabbed each of my arms and I felt myself being hoisted into the air. I lashed out, kicking at the robes I felt swishing against my sides, but their grip didn't let up until I roared,

"Let go of me God dammit!" They complied immediately, and for the second time today I crashed to the ground.

I immediately jumped to my feet and risked opening my eyes again. At least thirty Angels surrounded me, thankfully none of them appearing as balls of light, eyes and feathers anymore. All of them looked relatively the same to me. Blonde, brown or black hair was all cut and styled the same and set atop round faces with pale eyes. Some were standing on the ground and others hovered in the air. Each of them had at least two pairs of wings on their back, most of them more, in varying shades of white, beige and gold.

"She's armed, Gabriel," one quietly commented, and I found the group in front of me studying my face. No, more like over my shoulder. I turned but was met with more faces peering past me.

"You wear your mother's sword and shield." The original speaker, Gabriel I'm guessing, pulled my attention back to them. At my deadpan stare he sighed, raising a hand to tap his ear in the spot I wore my mother's ear cuffs.

"It's jewelry," I said flatly. He smirked.

"Sometimes."

"Where's my sister?" I growled and his smirk only grew wider.

"Straight to business, are we? Not even a shred of joy for being welcomed home."

"Welcomed? Home?" I repeated, before breaking out into laughter. "You're kidding right? You abducted my sister and think I'm happy to come up here and get her?"

"It would have been very easy preventing you from getting in. So believe me when I say we welcome you with all the joy and grace in our hearts," Gabriel said. I narrowed my eyes.

"Last I checked, God is the one who threw my Father out, and I don't notice him in attendance." I took a slow, measured step towards him, unafraid of the Angels surrounding me as I added, "Furthermore, I have the blood of two Angels in my veins. What could you have possibly done to keep me from getting here if I wanted to?"

The look he gave me was of sheer, burning rage. I set a glare of my own against him, watching his anger wither as he relented and averted his eyes.

"That reminds me, how did you get here exactly?" He asked, "We had the entrance guarded. Did you not fly?" I shook my head.

"Not that you deserve my honesty, but I don't know," I admitted. "I inherited the ability to Shadow Jump from my Father, so I manipulated that technique to transport myself through light instead." A quiet gasp echoed in the hall behind me, and the Angels began to murmur to themselves in small groups.

Gabriel, who had been hovering a few feet above me, slowly lowered himself to the floor in front of me. His eyes traversed my body, giving away nothing as he walked a slow circle around me taking me in for the first time. I shifted uncomfortably on my feet, trying to angle the point of the dagger out of my armpit where it ended up. Finally, he ceased his analysis, tilting his head and looking at me with what I could only describe as wonder.

"It seems you inherited a similar ability to that of your Fathers. One we haven't seen for centuries. In fact, your older brother was the last Light Walker to grace this Earth." I rolled the term around in my mind for a minute, ignoring the older brother comment.

"It didn't feel that different from Shadow Jumping. Just had to squint more," I commented, deciding to keep the whole feeling-like-I-was-burning-alive sensation to myself. Gabriel fastened his eyes to mine, a look of annoyance creeping into his features once more.

"I just told you that you possess the same abilities as the Lord's child, and you defile it by comparing it to your Fathers impersonation of it."

"Well, maybe that ability has to do with our Mother and not our Fathers?" I cocked an eyebrow, feeling another easy smirk slide onto my lips. Gabriel blinked, somewhat stunned by the idea but said nothing, turning on his heel and rising into the air once more.

"My sister?" I prompted, jogging along on the floor under him, hating the way my voice rose in pitch with worry. "I won't be leaving here without her. You can't cast me out, so you're stuck with me unless you give her back."

"Or we could just kill you." I stopped dead in my tracks, his comment hitting me like a truck.

"Why?" I ask, my shock letting the question slip out.

"Because as long as the two of you exist, you'll only grow stronger." Gabriel's voice was laced with malice, "In short term that is good. But undoubtedly, the darkness in your blood will win. There's no way to ensure you won't work against us and defile God's creations. The only way we can guarantee their protection is to eliminate any possible threats against them. Threats like your sister."

"And aren't I a threat?" I asked, fighting the urge to bare my fangs. Gabriel released a choked laugh.

"You my dear may find that by our healthy persuasion, have the potential of keeping your demonic tendencies under control. Rebecca I'm afraid will never have that capacity." He wrinkled his nose with contempt, "That child of the Devil and heathen God will never see the light of day again."

The room was spinning, and I felt like I was going to throw up. They wanted to kill her. Did they kill her? No, he said as long as she and I exist we'll grow stronger. He was still talking about her in the present tense, so I wasn't too late. I forced myself to swallow the bile creeping up my throat.

"Heathen God?" I prompted, trying to divert the conversation and buy myself some time.

Gabriel's eye twitched and all the Angels around us went silent. I fought the smile trying to creep its way onto my face. He hadn't meant to let that slip out. Feigning innocent interest, I tilted my head and pursed my lips.

"You said you wished to persuade me, and I genuinely don't wish to end up like the corrupted asshole my Father is. So, can't we find some middle ground? Like sharing why you referred to her mother as a God?" I kept a cool, neutral look on my face and pushed one step further, asking, "Isn't our God the one and only?"

Gabriel lifted a hand and in unison the Angels around us began to disappear in bold flashes of light. When we were alone, he reached that hand down to me. I worked a pleasant smile onto my lips and took his hand, allowing him to pull me with him skyward.

He flew us to the roof of the cave, entering a small crevice carved through the gold and set me back on my feet in the small chamber. This was the only space here so far that was dim, the room lit in a soft gold hue that my eyes welcomed after the harsh silvers and whites outside. Bookshelves were cut directly into the golden walls and were crammed with documents, scrolls, soft covers and hardbacks of all shapes and sizes.

"What is all of this?" I asked, peering around the room. There were no seats nor reading lamps despite the amount of written material bursting from every crevice of the room.

"History," Gabriel said landing beside me. "Documentation of and the practices related to all other Gods besides our own." My eyes shot to him.

"So, the heathen god comment about her mother—"

"Rebecca's mother is better known as the Egyptian Goddess Bastet."

He paced forward, sifting through some of the material upon the shelves before turning and holding out a weathered scroll toward me. I plucked it from his hands, unfurling it to examine the page.

'

> *Type: Goddess*
> *Region: Southern Egypt/North Africa*
> *Forms: Female/cat/black cat*
> *Abilities: consciousness projection, protection, good health, pleasure*
> *Relations:*
> *child of Ra— king/sun/creation*
> *sibling of Sekhmet— power/war*
> *wife of Ptah— creator/maker*
> *mother of Mihos— war*

'

I stopped reading and rolled the scroll back up into a tight tube replacing it with the others.

"So, if her mother is actually a Goddess, why is everyone under the impression that she's the daughter of the Sphinx?" I asked, eyeing all the other material in the room and noting how much of it there was. If all of this was cataloged information on other Gods, there must be a ton of them the Angels were trying to keep under wraps. Gabriel heaved a sigh, replacing the parcel on its shelf.

"Simple reason really. We can't have anyone knowing that other Gods exist when we preach about worshiping the one and only Father can we? The Sphinx is a mythical creature. A creature, Raven. Not a God, even if some people choose to believe otherwise. Her being the child of magic versus the child of a God makes what we are doing a whole lot easier." He grinned like he was sharing some type of amazing information with me.

"And what are you doing?" I ask, suddenly wary of our enclosed and high up environment. I shift one of my feet to face back towards the entrance of the chamber. Gabriel notes the move and flashes a blood chilling smile. With a sudden flare of his wings, he's on me within a millisecond, slamming my back against the shelves and holding my chin in a viselike grip.

"We're cleansing the world of those Heathens and their poisoned children to create the ultimate realm of light and worship. Help us rid our world of their evil, starting with your Father. We know you want to kill him. And it will be forgiven, because we need you to. This will be my only offer to you, Light Walker." He releases the hold on my chin, eyes searching mine.

He wants an answer now I realize. This isn't a proposal; this is a bargain. Will I agree to help them kill probably hundreds of deities, or will I refuse and be added to their hit list?

I replay his words in my head, how did we get so sidetracked? The scrolls my back is pinned against are bending under the weight. I need to start playing some of these pieces in my favor.

"You said starting with my Father," I point out, "I will need my sister to achieve that. So as a show of good faith in each other, release her and I'll send you a first-class package with the Devil's head."

"I can agree to that," Gabriel says. "So long as once her purpose is fulfilled, you finish the job. She was only kept alive to get you here." A rock drops in the pit of my stomach as he finally steps back. He strides across the room towards the entrance, glancing back at me in mild annoyance. "Would you rather not receive your sister?"

We do not fly slowly or easily this time. He shoots like a bullet through the air down that great, glittering hall. Down and down and down we go, until we catapult through another crevice in the wall.

This room is neon white and through the glare I can make out a giant silver cage. I swallow a sob seeing Becca inside. She's transformed, that great powerful cat of hers unconscious in a pool of blood. A spiked collar and muzzle dug into her skin, puncturing her face and neck from all angles.

The door swings open once Gabriel lands. I want to wrestle myself away from him, stab my dagger into his tiny cold heart and fight my way out of here getting her to safety. But I remember our bargain upstairs and focus on keeping my breaths calm as I pace my steps and I climb into that cage beside her.

The spikes of her collar must be made of the same silver as the dagger in my coat. Slowly I undo the buckle. I do nothing to stop it from tearing at her skin as the weight of it rips it free and turn my back to her to face Gabriel one last time.

"I'm sure you'll have eyes and ears everywhere, but I'll update you when she's healed enough to strike."

"Healed enough?" Gabriel laughs, "She doesn't have to be healed to be good bait. You attack the night of the full moon, when the Hounds and vampires are strongest, and your Father is weakest."

"That's in two days!" I sputter, shock coursing through my body. Gabriel nods.

"Indeed. I suggest using this time to master your mother's sword and shield. And for the love of God summon your wings. You're a waste in the future without them." I fight the urge to rip *his* wings off, and instead nod as if I'm accepting the advice wholeheartedly.

"Two days then," I agree, my throat dry.

I turn back to my sister, hating myself as I purposefully grip one of the holes in her neck before using the barely there shadow from the roof of the cage to take us home.

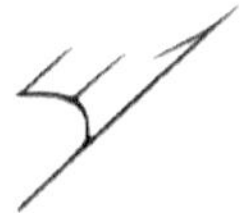

I deposit us right in the main hall. Becca's limp body falls to a bloody heap on the floor at my feet, and I can't help but bolt from her side to retch.

As the scent of her blood fills the room Silas materializes, throwing himself at her so viciously it takes both Kuma and Finn to keep him from blindly tearing into her. He's sobbing then, unable to control his pain, his shock, or his hunger. So, I do the only thing that I can for him.

I wipe the vomit from my mouth with the back of my hand before removing my jacket. The dagger dangling from its sheath swings against my hip as I slowly approach the struggle over Becca's body. I don't hesitate, freeing the silver edge of the blade and swiping it across my wrist in a single move. Finn's head whips towards the scent, eyes glowing ravenously, but he remains locked on his brother as a rumbling growl sounds from behind me.

"It's okay Akashi," I mumble under my breath, feeling the bulk of his Hound form brush against me. My eyes don't leave the back-and-forth patrol of the vampire brothers before me. "They won't try to kill me while I save his mate's life."

I step around them, Kuma taking advantage of their shock to push them both backwards from me and my sister. Akashi follows behind me as I kneel next to her, a solid barrier of muscle and teeth.

Gently, I pull her head into my lap and let my golden blood drip against her mouth. A puff of air races from me as she stirs, knocking my ribs with her paw as she begins to regain consciousness and lap at my blood of her own accord.

Akashi bristles behind me, prepared to leap into action if Becca's hunger takes over and tries to drill those pointed silver teeth into me. But she doesn't, and I knew she wouldn't.

Instead, her body slowly shrinks and with my free hand I motion for my jacket. Silas rips himself free, rushing forward to cover her naked frame with it as she transforms back into her human body.

Her blonde hair is splattered with blood and her eyes are dull, but thankfully the holes in her neck and face are gone, a sign my blood has done its job well. She takes a minute to get her bearings before tiredly asking,

"Did I at least get a pair of wings for a souvenir?" I grin and shake my head, standing but my legs quake out from under me, and I have to catch myself against Akashi's shoulder. She must have drunk more than I thought for that bigger form to heal.

"No, not a pair of wings," I say, scanning the room for Akashi's clothes.

Sure enough they're at the bottom of the stairs, proof he transformed the second he saw me in the room. To protect me. To help me. I grit my teeth and push him gently, allowing myself to use him as a crutch as we cross the room.

I bend and pick up his jacket, reaching inside the hidden internal pocket and pull out a small, weathered scroll. Gabriel, in his sick desperation to get me on board, must not have noticed when he pinned me to the bookshelves that we were directly in line with Rebecca's family history. So, I took the liberty of using the shadow my body created to transport that bit of information home. I hold the scroll aloft and muster a weak smile,

"Though I did make sure to grab something for my little sister before we left."

CHAPTER 27

I was at war with myself. Half of me wanted to rally everyone together and reformulate our approach. Considering how dramatically our timeline moved up, everyone needed to be on the same page, *now*. There could be no more bickering or trust issues otherwise we wouldn't make it out of this alive.

The other half of me didn't want to talk or think about it at all. That half of me was currently winning.

As soon as I handed the scrolls off to Becca I retreated upstairs and locked myself in my room. I needed everything about Heaven off me. The light, the bargain, the stench: off. So, I had run a bath, only tossing my boots aside before submerging myself in the water.

I lay on my side, braced against the ramp leading down into the pool. Gentle bubbles played along the surface of the water in time with my breaths and I closed my eyes.

I didn't want to imagine how everyone would react to everything I now knew. How many Gods there truly were, what the Angels had planned for them, what I had agreed to do. In a sick way it was kinda funny. In the span of a few hours, I went from being the most clueless person in our posse to the most informed. And I suddenly understood why Luna had spared me from the knowledge all these years. After all, I was sparing her now.

A knock echoed from my bedroom door, but I tried to ignore it. With a small wave of my hand, I send the bathroom door swinging shut on an invisible breeze to put another barrier between me and the outside world. The knocking came again, louder, and I groaned before shimmying towards deeper water and submerging my head.

Now this was nice. The silence of water is so prominent, it's calmness dancing against my racing thoughts as if it can give them some order. I hold my breath for as long as I can before resurfacing with a gasp that turns into a scream as the bathroom door gets kicked in.

"Raven? Are you alright?" Finn crosses the room in three strides, not even pausing to remove his shoes as he plunges into the tub to my side. He cups my face in his hands, frantic eyes looking me over. "Did they do anything to you? Are you harmed?" I'm about to ask him what the hell he thinks he's doing, but a memory clicks into place.

Right. Before this shit went down, he had brought me a gift, the most precious I had ever received, and was confessing to me. I blushed. I think I shut him down, but I can't expect his feelings to just disappear. I know firsthand just how pesky those feelings can be. Gritting my teeth I take his wrists in my hands, guiding his hands away as I take a step back.

"I'm okay. They didn't harm me." His eyes travel over me once more, disbelieving. I can't help but smile softly, "You of all people should be able to tell. There's not a scent of my blood right now, is there? I'm fine." I repeat. He blinks but nods, finally averting his gaze from mine.

I take another step away, wading up the ramp towards the sink. The slosh of water seemed to jar him, as if he hadn't realized he had jumped right in the bath with me and currently stood in waist deep water. I heard him quickly begin to follow me out.

"Why did you steal the scroll?" His question bounces off the tile, catching me off guard and making me pause. I throw a halfhearted smirk over my shoulder.

"Ah, that's just a little something I stole to make Gabriel's life harder." I thought the humor would lighten the mood, but at the mere mention of the Angel Finn's arm shot out, fingers gripping my forearm like a coiled snake.

"You spoke with Gabriel?" The edge in his voice is unmissable.

"Yes," I measured my words, "I'm assuming you know him? He seems like the ringleader up there."

"He personally told us to get you and your sister."

"That's not shocking," I mutter, keeping a cool mask of disinterest on my face. "He seems... unstable. Acting like he's literally in charge of Heaven and drunk on that power. Some of the things he was talking about..."

"What?" Finn's hand rises to my shoulder, the other again gripping my cheek. I frown but he persists, "Angel you know I recognize the best parts of you but please hear me when I say this: Heaven, as glorious as it sounds, is at war. And Gabriel allowed the Devil's child to not only carry a conversation there, but get so close to historical documentation that you could steal it."

I nod, understanding where he's coming from. He and Silas had been as close to forthcoming as vampires get, so I decided to share what happened and what I learned up there. How I was blinded by an Angel in its true form. That Rebecca is the daughter of a Goddess not a beast.

I kept the truth about my mother's ear cuffs to myself though.

When I began divulging their plans to eradicate as many other Gods as possible, he placed a finger to my lips and shook his head with a small smile.

"That, I promise you don't need to worry about. Gabriel has been dreaming of that for eons, but it won't come to pass unless God actually wants it to." I frown, wondering if that's the case then why was Rebecca's lineage changed, but say nothing.

Perhaps it was just an isolated incident because the Devil was trying to get to me and went through them first. The outcome just provided Gabriel the opportunity to act on his delusional plan.

"It's going to sound insane," I say with a shake of my head, "but it was just a feeling I had. And I even shot a jab out about it, and they didn't engage. But I don't think God was there." At this Finns smile drops completely.

Finn sighs, "Believe me, he doesn't go anywhere. I'm sure he had other things to attend to and put the Angels in charge of you and your sister. As the humans say, the Lord works in mysterious ways, yes?"

I can't help the flutter of laughter which escapes my lips and Finn's smile returns. But then he's twirling a strand of my wet hair around his finger and lifting it to his lips. I still as he tugs me forward gently, pressing a few soft kisses to my temple.

"Finn..." He ignores me, his hands dipping into the water on either side of me to find my hips pulling the two of us even closer together as his lips trace the shell of my ear. I place my hands on his chest pushing backwards, "Stop."

"She's politely asking you to get the fuck out of the tub Emo boy." Finn freezes as Akashi's voice rumbles towards us. My head snaps in his direction, his frame propped against the sink, arms crossed against his chest. How much has he heard? Seen? Finn sighs, releasing his hold on me and steps back, eyeing Akashi with absolute malice.

"That's right, I almost forgot. I did notice the two of you out in the garden earlier." Akashi visibly bristles against the implication, and I can't stop the blush that floods my face.

Finn wades from the water, shoes clipping the tile as he strides for the bathroom door. He pauses there, hungry

328

red eyes finding me once more, "Ya know, for a girl who claims to know nothing about desire you sure are twisted in a sticky web of it, Angel. And with your brother no less."

"I'm not her brother." Akashi's voice is deafening, "We aren't blood related at all, so stop making her feel disgusting."

"Oh," Finn chuckles, sizing Akashi up, "Do you really believe she feels disgusting after she moaned for you like that? Or do you feel disgusting for trying to imprint on your innocent little sister?"

Akashi dove for Finn but ended up splayed out against the tiled floor. The vampire had vanished once the cruel words slipped from his lips, yet I could still feel his mocking laughter clinging to the corners of the room.

"Chicken shit." Akashi seethes and rights himself, but anything else he has to say is lost beneath the steady drumming in my head.

Imprint. Imprint. Imprint.

"Yo!" Akashi's hands clap together, snapping me out of it. I blink in shock before yanking myself from the tub, crossing the suddenly small room to the linen closet for a towel.

"Little Bird, bathing clothed seems somewhat counterproductive," he mutters, trying to break the awkwardness with a little humor.

"I was relaxing, before you two buffoons barged in here." My heart races in my chest as I start wringing out my hair. Feeling his stare threatening to burn a hole through the back of my head I spin and bark out, "What?!"

Immediately he averts his eyes, shifting on his feet uncomfortably. I glance down at my body and curse. My white tank top is completely soaked through, and my jeans are hugging my thighs.

"I'll go, I'm sorry," he stutters, already halfway out the door.

"I don't hate you." My abrupt response to his earlier outburst in the garden makes him freeze in his tracks, "I also don't feel disgusting, as Finn suggested." I pause before asking, "Do you?" He takes a deep breath.

"No. I don't feel disgusting." His voice was strained.

"What did Finn mean about you trying to imprint on me?" I dared to ask. I swear the room itself was holding its breath as he slowly turned to face me again. His eyes were ablaze with want, but he was already shaking his head.

"Ignore him. You don't need to worry about—"

"The Angels demanded that I attack and kill my Father in two days," I cut him off and stride towards him. "They also demand that once the deed is done, I kill my sister. So please. If there is anything you want or need to tell me... tell me now." I demand.

Akashi was stiff as a board in front of me, his only movement being the short rise and fall of his chest with his breaths.

"Let me ask you something," his voice was thick. "Why do you find it so easy to share information with Finn?"

"I don't." I frown, not understanding why that of all things became the topic, "Though, I guess after years of being kept in the dark, it's nice to have someone willingly fill in a few missing puzzle pieces."

"But why *him*?" He pressed, eyes glued to my mouth, "Why not Silas. Why not the rest of us? I would have told you anything had you asked."

"It doesn't matter where or who I get the information from," I insist, "I just need it so I can decide what to do." A growl rumbles deep within his chest.

"You think I can't see what you're doing?" He shifts, angling us so that my back is pressed to the sinks counter.

"You never once have paused to think you're anything other than a burden to us. You cling to the idea of resolving this independently and take on all the pressure without entertaining the idea of support. Your whole life you've been desperately trying to keep us— to keep ME— out." His hands fell to either side of my hips, effectively caging me in as he lowered his mouth to hover inches from my lips, "And I'm going to punish you severely by forcing myself in."

Just as he was about to pounce, more knocking echoed from my bedroom door. Akashi's head snapped towards the sound, but he didn't budge.

"She's fine, we're busy." His voice was all business, not revealing a hint of the lust I saw lingering in his eyes.

"Why is the door broken?" Hikari's voice filtered to us. I could hear his feet padding across the bedroom floor, halting immediately when he heard the snarl that ripped from Akashi's throat.

"I said we're busy." His voice lowered to a pitch I never heard before, downright alpha, as he said, "Now get out."

There were no further protests and within seconds I heard my bedroom door click shut. Suddenly he was lifting me again, sliding me across the marble and pressing my back against the mirror.

"Akashi wait," I squirmed, Luna's voice ringing in my head as I slammed my hands on his shoulders.

His mouth was inches from mine, tantalizing me as I said, "You only get to imprint once. I don't want you to waste it. Not on me, especially when–"

"When we could both be dead in two days?" His hands found my hips, yanking me forward to be flush against him. My breath hitched feeling his wild heartbeat against my ribs, the only sign of his nerves as he pressed his lips against the shell of my ear, "How the hell could this be a waste if I'm getting exactly what I want?"

"Are you?" I released a flustered laugh, "Despite missing their mark, Finn's intentions are at least very clear. Meanwhile, you're toying with the lines between..." I trailed off.

I don't have a clue how imprinting works, or if he was just trying to satiate the near fire spitting energy crackling between us. If there was a difference between the two, he certainly never bothered to share it. My cheeks burned as I considered the fact that I could be the only one with these persistent feelings and that this encounter could just be purely physical for him. As if reading my mind, he flashed that cocky, all-knowing smirk.

His hands rose to cradle the back of my head, pulling me to him gently as he pressed the softest, brain melting kiss to my mouth. When he eased back, his gaze had darkened to molten emerald, sweeping downwards from my face to my neck, over my breasts to at last settle on where we were joined at the waist. His voice was dangerously low as he said,

"I think I'm being pretty fucking clear, Raven."

All my excuses and defenses evaporated. He grinned as I surged forwards, angling his head to catch my mouth again. His tongue expertly slid between my teeth as his fingers closed around my throat.

Vines erupted from my wrists and this time I let them do as they please. They slid under his clothes, caressing his skin. The careful placement of thorns had his shirt shredded from his body within seconds. He answered the move, grabbing the collar of my tank top and ripping it clear down the center.

I didn't have time to feel embarrassed before his mouth migrated to my now exposed chest. I moaned as his teeth dug into the soft flesh, immediately replaced by his tongue to soothe the small hurt.

His fingers left a streak of fire against my spine and involuntarily I jerked forward, releasing a sound I didn't even know I was capable of as he grazed the edge of one of the slits in my back. He paused, hot breath coating the damp trail of kiss marks he was leaving across my chest and locked eyes with me.

Slowly, deliberately, he traced a full circle around one of the edges. I tilted my head back, successfully trapping the needy whine in my throat but couldn't suppress the shudder of pleasure sweeping through me. Stars skittered across my line of vision and when I looked back down at Akashi, he was practically drooling at the sight of me.

But abruptly he pulled back, the cold dampness of the room slamming into me as his body heat receded.

"What the fuck!?" I hissed but he held up a hand,

"We aren't done."

"Good." I was beyond any point of argument, surprising both of us. A dark, satisfied smile spread across his lips, and he motioned towards the window with his chin.

"Go outside," he said, bending to untie his boots.

"Outside?" I asked, confused.

"I don't want any more interruptions." His eyes flashed and a hazy line of green spread across the floor from his feet encompassing me. With a wicked smile on his lips he repeated, "Now go outside. And run."

I never outran his spell, not even in the shadow realm. Flashes of green shone in my peripheral vision. When I glanced behind me the light was tailing me, like a trail being left for the wolf hunting me through the night. The echoes of Akashi's howls made me feel drunk on adrenaline, made my legs pump faster across the terrain so I'd beat him to where I wanted this to happen.

Akashi caught me right at the edge of the willow trees, arms encasing me against his heat and pinning me to the forest floor beneath him. He whispered all types of dirty promises against my skin as he undressed me with his teeth and braced me against the tree roots.

To my surprise, he tossed my thighs over his shoulders, lowering his head to drag his tongue from my entrance to my clit. I gasped when he caught it between his teeth, every nerve becoming a hyperaware blaze. The sensitive skin on my back was being scraped by the tree bark, the pull of pain and pleasure amplifying when a finger joined his tongue.

He was going slow, so slow. I jerked my hips upwards in a silent plea, but he just pushed me down again, forearm planted across my abdomen as he continued to work me in long, wet strokes. Then his finger curled, hitting a spot that made me quake.

"That's where you want me, isn't it?" He teased, repeating the gesture with a second finger. Intensifying the pressure, raising the speed. My fingers tangled in his hair as I hurtled over the edge, a crack of thunder above us swallowing my cry. He wasted no time shifting to hover over top of me, lips finding my neck as he settled between my legs. I automatically stiffened when he lined himself up against me, stroking himself against my soaked entrance.

"Breathe, Raven." My lungs forcefully snapped back into action— how long was I holding my breath? He chuckled, guiding my hands around the back of his neck before bracing a forearm on the ground above my head. "I don't plan on being done for a long while, so hang on tight."

Those first few inches were gloriously tight, the feel of his cock stretching my inner walls had my belly fluttering even as a hiss spilled from my lips. His thumb found my clit, the lazy circles easing the first hot flare of resistance, but it still had me jerking away from him. "I'm yours, Raven. I've got you." His voice was a reassuring caress against my baking skin.

I relaxed my clenched muscles, and he immediately rewarded me with hot, open-mouthed kisses delivered in a dizzying array of tongue and teeth. The next flash of pain had my fangs dragging his bottom lip, but before I could bite, he sank into me fully.

Fuck whatever Heaven or Hell could do to me, *this* was torture. Pure, delicious torture as Akashi slowly slid each hardened inch of him from me before slamming back in to the hilt. His control over himself was formidable, and annoying, especially since I could already feel the familiar itch of power in my veins wanting to be set loose.

I ignored it as Akashi flipped us, his cock anchored in my heat as he dragged me to straddle him. His grip seared into my waist as he guided my hips up and down, making my ass smack against his thighs and stars skitter across my vision. This time they didn't fade.

I gasped, pressing my hands firmly against his chest and halted. Shadows swarmed the space around us, but clinging to their tendrils were fractured galaxies of iridescent light. Akashi was utterly unbothered by my rampant powers, propping himself on his elbows to suck my nipple into his mouth. The stars flared a shade brighter when his tongue caressed the sensitive peak.

"Don't even think about holding it back." He commanded, driving me backwards to lay flat on the ground. He looped my vines around his wrist, using them to pin my arms above my head. His hair tickled my cheek as he punctuates each word with a kiss along my jaw, "Let. It. Go."

His mouth fuses to mine, stealing my breath and my sanity as his control slips, thrusts growing rampant and punishingly deep. Reality narrows to the coiling pressure between my legs, to the promised sweetness I can taste on my tongue. As if sensing I'm about to break he swings one of my legs over his shoulder, the new angle causing his shaft to drag against every perfect inch I need it to and I shatter.

The ground beneath us shudders and flickering, violet flames alight on my arms. His palms slide to the small of my back, out of harm's way, and arch me up to meet his final, aching thrusts. His own magic bursts across the ground then, enveloping the two of us in pulsing flashes of emerald as he loses himself in me.

Neither of us have the energy to call our magic back, letting it ebb and dull on its own time as we lay there tangled together. Akashi's attention had drifted back to my chest, and he was leaving extra gentle kisses against the suddenly raw patch of skin on my sternum.

When I finally shift, the ground under me is no longer damp sand, and my aching muscles appreciate whatever bed of flowers or moss my magic called fourth. A pleased shudder travels through me when Akashi's fingers slip from my waist to drag along it, as if he's admiring it as well. But then I stiffen. If those were flowers, I wouldn't be able to feel his touch as if it were on my skin.

"Well," Akashi lifts his gaze from the dark bed beneath us, his face a mixture of shock and fascination as he asks, "Should I take that as a sign that I did good?"

"What the hell was that?"

A howl had echoed through the busted-out windows of the house, waking Kuma from his sleep. Rising quickly, he first checked on Luna and Anzen in the room next to them, before returning to the room he was sharing with Hikari to shake him awake. As the howl sounded again Kumas eyes bugged, "Wait, was that—"

"There's all types of creatures in the wilds of purgatory." Hikari quickly interjected. Kuma frowned, eyes returning to his brother. Hikari lay there stiff as a board, the faintest of blushes coating his cheeks.

"Right..." Kuma muttered doubtfully, trying to figure out what he was missing.

"I wouldn't let your mind wander too much." Hikari gave him a pointed look before rolling over, clearly dropping the conversation.

Puzzled, Kuma left the room and quietly knocked on Akashi's door. The Alpha's bed lay empty. Ravens room was also empty, and what the fuck happened to the bathroom door? He crossed the space to examine it but froze when the thick scent of arousal hit him.

It was then that a third howl sounded, fading off in a guttural growl, and Kuma went red as a beet.

"For Hell's sake!" He returned to his room immediately, clamping a pillow over his ears. Hikari snickered, giving him a knowing look and Kuma flipped him off before rolling over and going back to bed.

CHAPTER 28

I woke up to the red sun blinding me through my eyelids. Despite the vivid glare of color, the room was cold thanks to the glassless windows letting the night breeze in.

I vaguely remembered Akashi carrying me back to the house after adamantly claiming it was too dangerous to sleep outside. Though I barely had the energy to shadow jump us back up to the busted windows of my room, the claw marks on the wall above the headboard sent my heart rushing as I recalled what we did before falling asleep.

Sitting up I rubbed my eyes, gaze snagging on my reflection in the mirror still propped in the corner of my room. I'm relieved to see that whatever darkness protruded from my back last night has made itself scarce.

Shifting my gaze, I raise a finger to trace the still sensitive imprinting mark that rests on my sternum just below the collarbones. It was a diagonal pitchfork of sorts, and just slightly paler than the rest of my skin. I caught a brief glimpse of Akashi's matching mark last night, his resting on his abdomen just above the left hipbone.

I should feel elated, but instead already felt dread threatening to stomp out any remaining highs of joy.

Officially, I had one day left before I was expected to march into Hell and kill both my Father and sister. Then proceed to kill any other entity the Angels told me to. With a sinking feeling, I realized I was about to be used as the weapon my family had tried preventing me from becoming my whole life.

Gabriel hadn't made any threats, but based on Becca's treatment I could only imagine what he planned to do to the Hounds if I didn't comply.

My heart thundered in my chest as I gazed down at Akashi, panic coursing through my veins as the image of that spiked collar digging into his neck sprung to mind.

I swung my legs out of bed, forcing the image from my mind as I tiptoed to the closet and pulled a sweatshirt over my head. I heard Akashi stir behind me but quickly donned a pair of shorts and slipped into a shadow before he could fully wake.

I wasn't avoiding him or unsatisfied, but I needed to see my sister before moving forward. And ideally, I wanted to see her alone. Without hovering boys, and not in a puddle of her own blood.

I emerged outside her bedroom door and knocked. When I got no response I traveled further down the hall, following her scent past Silas' door and found her in a makeshift gym that I didn't even know we had.

She was in the middle of doing pull ups when I entered the room. When she saw me, she dropped to the ground in a crouch, with all the grace and poise of a cat. I didn't know whether to feel reassured that she was healed enough to exercise, or to deck her for casually working out the morning after almost getting killed. I settled for the former and tossed her a half smile.

"And you had the nerve to make fun of our basement sparring area."

The room was filled with duct-taped together equipment. The walls lined with cardboard boxes proved how often they had to replace the current items. A ripped punching back dangled from the ceiling behind her, and several dented weight sets crowded the space. Even the ceiling hadn't been spared from the chaos I noted, eyeing the giant hole above my head where more than likely a spike of ice had impaled the stone.

"Yea well, it'd be a lie if I said we didn't get carried away," she muttered in reply, eyes flickering to the same gap over my head. "I'd also suggest from experience to give yourself more space while experimenting with any new powers you may have."

Silence swept the room between us. I haven't got a clue if Becca read the scroll I swiped or not. For all I know she could have just tossed it out. I shifted my weight from one foot to the other trying to figure out how best to approach the topic, but before I could come up with something witty enough to get the ball rolling, she released a sigh.

"You can just ask what they did. You don't need to dance around the subject for my benefit."

A rock dropped in my stomach. I knew how rough of shape she was in when I finally got to her. The image still had me checking her over for any fresh wounds, but... she was Becca. Probably the toughest of all of us. Definitely tougher than me.

So, I just healed her and left her to Silas. Gave her space. Got distracted by Akashi.

I hadn't let my mind wander to what the Angels might have done to her to make her that weak. And now, I was too preoccupied thinking about our next move to bother thinking of checking on her.

"I wasn't going to ask about that," I admit shamefully, "I was more so wondering if you read the information in that scroll?" Becca wrinkled her nose.

"You mean the crumbling Egyptian text? You expect me to be able to read hieroglyphics?" At my blank stare her eyes widened slightly, "Wait, were you able to read it?"

"Yes."

"Tch." After a short, annoyed glare, Becca rose from her place on the floor and pushed past me into the hall, "Fine, I guess you'll just have to read the damn thing to me."

I followed her to her bedroom, realizing just now that I'd never been inside her private space in my time here. I didn't know what I was expecting, but this wasn't it.

Three long tables were pressed against the walls, covered in pencils, brushes and bits of charcoal. Unstable stacks of paper, either pristine or stained in various colors, littered the floor. Large canvases covered in paint were propped up against any available surface to dry.

The walls, painted a pastel blue, were not void of art either. Various images from painted horseshoes to fiery dragons told a story around the room. I noticed how the images shifted from a child's scribbles to an artist's work, her years of practicing evident.

Up until this point she had always presented herself as gothic as the vampires. The absence of her usual bold reds and blacks was a shock, but even more so was the collection of cowboy boots and polished belt buckles I could see through her open closet door.

We crossed the room to her bed, which sat shoved into the corner of the room like an afterthought. Plucking the scroll from her nightstand she flopped to the mattress, extending the rolled parchment to me. Once I took it, it felt heavier in my hands now. Especially as I glanced between the ancient sheet of paper and Becca's expectant face.

"Keep in mind, if anything causes a possible outburst, I'm just the messenger. The last person I wanna fight is you," I said. She narrowed her eyes but nodded, before patting the space beside her.

I didn't read the scroll word for word as it was littered with material and smudged in many places, but passed along the basics I had previously gathered. Becca's face gave away nothing as I began listing off the true names and traits of her family, revealing that she was the daughter of a Goddess and not one of a creature. I read the detailed parts about her mother Bastet, describing the connections to her cat form and briefly mentioning other Gods in the family she was related to by blood.

When I finished, I set the scroll on the bed between us, bracing my elbows on my knees with a sigh. I heard the paper rustle as Becca rolled it back into a tight loop before the drawer slid firmly shut once more.

"So," she finally said, voice thick, "I'm the daughter of a God. Whose duties revolved around pleasure, protection, and health. Whose family has powers of the sun and the strength of war. Yea. That makes complete sense." She rose from the bed as if in a daze, "I need a drink."

"Becca—"

"He killed a GOD, Raven," Becca whipped around and I pretended to not see the tears in her eyes as she shoved a finger in my face. "They've all been killing Gods. What makes you think we even have a chance?"

Her words struck me like bullets. I didn't have an answer to that. I didn't have any reassurances or a plan. Instead, all I had to give was the truth.

"They want me to kill you." The temperature plummeted, ice spreading across the floor in every direction.

"What?" She snarled, claws replacing her fingertips.

"They want you dead and want me as a puppet." I leveled my gaze on her, not shying away from the brutal cold she was threatening to unleash, "And if people powerful enough to kill Gods are showing that type of concern, perhaps we have a better chance than you believe." I watched that icy glare of hers settle, and then begin to thaw as she contemplated my words.

"You really think we can beat them both? Heaven and Hell?"

"I believe we have a chance." My voice was hoarse. Her skepticism permeated the room, but she sat back down next to me. The heel of her boot vibrated on the floor as we both sat there and thought.

It was obvious I would be seen as a threat to whatever side of the war which couldn't use me to their advantage. If I were that powerful, then I alone should be able to end it. But regardless of my own standing, they tried to take out Becca too.

Sure, she could have just been a piece of collateral damage to our Father, but the Angels singled her out as well. I found it hard to believe they went so far as to drag Finn and Silas into this mess just to use her as leverage. They clearly weren't comfortable with keeping her alive, but maybe my growing hunch was true. Some part of her power might be tempting them, yet for some delusional reason they thought they could only manipulate me so would settle for her death.

Absently, my eyes drifted over the paintings on the wall again. I admired the detail of Becca's more recent work, the edges so sharp and realistic I felt like I could pluck the images from the stone. But something kept dragging my attention back to a small cluster of finger paintings a few inches from the floor. I noticed several of the images sported a small blue cat chasing after what appeared to be a purple butterfly.

"When did you paint these?" I asked, getting up to take a closer look.

"Oh, those stupid things?" Becca snorted, "Right after I got here. Silas said I was crazy worked up those first few months, so they gave my hands something to do. I shoulda painted over em a while ago huh? They bring down the rest of the art."

She laughed to herself a little bit, but I just kept studying those paintings. There was an eerie familiarity about the mountain range the two critters climbed in one image. That same feeling echoed in another picturing them swinging on golden tree branches.

I followed the images into Becca's closet and an audible gasp ripped from me. Rapid fire my eyes shot from one image to the next. A stone dais. A church. A cave. Two mermen. A castle with two queens. And a tall silver bridge. The butterfly and cat were shown together in all of them. I was vaguely aware of my shoulder slamming into the wall as my eyes began to blur.

"Rave what the fuck?" Becca's hands were on my shoulders, but I pushed her off, yanking an armful of her clothes from their hangers to reveal even more paintings on the wall behind them.

"You have no idea what you did, do you?" I started laughing. Her concern was replaced by confusion as she watched me throw all of her clothes out of the closet. "You didn't lose your memories Becca. You just forgot where you kept them."

Realization dawned on her face, and together we took in the images her child-brain painted of us. That butterfly and cat ran all over the world, played with all types of magic while living with their queens in the castle. The mermen were supposed to be Silas and Finn I realized, remembering we had only met them a few times out by the sea.

"But I don't understand." Becca traced a finger over the paint, frustration clipping her words as she said, "If I could remember all this then how could I not remember you?"

"You remembered more than enough." I pivoted her to face one of the last images. This one depicted just the cat, staring into the night sky, some of the stars warped to look like distant butterflies.

My palms are buzzing, and brain is itching, and her closet is suddenly way too small. Unquestioning, Becca follows me out of her room and down the stairs until I finally pause before the blasted-out windows of the main hall.

For the first time since Finn returned them to me, I remove just one of my Mothers golden ear cuffs. I roll it between my thumb and forefinger, paying more attention to the weight and undeniably smooth polish than when I did upon receiving them. Which is why I catch it this time— the slightest, most subtle crease in the gold. It's not even visible to the eye, so I run my fingertip over the crack one more time to confirm.

With a swift flick of my thumb, the base of the cuff rotates. For a moment I think nothing happened because the change was so swift, but my wrist dips under the weight of the golden sword now gripped tight in my hand. I don't know if I want to whoop or sob as memory after memory floods back. They aren't full or coherent, but they are enough.

"I told you I thought we had a chance. Now, I'm sure." I repeat the move against the hilt of the sword, shrinking the piece back into the cuff it masquerades as.

"What makes you say that?" There's uncertainty in her voice, but curiosity too. I turn, meeting Becca's expectant gaze, and grin.

"My mother told me how to win."

Everything had become much too serious, much too heavy. As relieved as I was having my brain unscrambled, and an actual plan, it just made the gravity of the situation all that harder to bear.

The bickering I had been tuning out escalated just as my eyes refocused the table where everyone was seated. None had reacted well to the news of how the Angels planned on using Becca as collateral since our childhood. It was an opportunity they thought they'd lost until I found my way here. Her abduction to Heaven had been a small play in a larger game, reinforcing to us both that they could easily harm her if I didn't comply.

Presently, the argument was about how to prevent that very scenario from playing out once Lucifer was dealt with.

"For the millionth time," Becca's voice had long since grown aggravated, "I apologize but we can't tell you every damn detail or it won't work."

"It won't work because we don't have the damn details!" Kuma pounded his fist on the table and turned to Akashi.

I was stunned that so far he had said nothing, just taken in what information Becca gave him with a locked jaw. Kuma's nostril flared, "Come on man! Don't let the thrills of imprinting blind ya!"

Akashi drew back his lips, and the snarl that echoed throughout the room was purely lethal. Becca groaned, exasperated, and turned in her chair to face me.

It was a wonder; how easy it was to read her now that I remembered her. We had been so close, and they took it. Just like they took our mothers.

We shared a few looks before I inclined my head towards the front door. With a small grin she rose, only pausing to place a kiss on Silas' open mouth before she left the house.

I ran a hand through my hair, suppressing my annoyance before I took her vacant seat.

"She's not telling you because I told her not to."

"Since when did you two get so buddy buddy?" The ice in Silas' voice rivaled my sisters. I ignored it.

"I'm not wasting a bunch of time here defending myself or explaining shit. We don't want to tell you because there's no way any of you can play our roles. And we don't want to spend the next twelve hours listening to the lot of you try to talk us out of it. It was my... it was Mary's plan." I swallowed, fighting the emotion bubbling in my throat before quietly adding, "It will work if you just for once trust us more than you fear them."

I ignored the multiple squawks of protests when I stood up and Luna's burning gaze. There was so much fear and love in it I nearly staggered to Akashi's side, giving him his own kiss before following my sister out of the house.

I'd known where she had gone of course. It was exactly where we needed to be. My clothes melted and reformed around me as I walked, a shimmering silver mask woven from spiderweb sticking to my face just as I climbed the rickety steps to the club and sauntered inside.

I made my way down the spiral staircase inside, spotting Becca in the middle of the floor. The music tonight had more bass to it than the last time we were here, and she was already dancing, a radiant smile lighting up her usual empty face. It was the first genuine smile I had seen from her since being reunited, and I would die to keep it there.

Her hand reached out, yanking me into the crowd with a laugh. We danced. We sang. We drank. We pretended to forget everything that was so heavily weighing on our minds and just lived for a minute.

And we silently promised to never lose one another again.

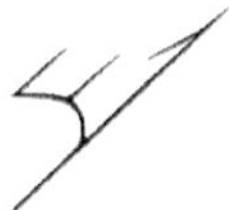

My head was swimming when I woke up. Vaguely, I remembered

stumbling back to the house. Akashi had been awake, sweeping me into his arms and into bed immediately. He was pissed but hadn't pushed me. And that just made what I was about to do so much harder.

Silently, I slid through the shadows in the still dark room to gather what I needed, before bending to press a featherlight kiss to Akashi's mouth. I didn't linger out of fear of waking him, and for the second time in two days left my mate to awaken alone.

Becca was already in the garden by the time I arrived, looking as ragged as I felt. Wordlessly, I pass her weapons and fighting leathers I'd conjured yesterday from the pockets of shadow under the bushes. We dressed quickly, and by the time the red sun peered over the horizon the two of us were gone. The danger today posed for our families hopefully retreated with us.

The vampire gazed out the window, his eye trained on the girls who were disappearing towards the eastern sunrise. He knew he had to follow at a respectful distance otherwise they would spot him

with ease and the day be ruined.
However, he was so focused on this fact,
he didn't notice the wolf far below
amongst the roses also watching them
leave.

CHAPTER 29

"So, are you at all confident in this plan?" Becca asks, side eyeing me with a subtly raised brow. I plaster a smile on my face, nodding almost to myself.

"What part of it doesn't make sense? It's his power after all." I hope I sound reassuring.

There was some anxious tension about how we would be getting to Hell. I had no doubt that it, like Heaven, would be complicated to get into. Since I only successfully got there while calling upon my mother's power, I figured the two of us combining our shadow jumping strengths would be our best bet at breaking open a gate to the fire. Becca shrugged her shoulders.

"All I'm saying is maybe there was some merit to Luna's warnings. I don't know about you, but I don't wanna be trapped in a shadow realm," she stated matter of factly. I grit my teeth.

My whole life Luna warned me about the dangers of shadow jumping, about how I could get sucked in too deep and not find a way out. But it was the warnings of giving my Father an avenue to find me which got my brain rolling on the whole idea of it. If it was a way for him to find me, then it should work as a way for me to find him as well.

"Well did the vampires ever warn you about it?" I countered and she shook her head.

"Nah. All they mentioned was Lucy finding me, never me getting stuck." She passed me a wicked grain, "But I am more skilled at it than you are, so I don't know. Maybe I'll get there just fine, and you'll be the one left floating through the abyss!" She doubled over belly laughing.

"Yes yes, by all means, make fun of my possible demise," I muttered, turning my back to her. Shadows pulse around my feet in dark tendrils, snaking across the Earth before disappearing into nothingness.

"I'm sorry, I'm sorry," Becca wipes away a tear as she composes herself, her own dark shadows wafting towards mine. "So how do you want to do this? My vote is to make a vortex of terror." I roll my eyes.

As our shadows swirl together, I pick out the subtle differences between them. Unlike how mine pulse in time with my heartbeat, my sisters move in more of a staccato movement. Mine also borders on a murky gray whereas hers are a shade of black deeper than the stormiest of nights.

We shift around the pit of darkness growing at our feet, the shadows beginning to crash like bound waves against the Earth. Silently, I hold my hand out towards her and without hesitation she takes it. There was no way we could risk getting separated from each other, despite it being our own power. A soft squeeze is my only warning before I'm being pulled into the fray, the flash of Becca's golden hair the last color I see before being plunged into darkness.

The shadow realm is darker than I've ever seen before. I can barely pick out Becca's eyes, gleaming at me through the dark like a cat. We begin to walk, taking care to avoid any blurry objects or pathways that pop up in front of us. We need to go further than any time before, deeper until only one destination is left.

Unlike light walking, the deeper we travel the colder it gets. Every inch of this place is a frozen tipped blade, the air assaulting our skin like we went swimming in the middle of the arctic. I can tell by the fragmented shivers crossing her palm to mine that even Becca is cold despite being used to the bite of her icy magic.

It's officially so dark now I can't see a thing and our pace has slowed to barely a shuffle. Suddenly, Becca halts beside me. I gently tug her in question, but she still doesn't move. I open my mouth to speak but the silence drowns out my words sending a bolt of panic through me. If we can't communicate, how the hell are we going to get out of here?

All of a sudden, a hazy orange light pops to life through the gloom. I freeze, my free hand gripping the dagger at my hip before I realize the light is coming from Becca.

Her golden hair is lighting up the space around us like the early morning rays of dawn. She and I both stand there for a moment, mouths agape before I wave a hand in front of her face.

I mouth the words, 'Mom's family,' and her eyes flicker with recognition. This must be a power she inherited from her grandfather, Ra.

She points to our feet, and looking down, I'm able to pick out the shape of cobblestones through the twisting shadows. I motioned my hand for her to dim the light if she could, and after a few minutes with just enough light to see we begin walking again, this time following the cobblestone path.

Through the haze a dull blue light, much like the shade of Luna's soul-searching spell, breaks through a crack in the darkness. As we veer towards it, Becca dims herself completely as it grows brighter. Noise begins to return the further we go. Finally, we shimmy out the hole in the wall, our feet tip tapping on the stones and both our breaths come in ragged gasps.

The landscape spread before us is red and gray, barren apart from the occasional towering stalagmite reaching up towards the cavernous ceiling. The only source of light is that faint blue glow, settled over everything like a thin mist. It clings to us in glittering folds, breaking and layering like a dead sea as I step further into it. The ground shifts beneath my feet like sand.

"So much for hell fire," Becca forces out, breath clouding in front of her. My own bones are quaking from the cold, the fire in my veins being my only savior. She smirks slightly, probably about to make a comment about how she's much better suited for this environment, but a laugh barks down from the rocks above us stopping us in our tracks.

Becca and I whip towards the sound, her claws breaking through her skin whilst I brandish my dagger in front of us. Perched atop an outcropping in the rock we had just climbed out of was a man.

Despite the cold, he wore nothing but thin cotton pants. As he stood, he seemed to take extra care stretching his arms over his head, effectively putting all the muscles packed on him on display.

"I've been guarding this door for over three decades, and you're the first two that ever made it through without getting stuck."

"Do we win a prize?" Becca's voice is razor sharp, and her smile is all teeth.

"Relax," he dragged out the word, grinning like we were on the outside of an inside joke. "It wouldn't be very professional of me to not recognize the scent of my Master's daughters, now, would it?"

"Hellhound," I muttered, immediately shifting my weight to press against Becca's back and drag my eyes across the landscape before us. Where there was one there was always another, and they kept themselves very well hidden in the empty space.

"Correct you are." In the mere seconds I had turned my eyes away from him he had hopped off the rock and now stood menacingly over us. Crossing his arms over his chest he continued, "We

365

have been awaiting your arrival for a very long time. So, if you wouldn't mind, sheath that dagger and follow me?" I raise my brow.

"And if I decide your pelt makes a better sheath than the one I already have?"

He doesn't miss a beat, "Then the kitty cat here will be roasted slowly on a spit."

"Dog," Becca spats, voice full of contempt. His smile only widens as he dares to lean closer to my sister.

"Something like that... but you'll find us Hellhounds to be far less obedient."

Her eyes shifted to mine, and I gave a subtle nod. She scowled, but her claws disappeared back into her knuckles anyway. I slid my dagger back under my leather arm band, eyeing him warily.

"Where's your pack?"

"Around," he replied nonchalantly, eyes focused on something over our heads. "In fact, you'll meet my Alpha right now."

"Oh, she's met me. Haven't you my darling sister?" My blood chilled to ice in my bones and Becca swore as we watched Anzen emerge from the gap in the rock behind us.

CHAPTER 30

I was in shock. My body was not my own as it pitched backwards and collided with Becca's chest.

I felt like I was going to bend over and vomit as I watched Anzen approach his subordinate. His usual warm doe eyes were now dark pits. His gaze brutal and unforgiving as the Hound between us dropped to a knee and bowed his head.

"I wouldn't have let her keep that dagger." His voice was sharp as my blade.

"Apologies sir." The Hound dropped his chin further, "You directed us not to threaten them. I figured allowing them to remain armed would de-escalate the situation fastest."

"Did you examine the blade at all?" The venom in my brother's voice made the Hound wince before shaking his head in admission. Anzen grabbed him by the hair and yanked him upright, "It's forged with Holy metal you fool." The Hound in his grip paled to near white.

"T-the blade was half black sir. I didn't realize–" The Hound yelped as he was sent flying from a backhand to the face. Anzen shifted his gaze to me, a mocking smile playing on his lips.

"Hand it over Raven. I won't hesitate to hurt her." He leveled his glare over my shoulder, where I assumed Becca was answering his stare with an icy look of her own.

"I don't have it," I hissed between grit teeth. His smile turned nearly feral.

"Should I strip you to find it instead?"

A shot of warning clanged inside my skull. Realizing Becca was still holding me upright I shoved her backwards, off of me. The subordinate Hound who just pounced at her back wound up tackling me facedown to the ground instead. The lacing on my leather arm bands was shredded in a millisecond– revealing no blade hidden beneath.

"What have you done with it?" Anzen snarled over me, the subordinate Hound still crushing me into the sand. I heard the crack of a whip before feeling something warm splash against the back of my neck.

"Bitch!"

"Becca put it away!" I screamed into the sand, sensing the approach of the rest of the pack. She ignored me, cracking the whip against the back of the Hound pinning me a second time. This time he got pissed off enough to release me and dive for her.

Panic shot through me seeing a massive grey Hound explode from a pit of sand behind her, but it immediately halted its attack seeing the whip Becca swung circling the first Hounds throat.

A strangled bark ripped from his lips, fingers clawing at the whip around his throat. His eyes widened, realizing that while in contact with the weapon he couldn't transform to break through. Becca meanwhile looked like she was on cloud nine.

The scent of pine and rain washed over me as I was hauled to my feet and pinned against Anzens chest.

"It seems you're all learning that my mate's sister is just as formidable as she is."

I could feel the weight of Becca's stare as the statement processed. Assessing. Calculating. Only then did I notice the black t-shirt, the jeans, the busted-up vans. All Akashi's clothes. What the hell was he playing at?

Subtly, Anzen tightened his grip on my wrist, and I dragged my eyes back to his. His gaze was just as formidable, but there was something quick and desperate there as well.

So, I let him lift my hand to his hair, which was washed with Akashi's shampoo, and styled with his gel. I pressed to my tiptoes, inhaling the scent of Akashi's body wash against Anzens neck.

My dear, sweet baby brother had covered himself head to toe in the scent that still lingered on my skin.

A pleased growl rumbled in his throat, one that to anyone else would sound lustful, but I knew it was a sign of his relief that I had caught on.

So, I bit my bottom lip and lowered my gaze, forcing the tears to be hidden by a front of shyness.

"Didn't we agree it would be safer not to tell them?"

I could feel Becca's eyes shooting daggers through me but blessedly she kept her mouth shut. Anzens lips tilted into a smirk.

"I didn't think he would so easily believe you sympathized with his cause, even after your trip to Heaven, without a permanent connection. It's best we don't hide it anyway."

I didn't know what to reply, but I didn't get a chance to as a growl ripped through the air that was absolutely blood curdling.

Immediately Anzen released me. I heard the dull plunk of the whip dropping to the sand before Becca gravitated to place herself directly between me and the Hound who appeared at my back.

Sensing an Alpha wolf was a thing I'd grown accustomed to, but even the average person would be able to detect the shift in the air when one was nearby. Wolves typically incited fear, or the feeling of being backed into a corner. An Alpha's presence had a cooler, sharper edge to reflect the control they held.

This Hound exuded neither of those things. Their presence held absolute power.

"Commander," Anzen only dipped his head in submission while the other Hounds around us either dropped to their knees or, if transformed, laid flat on their bellies.

The skin around my imprinting brand tingled, something in the mark able to identify the Commander for who they were before I could. Despite my senses flaring incessantly at the Commanders presence, there was a steady beat of calm inside my chest as I turned to face them.

It wasn't their massive size nor the bared teeth which elicited the shockwave that crashed through me. It was the eyes, warm and green like the spring. The Commanders vermillion coat reflected the bursts of red I was used to seeing against black fur. And then he barked a laugh into my face in the same way my mate had all my life, and I knew with absolute certainty that I was in the presence of Akashi's father.

"You mated with the child of our master? Have you gone mad?" The Commanders voice had a thick accent similar to Silas'. His gaze rifled down me and then back up, "I don't see an imprinting brand on her."

"Her's is in a place I'd rather keep all to myself." Despite the power difference between the two, Anzens voice remained steady as he reached for the hem of his t-shirt, "Allow me to show you mine instead."

There were murmurs amongst the growing crowd of Hounds as Anzen lifted the fabric to reveal a pattern of circles and leaves on his ribcage. The mark did not match mine, but it was undoubtedly an imprinting brand he had shared with someone. I did not meet his eyes as he lowered his shirt back into place.

The Commander snapped his teeth, pacing before us. Eventually, his eyes slid from me to Becca, still standing firmly between us.

"And what am I supposed to do with you, Cat?" He sneered. Her answering smile was sickeningly sweet.

"She's not going to be a problem. In fact, she's here because Heaven wants her dead," Anzen says.

"Well so did Lucifer." The Commander stops pacing, "Bring them both. We'll see what he has to say about that one." He snarls at Becca before turning away, "Make sure to disarm them."

Three Hounds make a go for her at once and I react without thinking. Shoving Anzen off me, vines with curling red thorns spring from my wrists and weave a barricade around her. The first two Hounds don't pay heed, and limp away once their paws were shredded.

"Disarming us will do nothing for you." My voice is shaking, from fear or rage I don't know, but I hold the Commanders gaze as I say, "You can take us to Lucifer with or without your dignity intact. It's up to you."

He eyes me for a moment, his expression blank until he finally growls in frustration.

"Very well, Princess."

Becca and I walk side by side, surrounded by Hounds on each side at least five layers deep. Anzen had placed himself in the innermost layer directly behind us. I had so many questions, and concerns, but they could wait. For now, despite my confusion, I was glad he was here and on our side. At least I think he was.

Not much changed about the bleak landscape, the sand and mist stretching for miles in any direction. The further we walked the thicker the latter got, which was why I almost slipped and fell on the sudden ice under my feet.

I whipped towards Becca, hoping she hadn't done something haywire, but found her staring at the ice beneath our feet with an arched brow. I didn't have the luxury of feeling relieved as I followed her gaze and eyed the distant light beneath the surface. Wait, that wasn't light that was—

A gasp ripped from me, and I dropped to my knees, fingers clawing against the ice of their own accord trying to reach the silver flames far below. I feel a hand on my shoulder, but I ignore it. Gold splatters the ice as I lose control of my body, my fingers being sliced by shards of ice I can't crack. Anzen rips me backwards, pinning me on the sand and slaps my face.

"Get your shit together." He rears his hand back to slap me again and I glare up at him, making him stop short. He lets out an annoyed huff, yanking me back to my feet.

"Angel blood." Someone sneers over my shoulder, laughter piping up from a few others. Becca's gaze is still on me, perfectly empty, perfectly calm. I dip my chin and she looks away. My eyes go back to that ice, fingers twitching in anticipation, wanting what's below.

"Get on." Anzens nose butts my waist.

"What?" I ask, still half in a daze. I hadn't even noticed he transformed, my obsession with those flames returning as soon as he stopped distracting me. He snorts, butting my ass this time.

"You're going to ride me across this lake and you're not gonna bitch about it. Get on." He repeats. Fucking hell when did he become so vulgar, or was that an act too? I shake my head, ignoring the snickers from around us as I climb on his back.

We begin moving again and I remain out of contact with the ice. I keep my eyes on Becca, trying to prevent them from drifting back down to those flames. Which she is making increasingly difficult as she does not break her gaze from them once.

Finally, the ice disappears, but instead of sand now there is stone under foot. Polished black onyx weaves a pathway through the mist, coming to a halt at an outcropping of rock. There's a door carved into the wall, much like the one at our home in Purgatory I note, but this door is connected to something much darker.

Jutting out of the cliffside is an obsidian palace, the delicate stone carved into dangerously sharp edges and peaks. Red flames of candlelight flickered out of what I assumed were windows high above where we stood. The place seems barren. Dead.

In the few books I've read, the hero reaching the villain is aways some dramatic scene drawn out over several hours or sometimes even days. But in reality, it's depressingly fast.

Becca and I are marched through the doorway and up the adjacent staircase, only pausing once before a wide set of doors.

I should have looked at her then. I should have looked at Anzen. I should have waited for Akashi to come with me. Because those French doors swung open much too soon, opening to a throne room and I was face to face with my father far faster than I was prepared for.

CHAPTER 31

Akashi ran faster than he ever had in his life.

He trusted her. Against all his instincts screaming not to. He let her keep her secrets. Let her leave with her sister, her TRUE sibling. Everything he couldn't be for her anymore.

He didn't ask questions or bark concerns when she arrived home at 3 in the morning absolutely plastered. He was just patient. Kind. Trusting. He owed her that much. She practically begged for that much the last time they spoke.

But then the bitch fucking left him here to wake up to an empty bed knowing exactly where she was without his help.

The thought had a fresh batch of adrenaline pumping his legs faster to near impossible speeds. He didn't bother to collect everyone; he just threw himself out of bed and howled as loud as he could. It was up to them to get their shit together and follow.

He didn't slow for anything, not until his claws left valleys in the cobblestone path he hadn't tread upon for nearly a century.

CHAPTER 32

I've seen art of Lucifer before. Several years ago, I got on some kick of wanting the bastard to be ugly, thinking it would make me feel better. Instead, it just made me fly into an immature rage after finding all the beautiful paintings and drawings of him.

I even found two sculptures, commissioned by the same church. The church was unsettled by the first sculpture, afraid of what its visitors would think seeing the Devil portrayed so tastefully, so they refused the piece. Instead, they commissioned the original sculptor's brother to re-create it more appropriately. The second sculptor had outdone his brother's work on all levels of sexiness, but not appropriateness.

None of the art I'd seen compared to half of the reality.

A stone dais rippling in red flame rose from the center of the otherwise empty room. The man sitting in the plush throne atop it had the flawless complexion of porcelain. His eyes were all pupil, and his snowfall hair contrasted sharply with the shadows quivering on his shoulders. Lips that put rubies to shame parted in a welcoming smile, pointed canines flashing.

"I haven't had a reaction to the fire like that in a long time." Lucifers voice wasn't short of elegance, each syllable perfectly pronounced. He leaned forward in his seat, pursing his lips, "Though I'm intrigued by just how desperate you seemed to get to it."

Words failed me. I just stood there silently, hoping I wasn't staring at him with a dumb face. As my silence persisted, the smile on his lips dipped into a smirk.

"One could think you were planning to kill me with it." The accusation hung in the air, a fist waiting to fall.

"I'd prefer to use my hands." Silence. Except for Becca, who couldn't help the short laugh that sprung from her mouth before smacking a hand over it. Lucifer seemed unfazed.

"Intelligent and silver-tongued. You are my daughter indeed." He rose from his seat, boots clicking on the steps as he descended towards us. Becca took a step closer to me. I flicked my wrist, and she froze. We didn't know if he also planned to use her as a hostage just as Gabriel had done. As if reading my mind, he snickered.

"Ah yes. My brother has the tendency to default to the most extreme tactics to get what he wants." His dark eyes scanned Becca from head to toe, "I would have come for you myself but, well. I don't exactly have a key to that particular gate."

Neither of us said a word, and I fought the urge to sidestep in his path as he passed me and walked a slow circle around her.

"You're the spitting image of Bastet you know? She was all the rage with her golden locks. A rarity amongst her kind for that alone."

"The rarity is how she ended up fucking you." Becca's voice was cool and even. Zero reaction at the mention of her mother. Lucifer smiled.

"I'll correct myself: two silver-tongues."

"You seem pretty comfortable for a guy who's on our hate list," Becca

381

drawled. I leveled a glare at her and she shrugged, "What? It's not like we're here for a family picnic."

"Regardless," I said through grit teeth, "we need him to stop Gabriel. Or did you forget that there's a legion of Angels willing to murder anyone and anything not of their faith?" Becca crossed her arms releasing a huff but let it go.

"So, you have learned what's going on up there?" Lucifers dark eyes glittered as he turned to face me again. "I will say that is a relief. Perhaps now you can understand many of my past actions without me needing to persuade you."

"Hold up." I frowned, "Just because I realize your brother is a homicidal maniac, doesn't mean I agree with a single one of your tactics." Fire laced my words. As if sensing it Lucifers grin melted. A flash of displeasure clouded his handsome features.

"Should I have joined them in the killing?" He challenged, arching a perfect white brow.

"You started your own track record anyway, so I don't see a bit difference." My hands were shaking now but I kept my head high. "Killing our mothers makes you no better than those you tried to rebel against. In fact, to us, it makes you worse." Lucifer released a cruel laugh.

"I did not kill Bastet. I believe Uriel had that pleasure. Now as for your mother," his mouth curled into a sneer, "Mary lost her nerve. And she paid the price for it."

The urge to kill him where he stood amplified by a thousand: because he was right.

I remember finding my mother in tears many times. I was an accidental birth, and too young to understand what change she thought I could bring. Change that I never had the opportunity to bring because neither side wanted to nurture me, just use me for their own gain.

Use me to kill anyone who opposed, not to save anyone who followed. She died trying to ensure neither of them had the opportunity.

And here I was on that precipice I was so familiar with, my emotions ready to consume me, ready to explode and take the world out with me.

Flames danced under my fingertips, aching to be set loose upon him. Unshed tears threatened to release tidal waves in the room. Even my racing breaths promised a tempest. But I took a moment, and mastered my composure.

"My mother's sympathy and understanding of your overall goal was not her consent to make me, or use me." A hint of malice shone in his eyes, reflecting the defiance in my own gaze. He stepped forwards and dropped a hand to my shoulder.

"I know full well you want to kill me. But you can't, can you?" There was nothing beautiful about his voice now, just plain cruelty. I stiffened as he lowered his lips to my ear.

"You haven't completed a few very important steps to unlock your powers, so you're settling to use me for your own gain. A mighty fine move, but don't forget," his nails dug into my skin so hard I saw stars, "I will kill you the second you are of no use to me. So, play your cards wisely, and slowly."

He released me, stomping back up the dais to his seat.

"Report, Anzen." His voice remained dark, his welcoming atmosphere thoroughly extinguished. Anzen stepped forwards, thankfully re-dressed, and cleared his throat.

"As you can see, I secured not just one but two of your daughters and returned them to your control at the most opportune time. Raven has recently completed her Reformation, and Rebecca has long since perfected her skills. I have kept calculated logs on all their capabilities, both physical and magical, as well as formed a permanently deep bond with Raven in particular."

"What kind of bond?"

"I've imprinted on her."

Lucifers face gave away nothing as he spoke to the Commander.

"Did you know of this?"

"Not until their arrival I'm afraid." The Commander stepped out from behind a Hound, transformed into his human body. His red hair was in a braid and those green eyes of his were no longer powerful, but somber. Obedient. He shifted towards Anzen, "We have seen his imprinting brand. It's real."

"And my daughter's?" My stomach rolled hearing him address me that way, but a flare of panic quickly took precedent as the Commander shook his head.

"Anzen prefer we not view it as hers is in a more, intimate of area, sir."

"Now Aengus, that was thoughtful of you." The Commander, Aengus, bristled as Lucifer added more sharply, "But is that your job?"

Anzens eyes met mine, a flash of warning crossing his features before being replaced by enraged possessiveness. He growled, taking a step closer to me.

"I'll show mine."

"It's okay!" I quickly interject, my hand shooting out to catch his before he could raise his shirt again.

My brand didn't match his. The Hounds would know that, but it was a gamble I was willing to take. If Lucifer saw Anzen's brand but then still demanded to see mine, we would be fucked.

"I'm not shy. He is just my Father." I fought the bile in my throat. I hid my face against his shoulder, trying to appear bashful as I asked, "But would a few of them mind turning around?"

For emphasis, I raised my hands to untie the back of my leather corset. If I had known getting undressed was on today's schedule, I wouldn't have chosen the lace-up fighting leathers.

Anzens growl was full of possessive prowess, and I did not have to repeat my request. All the other Hounds, save for the Commander, turned to face away.

"Becca, help me please," I muttered, only getting the laces halfway undone. I could do it myself, but I didn't want Lucifer to have a direct shot at her any longer. She circled behind me, releasing a few more inches of tension before helping me shimmy the corset down far enough that the top of my chest was exposed.

Lucifer said nothing as his eyes latched to the brand on my skin, assessing it from his view on the dais. Unimpressed, he averted his eyes and waved a hand.

Becca wasted no time and yanked my corset back into place, sparing not a second more to possible straying eyes. The Commanders molten gaze on us was enough.

I glanced in his direction, intending to meet his gaze, but was surprised to see him staring over top me at Anzen. He stood stock still beside me, his mouth pressed into a thin line.

"And what of the Nightshade pack?" Lucifer asked, calling our attention back to the top of the dais.

"I left that to Anzens discretion." The Commander's voice was like iron, each word slow. The underlying message clear: he would have no part in what we were trying to pull off but wouldn't stand in our way either. Impatiently, Lucifer turned his expectant gaze back to my brother.

"Eliminated," Anzen said, his voice wavering for the first time since we arrived. "Every Nightshade Hound lies dead, along with the vampires in their lair. Their bodies can be retrieved from the Purgatory morgue in a day or so." My blood ran cold.

"What...?" I asked, unable to mask my horror, "What did you just say?" He looked down at me blankly.

"It was the only way I could ensure they would not follow and attempt another kidnapping." His voice held no emotion, "You understand, don't you, my mate?"

The world turned to ash around me, and I swayed. The Commanders hands swung under my arms as Becca lunged for Anzen, silver claws whistling.

Akashi was dead in my bed, and it was my fault. I left him. I kept so many secrets the past two days. I didn't trust him. And now, Anzen had killed him. That would make sense as to how he suddenly became an Alpha.

How could he? How could he kill his brothers? How could he make me motherless yet again?

"Luna..." I shoved the Commander off me, his face paling at the name I uttered under my breath.

My Mother had died in a puddle of golden blood. Luna's would be red.

My last tether of restraint snapped.

With a single flick of my wrist, a bolt of lightning shot Anzen away from my sister. He collided with the stone wall so forcefully it cracked on impact. I would have torn him limb from limb right then and there, but the sound of Becca choking made me freeze. Slowly I turned to find her pinned to the floor, straining against an imaginary force holding her down.

"Oh dear, did the excitement start without us?" A graceful figure swept through the double doors, uttering phrases in a foreign tongue. The Hounds around me fell in similar fashion as my sister. Disturbingly, I noted that only Lucifer and I remained standing.

Lucifers power made the floor shake, but the newcomer paid my Father no mind. His confident strides came to a stop before me, burgundy eyes reflecting the flames roaring beneath my skin. When he spoke, his usual honey filled voice dripped with acid over Becca's pained gasps.

"I fear you've run out of time to join me, Angel."

CHAPTER 33

Finn's smile was all teeth, his lips and fangs stained with fresh blood. The lack of Hounds pouring through the door was enough evidence of what he'd done.

Behind him Becca wheezed, but I didn't dare look away. I knew how fast he could move from our training. Yet, if he was here to kill me, he wouldn't have given up the element of surprise.

"What's going on Finn?" My voice wasn't shaking but my body was. I wasn't recovered from Anzens sudden appearance, and now this?! As if reading my mind his gaze drifted past me to where my brother lay unconscious on the floor.

"I thought dogs were supposed to be loyal." Finn's voice was pure mockery, "At least I don't need to feel as guilty now, since my plans never included *purposefully* betraying you."

Before I could react, his fingers dug into my shoulder and we moved, a blur as he dodged the first of my Fathers attacks. Lava sprayed the floor where we just

stood and stones rained down on our
heads, but Finn kept dragging me along
at an unnatural pace.

"I wouldn't do that if I were you."
Finn sounded downright gleeful as he
shouted over the chaos Lucifer unleashed,
"What if you hit your precious daughter?"

"I don't care." The words were deep
and cruel and malicious, and I don't know
why they cut me like a knife.

Panic flared through me. I couldn't
see Becca. I didn't know what end of the
room I was on. It was pitch black now
from Lucifers shadows, the only light
being from the mute flashes of molten
rock he flung in our wake.

When a third wave of heat and
rock hit me in the face, I realized Finn
wasn't dragging me around as a pawn. He
was shoving me ahead of him as a living
shield. As leverage that Lucifer clearly
held less regard for than he planned.

So, I raised my hands to his
forearms, caressing him. And lit his
jacket on fire.

My wrist slipped from his grip as
he yanked it off, throwing it away before
he could be burned. Not only was it an
attack, but also a beacon to Lucifer of our

exact location. I slipped into a shadow well before the column of red flames reached us, but Finn wasn't so lucky.

The sleeve of his shirt was completely gone, the once pale skin of his left arm now a vicious red and black bubble.

I re-emerged behind the dais; the smoke on this side was less thick. I could just make out the back of my father's head.

"I don't care."

Flame upon flame, explosions of lava, hovering shards of obsidian shot like arrows. Lucifer didn't so much as blink as he continued to rain down his assault where he thought Finn and I would land next.

"I don't care."

My temper flared, vision blurring at the edges. He didn't suspect at all that I could shadow jump like him. He imagined me far too weak.

I placed my foot on the bottom step, hands reaching for my mother's ear cuffs.

But a flicker of movement caught my eye. The smoke and shadows parted just enough for me to see Anzen crawling

across the floor. No, he wasn't crawling.
He was dragging my sister.

He had already been unconscious
once Finn arrived, which must have left
him immune to Finn's power to paralyze
the rest of the room. His arm was broken
and face bloody, but his grip on Becca
didn't waver as he continued to drag her
further and further out of harm's way.

He wasn't the only Hound up and
moving now. I noticed others dragging
their still paralyzed comrades out. The
Commanders Hound appeared; his red
fur barely noticeable under the pile of
fallen Hounds on his back.

The longer Finn was distracted,
the less powerful his spell was.

I was at a crossroads. Lucifer was
right there. In my head, all of this would
be over. All my rage and pain, all the
screams I had to swallow. But ironically
painful as it was, he wasn't the greatest
danger.

With a frustrated growl that I
knew he heard, I turned from the dais
and sprinted to my sister's side. Anzen
flinched as I shoved him off, taking over
and dragging her out of the way faster
than he could have in the state he was in.

"I'm so sorry Raven." His voice was raw as he rounded to lift her legs, "I didn't have a choice."

"Enough. We have bigger problems." My eyes hadn't stopped darting around the room. They skimmed over Finn, still a golden blur against the dark. I avoided latching my gaze to Lucifers whose dark eyes now bore into mine as if he was contemplating killing me where I stood. But I was more focused on the shadows. On the cracks in the rock high above us. On who was hiding, because someone else was here.

On arrival, Finn had mentioned *'us'*. Clearly, he wasn't working with Lucifer, so that meant there was still a hidden third party.

After resting Becca behind a pillar of stone, I summoned my shadows to my feet. The blacks and greys mixed with Lucifers as I shot out across the room. His flames were a monster at my back, exploding against my own violet inferno.

My hand slipped into the shadows, pulling my silver dagger from within. I slashed upwards for Finn's throat, intending to use him as leverage as he planned to use me, but the strike never connected.

The darkness abruptly vanished against a blinding light. All shadows and flames scattered, leaving utter silence in its wake. My body went completely numb, and I dropped the dagger.

Gabriel bent, retrieving the dagger from where it lay on the floor.

Whatever blast he'd unleashed subdued Lucifers power enough that Finn regained control of the room. Each of us, myself now included, were frozen in place. Lucifer seemed to be the only one Finn couldn't affect, but the flaming sword held to the back of his neck by another Angel kept him from making any rash moves.

"Miss Nightshade, I thought we had come to an agreement?" Gabriel's demeanor was of relaxed confidence, but there was something chilling in his tone, "I see your Father is still alive, even after having a clear shot at him." He released a heavy sigh, like a disappointed parent.

"So then why don't you do it?" I choke out, "You had no problems killing Gods. I can't believe he's harder to kill."

"You are missing the point." The tip of the dagger caressed its way up the side of my neck. "You are what we are after. Killing him is just icing on top of the cake." Snickers filtered down from the ceiling above as he circled me.

"Let me paint a very clear picture with those muddled memories of yours. Mary decided that despite his fall he was deserving of empathy. All this did was earn her chained to a bed until she was impregnated with his key back into the Silver City. You." Chills racked down my spine and I strained to move but Gabriel continued, completely unbothered.

"When you were born, she vowed she would bring you up to be Heavens Pearl, a compliment to your half-brother. You see," I felt blood trickle down the side of my throat as he dug the blade in a little deeper. "Your brother is the pure-blooded child of a God. You are his by product. What was left of the Lord in your mothers' womb. Barely anything of worth, but mixed with your Fathers unique makeup, well, you became very valuable indeed. You can do things the rest of us can't. And you will. But first, you must kill. Without blood on your hands, you're useless."

I gasped as my lungs once again lifted and fell freely. To my surprise, Gabriel slapped my dagger down into my palm before turning me to face Lucifer.

And just for a moment, I felt sorry for him.

He was on his knees at the foot of the dais, the flaming sword poised above his neck execution style. In this position, cast out from his family and home, because he dared to question, dared to *think* independently.

Dared to not kill even when directed to.

But those empathetic thoughts were swept away as fast as they'd come. There was nothing but hate and rage in his black eyes as he stared up at me. Maybe he hadn't actually killed my mother, but he had raped me into existence. He had cornered her in that church in the first place.

At my feet was a Devil who tried to kill me multiple times. And at my back was an Angel wanting to kill thousands more. I twisted the dagger in my palm, the hilt feeling like ice in my hand. My fangs pressed against my lower lip.

"Finnegan Esmeraldas Hagan!" A voice boomed through my bloodlust, literally knocking me back a step. I whirled, eyes falling on Silas who was stalking through the open double doors like a monster. Out of the corner of my eye I saw Finn go eerily still. His mouth dropped into an 'O' as his back slammed into the wall, Silas' hand closed around his throat.

"Release." He commanded.

Lucifers fingers flexed. I heard the crack of ice at my feet as Becca awoke. And all hell broke loose.

CHAPTER 34

The force of the blows Gabriel and Lucifer rained on each other threatened to bring the castle down on top of us. As lightning struck ice I dove into a shadow, leaving my Father and Uncle to preoccupy themselves with each other.

Even in the shadow realm I could sense my sister moving again. I wanted to go to her side, but we ran out of time as soon as Finn walked through the doors. We had to play our hand *now*.

Hounds were pouring through the double doors, jaws clamping around Angels who were dive bombing us from the ceiling. I threw myself back into the fray, twin black blades in my hands and sunk them into the first pair of wings within reach. As their body sunk to the ground, I got a view of Kuma's Hound. I let out a cry, fear pulsing through me as I watched a silver blade connect with his neck.

It was split in half before the cut could be fatal, the shredded metal dropping from Akashi's maw. His coat was stained with both red and gold splatters of blood, and it took everything in me to not sprint to his side.

I didn't have time to let my eyes linger as I dodged a brilliant column of light, presumably Gabriel's power. It grew and thrashed through the room like a twister, already rounding the room to barrel down on me again.

Its sheer brightness made it impossible to shadow jump so I did the only thing I could do and sprinted in the opposite direction. Hounds had fled to the edges of the room. Even Angels had risen towards the ceiling to avoid being directly hit.

Run and never stop. My mother's voice pounded in my skull. *Run. Run. Run!*

Fuck this.

A vortex of amethyst flame exploded from my chest. My flames did not die until long after the light storm was reduced to glimmers. They raged from purple to red to black, everything I had bottled forcing the rest of the room to shield themselves from the force of my unrestrained emotions.

When I finally did call my fire back to me, I was standing alone at the top of the dais. Lucifers plush throne had been reduced to a pile of ash. The obsidian under my feet had boiled down into sharp, slippery waves where there were once stairs.

Ice splintered through the melted stone, my only warning before Becca was at my back. She didn't hesitate to place my dagger, half cursed and half holy, to my throat.

I dropped my twin blades, their clatters sounding like gunshots in the eerily silent room.

"Raven..." I didn't look towards Luna's desperate call. Didn't search the crowd for Akashi despite feeling his panic beating in my chest.

Lucifer, now with a sword in hand, stalked towards the frozen steps of the dais. Becca's ice began to melt under his pressure as he climbed towards us.

"We can still end this. Together." I didn't react, but Becca guffawed.

"In order to do that I believe she needs to fully reform, right?" She pressed the tip of the dagger a little deeper and I felt a trickle of blood slip down my neck.

Lucifer halted, head cocked. Behind him Gabriel looked equally perplexed. Becca rolled her eyes.

"What geniuses you are. She's killed before, you morons." Her lips split into a feline grin as she eyed our Father, "One of your puppies I believe."

I took a breath, refusing to shake as I met Anzen's eyes. My nightmare replayed in my head, a piece of it which I hadn't remembered clearly until seeing his imprinting brand.

There was a sixth wolf that night. He was the fastest and caught up to me first. He was the one I slashed at so quickly I wound up covered in his blood. And as he lay dying Akashi wrestled the blade away from me and carried me home.

I had killed Anzens mate.

Realization began to set in for the Hounds in the room. Anzen looked like he wanted to disappear. I cleared my throat.

"Correct me if I'm wrong," Becca's sing song voice clanged through my ears, "but killing is just half of it. As a Shadow Walker, she's as strong as she's going to be. But as a Light Walker, she must rise."

She did not hesitate. It was fast, and anti-climactic really. The dagger was already poised, so all it took was the quick sweep of her arm to open my throat.

Lucifer broke into a sprint towards us, Akashi hot on his heels. I think Luna screamed.

But I was fixated on a sight at the far end of the room. On Gabriel, who had notched a silver arrow into the bow he pulled from beneath his robes.

From his angle, if his shot was true, he would strike not only Akashi but Becca as well.

I opened my mouth to scream a warning, but it was far too late for that. My vision was blurry, my body was far away.

And the last thing I saw was Anzen falling, the arrow sunk deep into his chest.

CHAPTER 35

Akashi wasn't able to process what was happening, but his body reacted anyway. The room had launched back into a full-scale war, but he couldn't be bothered to pay any attention to it.

Hikari tackled Gabriel the second after he loosed that arrow. That arrow which, from Akashi's angle, had been flying towards Ravens heart just a second ago. She too had fallen, from what he wasn't sure. He sure as hell wasn't about to take his eyes off his brother to find out. If he did, he didn't think he would recover.

The pungent smell of Alpha blood flooded his nose as he caught Anzen before his skull cracked on the floor. Blood that was spilling at too fast a rate down the steps of the dais.

"Anzen you idiot!" He hissed, pressing both hands on either side of the arrow protruding from his chest. He wanted to rip it out, but he knew it would just kill him faster. Kuma rushed up the stairs to them.

"Akashi, the fuck do we–"

"Shut up and give me something to stop the bleeding!" Kuma took off without hesitation. Weakly, Anzen raised a hand, giving Akashi's hands a soft push away. He shook his head roughly.

"Stay still. I've got you."

"Raven," Anzen wheezed, and Akashi went rigid.

He still hadn't looked towards her, though his body was *very* aware of the river of blood trickling down the stairs at his back. Too aware.

"She needs... you to–"

"Stop talking," Akashi was shaking, his pain and fury threatening to take form. But Anzen squeezed his hand again, his voice firm and his eyes clear as he said,

"Trust. Her."

And then he was gone.

Rebecca barely caught Raven before her skull hit the floor. Her sister's river water eyes had widened just slightly, before rolling back in her head as

she dropped to the floor like a sack of bricks.

She didn't want to touch her, didn't want any more blood staining her than there already was. It shone against the floor, a rushing river of gold against the black stone.

She double checked that the artery was severed before removing her hands from her completely.

The smoke and flashes of light in the room made it impossible to tell who was who. But there was one set of eyes, like cauldrons of green fire, promising death.

"What have you done?" The growl was pure monster. Akashi had transformed again, his black Hound easily pinning Rebecca to the floor.

"She'll need me when she's back." Rebecca voice cut through him like the blade she'd just used to sever his mate's neck. She didn't bother to fight him, her icy eyes staring up at him bored. Empty.

"I'm going to kill you," he whispered. She didn't blink. Just repeated in a dull, flat tone,

"That's fine. But after she's back. I need to go melt that lake."

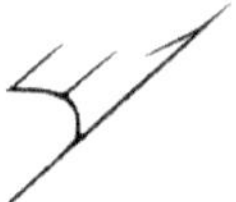

Hikari didn't stay in Gabriel's range after stealing the bow and snapping it between his jaws. He could feel his mother hot on his heels, the pair defending Silas' back.

The vampires were in a mental war. If Silas was distracted enough or killed, his puppet spell on Finn would lift. That would leave everyone in the room vulnerable to Finn's paralysis once more.

Finn's complexion was flushed, the veins in his neck popping under his brother's grip. Dark hair clung to Silas' brow, his entire body shaking as he continued mumbling commands over and over.

Finnegan Esmeraldas Hagan, remain still.

Finnegan Esmeraldas Hagan, you may not move.

Finnegan Esmeraldas Hagan, Finnegan Esmeraldas Hagan, Finnegan Esmeraldas Hagan…

A roar perforated the room. Where Rebecca had lain seconds before was a formidable black hellcat. It was nearly Akashi's size, giving it the leverage to throw him off the dais. It released a raspy scream before darting through the room to disappear out the double doors.

"Akashi!" Kuma was at his side, eyes bugging out of his head. Akashi did not follow his gaze.

"She's going to the lake." The calmness of his voice clashed severely with the chaos around them. However, the urgency of the situation was not lost as he said, "See to it she gets there unscathed."

Kuma nodded, but before he did so he lowered his muzzle to drape his torn shirt over Anzen's face. Then he stood and took off after Rebecca at an untamable pace.

Then and only then did Akashi
finally let his gaze drift to Raven.

Her blood was smeared all over the
floor, hundreds of feet leaving golden
footprints or skid marks as the Angels
and Hounds continued to rage around
him. But it wasn't the sight of her blood
that made him want to scream.

It was the thin white scar across
her neck where a gaping wound should
be.

"You realize if she does indeed
wake, it's over for you brother?" Gabriel's
taunting laughter sang over the crack of
Lucifers' whip. He'd summoned the
hellish thing, a wriggling snake of
shadow dripping lava, as soon as Gabriel
loosed his arrow. Not in defense of his
daughter, but in defense of himself.

"Wishful thinking." Was his curt
reply before snarling as again his brother
dodged the blow. "Even you would not
rise from a slice of that blade."

All Gabriel did was smile before releasing nothing short of a canon of light from his chest.

Akashi had just picked up the fallen dagger with shaking fingers before being blasted to the floor by an explosion behind him. He slammed into the floor at the base of the dais, almost impaling himself on the blade but twisted at the last second, making his head connect with the bottom step. Blood trickled from his ears, and he groaned, turning to view a new hole in the side of the throne room opening to... he stopped breathing completely.

There must have been thousands of Angels in the skies outside, all armed with silver bows or golden swords. By the way they were firing and diving at the ground he could only assume that the Hounds outside were being absolutely demolished.

A yelp drew his attention away from the army, and he struggled to his feet seeing his mother pinned by a large red Hound. All the pain in his body faded as he sprang to his feet, sprinting to tackle the assailant off of her. He placed himself in front of her, all snapping teeth and claws.

"You abandoned us all, abandoned me!" The red Hound didn't even spare Akashi a glance, his eyes burning Luna to the spot she lay. She released a low whine but said nothing.

"Mom who the fuck is this guy?" The scent the red Hound let off made it clear *what* he was, but Akashi didn't care, "If he touches you again I'm ripping his fucking throat out."

"Akashi please—"

"Akashi?" The Hound before them seemed to freeze, the clear rage he dispelled moments before shifting to cold shock.

A pained feline scream broke whatever moment the trio were frozen in.

And distracted Silas just long enough for Finn to slip free.

As soon as Rebeccas paws hit open ground she dispelled thick black shadows from her in every direction, providing at least some cover in the otherwise open space. The Hounds had been suffering under the endless assault of silver arrows, the Angels being too high and their Master unable to provide cover with his own shadows.

She had felt her heart drop in her stomach when they initially bolted for her, but quickly realized they just sought refuge to regroup. As her shadows swelled and spread the arrows from above slowed. The Angels soon had no clear target under the pulsing black sea.

"Rebecca!" She whirled, finding Kuma by her side.

"Get your people off the ice. It's not going to be there for long," she hissed and he nodded, taking off while releasing a high-pitched howl. *Fall back.*

She ran further into the abyss, Hounds flying past her back the way she'd come to the palace doors or other cracks in the stone.

Suddenly the ground pitched under her, the earth erupting against her back being shattered by a column of amber light. The light scorched the ends of her fur, the blast obliterating her shadows.

She hit the ground, teeth snapping together so hard blood dripped from her maw. A shadow flew past her, smashing into the sand a few steps away.

Lucifer coughed up black blood, the shadows around him flickering, trying to recover from that direct hit. He raised the whip in his hand just as the first Angels dove.

Rebecca surged forward. Somersaulting over the hoard of Angels that buried him, her tail swept out and knocked many of them to the ground like broken toys. She plowed on, the army dropping like missiles between her and the ice. In her peripheral, she could see the Hounds charging as the fight was brought down to a level they could reach.

It felt as if she had run a mile before her paws hit ice and she skidded to a stop. Mistake. A golden blade sliced through her shoulder, and she screamed, claws shredding the assailant to pieces. She limped a few feet further before rearing back and slamming her two front paws down into the ice.

And her magic exploded.

CHAPTER 36

There was no heaven or hell here. There was no peace or war. There was none. Nothing.

Nowhere.

Because that's the only place a demonic angel could go if they died, wasn't it?

At least now Raven knew what she had to look forward to. She didn't have to fear the beyond like she had for most of her youth. Didn't need to panic about meeting her mother's ghost. Mary would not be found here. This place of nothing.

Her lips parted in a silent laugh. At least she thinks they did, it's what she wanted them to do.

How cruel and comical it was. A being supposedly sought by all, to end up utterly alone.

But she was not alone here, she realized. Something had to control this nothing. Something had to pull her into it. She flailed, wanting that Something to come closer. And it did.

It curled against her like a cat, it passed through her like a breeze. Something did not stay in one place long enough for her to truly see or feel it.

'You're here early.' Something said. Raven just continued to wheeze her soundless laugh. Her nonexistent tears floated through the nothing to land on Somethings cheeks.

Something was perplexed. Something was happy. Something was anxious. Something shifted, and gripped Raven by the back of the neck with its teeth.

'The Creator promised me you'd come.' Something said. 'You must decide. Do you wish to stay with me now, or return later?'

Ravens silent fit stopped as she hung there, thinking. She couldn't see anything though there was nothing to see. But still, she passed her hands where her hair would have been. Moved it out of the space that would have been her face. Her thumb grazed the space that would have been her temple, her ear, and froze as it connected with something tangible. Cool. Heavy.

Gold.

Her mothers Golden ear cuffs were floating in the space of nothing, the only thing besides herself and Something. But they did not stay. They were floating up, away. Back.

Everything came back to Raven then, her body, her brain. Her hands reached for the cuffs, so high up, so far away that a part of her thought she ran out of time.

'We will have plenty of time.' Something repeated, their teeth releasing the back of Ravens neck. Raven kicked, and pulled, and reached. She did not look back at Something, did not wonder why it didn't force her to stay once she arrived.

Something watched her for just a moment, before it slinked away back into nothing to wait for her, for anything, to arrive.

Finn's fangs were in Silas' throat, draining him. Tears streamed down both of their faces, though Silas was long unconscious.

The last thing Silas had been able
to do was teleport all four of the Hounds
aiding him outside, out of range of his
brother's voice. The throne room had long
since emptied after Gabriel's blast
anyway. There was no reason for them to
stay and die with him. Which was in fact
happening now, the promising spark of
light already shining out of the gloom
surrounding him.

He would have cried out in relief if
he could, but his soul settled on a
thankful prayer. He had done enough to
get into Heaven after all, despite what
he'd become, despite what he'd done. He'd
repented enough. Done enough. At least
Gabriel kept that promise. He let his body
go lax, waiting for his mother's embrace.

A flash of light and then he felt
her. Her gentle hands, her soothing voice.
It was still much too bright to see her.
But she was warm, and that heat flowed
into him. He released a sob, when was the
last time he'd been warm?

But as the light dulled and he
opened his eyes his heart released one
thundering beat inside his chest.

"Welcome back." A hand smoothed
his dark hair, gently gripping to pull him

away from the body he clung to. To remove his fangs from her throat.

"Finn won't be coming back for you," The female rose back to her feet, being sure to not let him slip to the floor as she helped him stand. "Regardless, I'd appreciate if you would prioritize keeping him in your mental trap for me?" A question he realized, not an order.

He nodded, then followed her gaze to see his brother wedged into a crack in the wall. Presumably where the female had thrown him.

Finn hung limp against the stone, unresponsive. Flickering vines of red fire laced in and out from under his skin, holding him tied inside and out. Silas' stomach rolled. The pain must have been excruciating.

"How did you—"

"Silas," Ravens voice did not waver as she settled him down onto what remained of Lucifers throne. She strode past him to retrieve her fallen dagger left abandoned on the floor, the blade still slick with gold. "I'm counting on you if he wakes, okay?"

She slid the dagger into the sheath hanging from her waist before descending

the throne, striding across the blood-
stained floor and stepped directly out of
the hole in the rock into open thin air.

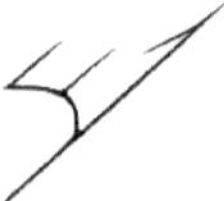

    After unleashing such an attack on
his younger brother, Gabriel needed to
recover his strength. As his legion fell
upon the Hounds and their Master, he
rose to the cave ceiling to watch the
spectacle from a safe distance.
    A few of his officers made to dive
for the raging feline below, camouflaged
in the shadows that spilled from her save
for the flash of her claws and teeth, but
he called them off with a wave of his
hand. He would much rather tear her
limb from limb after she exhausted
herself. Though the power currently
radiating from her was impressive, he
had to give her that.
    The ice her claws shredded at was
reflecting a fierce blue, responding to the
magic flowing in her veins and melting as
she willed. That ice was thousands of
years thick, even the Devil himself was
unable to melt it now. He had been that

desperate to keep the hell fire for himself that he had fucked himself out of being able to use it.

Gabriel's face hurt and his jaw ached, the manic grin on his face threatening to pull tears from even him. He just couldn't help himself, the display below him was too brilliant to not appreciate. Though he was disappointed as the Hounds assassinated the mountain of his officers that buried his brother.

So be it, he would just have to be a little more patient. Either Raven would wake, and if she did not then as soon as that ice melted the fire would be his to reclaim and he could finish his brother off with it. His brother, who was too distracted by a personal vendetta to realize what his youngest daughter was trying to do.

Akashi felt the throws of teleportation moments before Silas forced their abrupt exit. He, Hikari, Luna and the red Hound all rolled in the sand, the impact knocking the wind out of him.

Immediately, he turned to search for his mother, but found the red Hound nudging her to her feet, taking a protective stance before her now that they were in sight of the Legions silver arrows.

"Akashi!" Hikari's voice jarred in his head, "Kuma needs our help!"

Indeed, Kuma had led a small charge against a line of Angels who were brave enough to descend upon the ground, and it was not going well.

Silver arrows rose from his brother's strong, muscled back. No vital points had been hit, but he was slowing down enough that the never-ending wave of golden swords arching for his throat were swinging uncomfortably close.

Akashi and Hikari hurtled through the sand, leaving a river of golden blood in their wake. Hikari's teeth snapped, slicing an Angel swinging for his brother's head in two. Akashi took out the three divebombing them with a well-timed jump, claws raking feathers and skin.

"You need to fall back, now!" He roared over the clamor. Despite his state Kuma glared.

"I will not abandon our comrades for a second time!"

"Fall back now!" Akashi ordered, hip checking his brother towards the hidden caves etched into the cliffside, "Hikari, sound off."

Hikari threw back his head, the howl to retreat echoing through the black. Any lingering Hounds turned and fled, not needing any more prompting.

"Where's Rebecca?" Akashi panted while they ran. He kept Kuma between himself and Hikari, the latter in the lead.

"She's trying to melt that blasted lake!" Kumas growl reverberated through the sand, "I was out here backing her up."

"Is she still out there?" Akashi's stomach flipped and he damn near turned around to go check.

"To hell if I know. Hopefully she kept most of these shadows close to her. I lost sight of her as soon as she said to get everyone off the ice."

Akashi cursed but kept running. The flash of Luna's blue soul-searching spell drifted to them through the haze, and they adjusted their angle to reach her faster. The shadows were especially thick around this part of the cliffside, but Akashi took that as a good thing. Of course, his mother would find the best place to regroup, she was a far better Alpha than he would ever be.

But any hope of rectifying the situation evaporated as he and his remaining brothers skidded to a stop a few feet away from her.

The red Hound was flat on the ground before her. A silver arrow was lodged halfway into his throat, a breath away from killing him. Lucifer turned and grinned over his shoulder, the hand holding the arrow in place hissing against the Holy Metal.

"Be a good pup like your Mum, and come. Or her mate will die in front of her."

The first hole in the ice finally appeared and Rebecca descended upon it ravenously. She didn't know if she would be able to melt this whole lake or not, but at the very least enough of the ice needed to be weak for Raven when she came. When, not if. It had to be when.

Once she could fit her whole upper body through, she pulled back, the top layer beneath her feet now just slush. Carefully, she maneuvered her way back onto solid ground, not wanting to hang out and flirt with falling completely through. But she did not call her magic back, the blue flashes in the ice were still hard at work to melt it from the inside out.

She turned, sharp eyes searching through the smoke. All the Hounds had fallen back to the cliffs, and it seemed the Angels also took this moment to flock back to the top of the cave to take refuge and account of their wounded. And dead. Her gut twisted with sick satisfaction seeing so many broken wings and mangled limbs.

Out of her peripheral, a faintly glowing blue bubble drifted towards her. She reared back, cautious. When it just floated in front of her, she batted at it, but it just shifted and rose to hover over her shoulder. It reeked of Luna.

As it bobbed away towards the cliffside she followed it at a distance, still unsure but prioritized finding Ravens pack. And find them she did.

Lucifer had the Commander under his boot, that flickering black whip of fire back in his hand. Hikari, Kuma and Akashi had barricaded Luna against the cliff wall behind them, teeth bared. But it was clear what would happen as the Devil rose his free hand, aiming the killing blow at the remainder of the pack who betrayed him.

She broke into a sprint before she realized what she was doing. Was she really going to risk her life for those Hounds even though Raven wasn't with them? Would they have done the same for her?

But then there was a drop of light, and her racing limbs slowed. From above, a single white rose petal drifted down between Lucifer and the Hounds, alighting soundlessly on the sand before dissolving into nothing. Seconds later a shadow from overhead had Rebecca spraying sand in her effort to halt. That shadow disappeared in a flash of light, in a comet hitting home with a boom in front of Akashi.

The ground was covered in so much smoke and dust she couldn't see anyone anymore. She could only make out the blaze in the center of it all, glowing a brilliant gold. Her keen eyes focused on

the figure radiating the blaze. One fist
was braced in the sand, their opposite
hand brandishing a long, golden sword. A
sword that until now only she and the
Devil had seen.

Ravens skin was pulsing gold while
shadows rolled off her legs. She had a
jagged scar glittering around her throat
like a necklace. One of her eyes was an
iridescent mirage, the other a pit of
charcoal black. Above that eye, a singular
curved horn rose from her temple.

As she stood, a whiplike tail
thrashed behind her, scales glaring as she
gained her balance. But it wasn't any of
those things that stole Rebecca's breath.
She could only stare in fascination and
relief at the four ebony wings rising from
her sister's shoulders.

CHAPTER 37

Everything was happening in slow motion since I awoke on that dais. The first thing I did after bolting upright and grabbing my throat was stop Finn. I had shaken with the effort not to kill him. My magic had a mind of its own, abilities molding and appearing with each breath, and I didn't exactly have the luxury of time to sort it.

Silas to his credit had held himself together quite well, and I was relieved to say the least when he didn't protest to follow me. I had tasked him with holding Finn to keep his mind focused on something, but Finn wasn't going anywhere anytime soon. Not with thorns and flames and nightshade roots in his veins.

As soon as I stepped out of the hole in the wall, I realized something was different with my body. I didn't fall as I expected to. I was hovering in place. And my back was fucking *screaming*.

But my brain was screaming louder. Below me there was a raging cyclone of shadows, at their center an iridescent blue. At first, I thought it was Rebecca, but seeing a flash of white fur I quickly realized it was Luna. And those shadows most definitely were not coming from her.

So, I tucked my wings, and I dropped. My fingers graced my mother's sword, pulling it fourth from its hiding place as I landed. The impact sent a shudder through my whole body, but my wings shifted, keeping me upright.

And now I was face to face with my father who held an arrow in the Commander's throat.

"One step, and your mothers mate dies." Lucifers growl was laced with pure joy, the bastard vibrating with excitement before me.

"Yes, he will." I paused, standing upright and angling the sword in front of me. "But I don't think we mean the same one." A muscle in Lucifers jaw ticked and he said nothing.

"I'm not typically one for dramatics," I said, free hand drifting to my dagger to pull it from its sheath. I positioned it in my hand holding the sword, my grip loose and awkward around the two hilts, but it wouldn't be for long. I arched a brow.

"I take it that the ability to manipulate natural matter did not come from you. You might have been the favored Angel, but that gift was reserved for God's actual child. A gift developed in my mother's womb, and later passed on to me."

As I spoke the two blades withered, melted, and merged in my hands. Half the sword's blade remained gold, the other shifted to silver. The obsidian etched itself in a vinelike pattern through each side, and wholly blackened the pointed tip. The hilt became a swirl of all three metals, with small, pointed shards biting my palm. They drew my blood, my *magic*, into the weapon, making it vibrate with power in my hand.

With the new weapon complete I freed my mother's shield from the other cuff. Also plated in gold, the titanium and silver cylinder was large enough to cover half of my body, possibly all of me besides my wings if I was crouching. I couldn't help my smirk as I said, "You see, when Gabriel told me what these were I realized something."

"What did you realize?" Lucifers whole body was rigid, but his voice was still as smooth as silk. I resisted the urge to rip his vocal cords out with my fingers.

"You can't be killed by pure holy metal." Silence fell, the statement dropping like a bomb. Lucifer blinked; his eyes flashing to the weapon I held was all the confirmation I needed. I took advantage of his shock, striking faster than even my eyes could register.

My vines curled back into my skin after they struck. Gold blood stained the thorns, matching the blood dripping from the cut on his cheek. I hissed, "You might be a devil now, but you were an Angel first."

We exploded at the same time, fire meeting fire, shadow meeting shadow. Lightening jumped between my wings; the feathers individually electrified.

I launched into the air, the flap of my wings sending bolts lighting and fire toward him. The coward shadow jumped away before he was struck and landed a blow to my back right where wings and skin met.

I screamed, falling back to the sand as lava rolled down my spine. I heard the sing of his whip coming for me seconds before the first lash hit. I rolled before he could land a second one, sword slicing for his head. His laughter mocked me from the shadows.

Furious, I followed him into the shadows. On this side of the veil, his powers were amplified. Rather than sprays of lava or columns of flame it felt as if he dragged me into a volcano. I lashed my wings back and forth again, lightning crumbling the onslaught of this hell trap, but it just manifested again as soon as the blasts stopped.

A feral yowl ripped from over my head, and I whirled to see Becca diving into the pit with us. Ice exploded from her in every direction, seeming to halt the lava for a moment. From the darkness Lucifer pulled twin silver daggers, abandoning his whip as the Hellcat descended on him. I threw my mother's shield, invisible hands in the wind guiding it to block her neck as he swung the blades for her.

He shifted, one blade adjusting to parry the shield and the other expertly catching Becca under her outstretched arms. She hissed but drove her shoulder forward, the blade disappearing under her fur completely and wrenching it from his grip. Both sets of her silver claws connected with flesh. Lucifer roared as his robes were shredded along with his ribcage beneath.

"I'm gonna draw him out," Becca's voice sliced between my ears. She dove for him again. He had one blade left, catching her in the same spot he did last time to deepen the wound.

He twisted the hilt and the Hellcat staggered, back legs slumping back to take the weight off her front right leg. He dove for her, black flames on his hands. If a cat could grin, that's exactly what she did.

Spears of ice impaled him midair, one through each limb, his gut, his neck.

"Time to go!" She urged and I didn't need to be told twice. We slipped back into hell, the inferno he released behind us trapped in the shadow realm with him.

But he was right alongside us, cutting through space, time, charging to cut us off as we sprinted towards the cliffside.

Akashi was in a full sprint himself, flanked by Luna and the Commander. The full army of Hellhounds had regrouped and were charging for us. At this angle, Lucifer would emerge from the shadow realm directly between us. I stopped running, wings flaring to halt my momentum.

"What the hell are you doing!?" Becca hissed, my sudden stop catching her off guard.

"Keep going," I turned, bolting in the opposite direction, "he's gunning for you after that trick anyway!" Despite the situation I could have sworn I heard her high trilling laughter as she once again took off, leaving me.

As suspected Lucifer shifted, his rage blinding him to all but revenge as he chased her down. Leaving me just enough room and time.

My boots skidded on the ice, but I didn't slow. I tucked my wings and dove through the crack Becca made. I fell quickly, body swallowed by those silver flames it ached for far below.

Lucifer ripped back into existence as a tempest of ice and flame. Leathery red bat wings now sprung from his shoulders and a vicious pair of black horns curled off his temple. His Angelic face was screwed up in a rageful glare, wings beating bullets of ice down onto Rebecca's head.

He released a roar as most ricocheted back at him, Mary's shield still perched atop the Hellcats vulnerable neck as she half limped half sprinted into the cover the Hounds now provided.

Being born from it themselves, the Hound army was equipped with every advantage against Lucifers magic. Their fur absorbed flames that would incinerate others, and their vision was designed to navigate the shadows pouring from their rageful master. Many with gifts similar to Luna's and Akashi's combined their spells, building a protective barrier against the ice, the lava, the crystal bullets.

Hikari appeared at Rebecca's side. His teeth grabbed the exposed hilt of the last dagger and pulled it free. The second was too deep, but enough pain was relieved for now.

Together they turned, sprinting stride for stride, before leaping into the air straight into the fray. The wound in her shoulder was gushing blood but that didn't slow her as she and the Hound collided with Lucifer midair, each tearing into a wing and forcing him to the ground.

The ground was rolling now, the groan sounding from the center of the Earth itself. The lake behind them shuddered, its frozen surface going grey before collapsing in on itself.

The fire did not burn. It felt cool, like water. And functioned like it as well. I hit with a splash, the silver flames skittering away from me in ripples.

My body absolutely *sang*. This was like being drunk, high, and orgasming all at the same time. My body was threatening to betray me and just let itself be swept away. In desperation I gripped my sword tighter, the thornlike teeth in the hilt digging deeper, the pain pulling me back.

I plummeted to the bottom, skull smacking stone making stars shoot across my vision. With a groan I forced myself to my feet, beginning to feel the heat now that the flames recognized me as an intruder rather than prey.

The air and ground hissed where my blood dropped, no doubt whatever magic that fueled these flames reacting to the demon half of my blood.

"I'm not him." I whisper to the flames, but it does nothing to quell their mounting rage. The heat is suppressive now, coating my body like burning oil as the remaining ice above me cracks.

"Take my wings as payment!" I scream into the fray, "Take my wings as proof!"

Everything freezes. Literally, everything. The plummeting slabs of ice are unmoving, aloft above my head. Each flame is standstill. Even the air around me does not shift.

"Raven Nightshade, daughter of Lucifer."

A faceless voice purrs in my ear and I feel a presence over my shoulder. I don't move, I can't move. Whatever is behind me is older than time itself.

"Hmmm," it drawls. I shiver, feeling invisible fingers tracing the arch of my upper left wing, *"daughter of Mary. Why would you give up your redemption for the fire?"*

"My redemption is worth nothing if it only benefits me." I whisper, a single tear escaping and sliding down my cheek. I think of my family, above me on the battlefield. Of Mary, a mother taken from me. Of Finn, a friend who betrayed me. Of everyone who already died at the Angels hands, all of them including my brother. I close my eyes against my overwhelming emotions.

"I'm not manic enough to believe I can save everyone. But saving as many as I can is worth everything to me."

"But how long will that be enough? "I blink, not understanding but the voice cackles and continues, *"You shall keep your word. Your wings will be payment, just as your fathers were. The day temptation overpowers your aspirations will be the day we take them from you."*

One sharp yank pulls a cry from my lips. A single black feather is held aloft in front of me.

"A sign our bargain has been made. We are in your charge, Raven Nightshade, Angel born."

And then, agony. The pain is so overwhelming I can't even muster a scream. My sword drops, body following, silver fire covering me, filling me.

And as suddenly as it started, it was over. I glance around me, the vacant lakebed echoing nothing of what just transpired.

My wings flap of their own accord, the pain they caused me before now nonexistent, and from the glow surrounding the space around me I know they are on fire. My hand finds my sword and then I'm airborne once again.

Lucifer is pure demon now, black skin and burning sockets where his eyes once were. Tattered bat wings dragged on the ground behind him, getting caught on the razor-sharp tail he swings around himself. He is surrounded on all sides by Hounds, each attacking in fluid succession before diving out of the way.

I hear cries from the Angels above me, no doubt in shock and horror that I claimed the hell fire. But I'd deal with them in a minute. By now, many of the

Hounds had noticed my appearance above them and began herding their comrades out of the way. I locked eyes with Becca for a moment before she threw herself forward once more.

Lucifers tail ripped into her side and she visibly winced, but she got enough of a hit on him to rip both his arms clear off. Lucifer staggered back from the fallen limbs, unable to balance, dropping to one knee.

For decades I dreamed about what this moment would look like, would *feel* like. But as I adjusted the angle of my sword and dove, barely any of it was registering.

Lightning shot from my chest, plastering Lucifers broken body to the ground. Purple flames swept from my arms, incinerating his fallen limbs. And the sword, all blended holy and cursed metal, plunged through his chest to the hilt. He opened his mouth, but the bolt of hell fire I laced within the blade had already enveloped his heart and before our eyes the devil withered to nothing but ash.

CHAPTER 38

I was frantic in the first few moments of utter silence following what I had done. I believed my mind was playing tricks on me, like I was hallucinating the whole affair. But the heaps of dead bodies and bloodstains in the sand were a harrowing reminder.

I immediately turned towards the roof of the cave, bracing myself for the Legions assault but was stunned to find the space void of any Angels. When and why they fled, I was unsure. Maybe it had something to do with Lucifers devilish body. Or the fact that hell fire now pulsed in my veins. Perhaps it was just as simple as God calling them back.

Wind and rain and sleet were whipping around me haphazardly, my sword shaking in my hand, my breath rasping in and out of my lungs. I was only able to calm my magic and myself when Luna appeared at my side.

The man's shirt dangling off her petite frame was ridiculous, and at another moment I would have laughed.

But her skin was stained with blood and her hair seemed grayer than before. But that spark in her eyes was stronger than ever. Those small, strong hands of hers wrapped around my body, wary of the wings hanging off my back, held me in an embrace until the tremors stopped rocking down my spine.

Beyond her, Akashi looked about ready to split himself in two. Clad in only thin cotton pants, I choked back a sob as I took in the cuts and bruises littering his body. Hikari and Kuma were not by his side, so I assumed there went inside to recover Anzens body. His body.

I had no doubt Akashi wanted to be with them, but his wild eyes were searching mine. I extended an arm towards him, a welcome into the safe space Luna had created. It took him all of three steps to reach us, enveloping the two of us and squeezing until Luna finally protested. As soon as she stepped to the side his hands were on me, tugging at my clothes and turning me around.

"I don't understand," he muttered and I gasped as I felt the laces on the back of my corset coming loose.

"Akashi!" I hissed, jerking out of his grip. He yanked his hands back as if they had grabbed me of their own accord.

"I don't understand how you don't have a mark on you. Even your neck is healed." His eyes flared; his confusion clouded by delayed rage.

"She followed my mother's plan perfectly." I said, my tone making it clear that confronting Becca over the move was off the table. He stood there for a minute, his temper shaking his whole body, until he regained his composure and gave a curt nod.

"Never," he growled, hands reaching for me, "do that again."

"I don't plan to." He tucked my head under his chin, arms clamped around my shoulders. I shifted my wings, trying not to throw myself backwards with him hanging on but needing to create space. There was too much blood on us. In the air. My head was spinning like a top and I could feel my canines ripping into my gums.

"We need to go to Anzen." I force out, successfully unwinding myself from Akasi's grip. His face was grave, but he didn't protest. I slid my fingers into his to shadow jump us, not trusting myself to fly us both up through the crack in the cliff.

When we step out from behind the dais the first thing I see is Becca. She's sitting on the bottom step, Silas unconscious in her lap. I start for them, but she shakes her head before gesturing to Finn who's exactly where I left him. Theres a small crowd of Hounds gathered before him, gawking at what I had done.

"Raven!" I turn just in time to catch Hikari as he launches off the steps to wrap me in his arms. I suppress a yelp as his arm knocks a lower wing, tucking them just in time for Kuma to replace Hikari, his strong arms nearly swallowing me whole.

Before I can say anything there's a flurry of voices echoing from beyond the double doors and the Commander enters the room. He's flanked on either side by massive soldiers, all young Hounds in their prime.

Their human forms resembled nothing short of Vikings, leading me to imagine they were probably some of the most powerful Hounds here.

Akashi shifts in front of me a snarl already tearing from his lips, but the Commander only smiles and holds up a hand halting the men beside him. He reaches his hand back, for Luna I realize, lips moving but I hear nothing.

My eyes snap back and forth between the three of them. I thought there were similarities before but now with the two men side by side and Luna there…

"You're his father." It's barely more than a whisper but the room goes so still you could hear a pin drop. Akashi isn't moving, isn't breathing even. The Commander looks as if he's struggling for words. But it was Luna who stepped forward, her face blank and voice calm as she said,

"It was customary for female Hounds to be bred with only the strongest of Alphas. I was a rare female Alpha, so our pairing was determined long before we knew one another."

Akashi jerked back as if he'd been shot. Venom was dancing through my veins. Luna had been bred as if she were cattle.

"That matter can be discussed at a later time. As I was saying," The Commander interjected apparently finally finding his wits, "what will you have us do with the bodies, my Queen?" It took me a full thirty seconds to realize the question and title were pointed towards me.

"Huh?" I blinked, "I'm sorry, what?" The Commander released an awkward cough.

"What shall you have us do with–"

"No, I heard you, but why are you asking me?" My brain was short circuiting, "And what's with the title?"

"You killed Lucifer." The Commander said pointedly, "And as far as we are aware you are his eldest, making you, his heir."

The hell fire in my veins began humming, as if trying to assert that what the Commander was implying was true. I could feel Becca's gaze boring into me, but I was frozen to the spot. I didn't want any of this, I didn't do what I did to receive it.

"All I want to do is recover my brothers' body." I said quietly, taking a step back. The Commander's gaze was soft, understanding, but it didn't lighten the blow of his next words.

"Yes. That's why I was asking what you want done with it. Before, the common practice was to burn the dead." A flare of panic and disgust went through me, but the commander added, "We would prefer not to do that anymore, but need your permission."

Becca's cool hands landed on my shoulders then, steadying me. She was all cold grace and authority as she addressed the Commander.

"We wanted to kill him for revenge, not power. After learning what the homicidal doves have been doing, our cause and actions became more noble. Taking a throne was never a part of the plan. Losing her brother was never a part of the plan." Frost coated her final words, "If you sincerely see my sister as your master, then back the fuck off and give her a moment to grieve."

Gently she turned me around, out from under the heavy, expectant gazes of the Hounds in the room. Through blurry eyes I noticed that Luna had moved to Silas' side, the vampire beginning to stir.

The pounding in my head slowly increased as we climbed the dais.

Anzens body still gave off some warmth, but his face was utterly pale. The strong pull of his alpha aura was no longer present.

My mind was moving too fast, the thoughts piling atop one another and threatening to drown me. Even after killing his mate, he devoted his life to me. Had hidden what he was from us for decades. Had devised his own scheme behind the Devils back in order to protect me once I found myself here.

I knelt over his body, wings shielding us as I pulled him close, and cried more than I ever had before in my life.

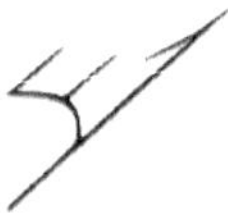

Rebecca was a forcefield before her sister. As far as she was concerned, these dogs could sort their shit out themselves. The only ones she let approach were Hikari and Kuma.

Ravens tail, horn, and that ethereal glow to her skin had all but faded once the tears started. Still, the two knelt cautiously by their sister's side, before gathering her into their strong arms and doing what they could to soothe her. Doing what Akashi should be doing.

Instead, he had crossed the room to the group of Hounds gathered beneath where Finn dangled.

When Rebecca first saw him, she had nearly thrown up at the sight. The wiggling red flames slithered in and out of his body like snakes. Blood dripped from the points of his shoes, and the vessels on his neck and forehead were stained purple against the pain. Her memories of her sister may still be fragmented at best, but she knew in her soul that there was no way Raven would have done something that brutal just because of his betrayal.

Silas had said nothing about it before passing out in her arms. Given his weakened state and the jagged puncture wound in his neck, she could only be grateful that her sister awoke in time.

She stomped down the dais, casting an anxious glance his way. He was sitting upright now, laughing gently at something Luna had said. The she-wolf met her assessing stare, giving her a reassuring nod. It eased Becca's worry enough for her claws to stop threatening to spring out from under her skin.

She padded across the room aiming for Akashi's side, preparing to give him an earful for ignoring what was happening at the top of the dais but bit her tongue when she caught a glimpse of his face. His skin was a sick shade of grey, eyes hollow and empty as he looked up at what his mate had made of the man dangling from the wall.

"He's alive." Rebecca said, sidling up next to him cautiously. He didn't react, but a few of the other Hounds in the group were startled by her sudden appearance.

Though they towered over her in this form, they studied her warily. No doubt their sharp sense of smell easily paired her with the Hellcat that had rampaged outside. It filled her with a shamed sense of pride. She swallowed any comments she had to say about it.

"When a vampire dies, the decades or centuries of rot catch up with them all at once." She explained, "Sometimes they just fall into a lump of flesh and bones.

Since he's still in one piece he's very much alive, but it will take him a hell of a lot longer to recover than he's used to."

"How do you suggest we get him down?" The Commanders voice rose from behind her, and Akashi visibly flinched beside her. Subtly, she shifted to place herself between the two as she faced the man who fathered the young Hound beside her.

"Your name is Aengus, right?" She asked, cool eyes flicking over him from head to toe. He hesitated, as if he wasn't used to being called by name, but nodded once. She pursed her lips, "Well since your so obsessed with Raven making all the decisions here, I say we leave him there until she decides what to do with him."

It was a front. Rebecca couldn't even begin to imagine how to safely remove those flames, but it was convincing enough for the crowd to start to disperse. She released a breath she hadn't known she was holding.

"Is she okay?" Akashi's voice was low. Raw. Rebecca didn't turn around, her tone unforgiving.

"I understand you've been through a lot today, but I'm the one who actually killed her. I turned her into this... new her. So, the least you can do is manage to look at her."

"You're the one I'm having a problem looking at." The snarl was so vicious that Rebecca actually took a step back.

So that was it. He was disgusted with her, not her sister. Rebecca said nothing else as she stepped away.

He could hate her as long as he needed to, it didn't make a damn difference to her.

CHAPTER 39

I don't know how long I laid there with Anzen, Kuma and Hikari by my side. Snot was running from my nose, and I could feel how swollen my face was from crying just by blinking. I looked anything but queenly, but thankfully Akashi and Becca seemed to have cleared the room. Save for the Commander, who made it clear he would not be leaving Lunas side unless she ordered him to.

Despite my appearance Akashi cupped my cheeks, brushing any remnants of my tears away and placed soft kisses across my temple. I didn't miss the tension lacing the air between him and my sister but didn't comment on it. Whatever they needed to hash out, it could wait.

"I don't want to burn his body." I finally said, looking at each of my brothers in turn. I swallowed the urge to throw up as I added quietly, "I don't want to burn any of the bodies. Their families should get to bury and mourn them properly."

The Commanders gaze on me was electrified with anticipation as I stood. I winced as I stretched my wings out, the angle I had them at before doing horrible things for my spine, before tucking them in tight and bending to retrieve my sword.

Descending the dais I pressed the subtle button on the base of the hilt, the weapon shrinking back into a cuff. With the extra metal, it was now adorned with drooping silver and black chains. Becca was by my side in an instant, the cuff containing my mother's shield held in her extended palm. Akashi's gaze was heavy as I reached for it, reached for her.

The Commander followed silently at my back as I approached the blown-out section of wall, "My Queen—"

"If you can't manage to use my name, at the very least address me as my pack name." The bite in my voice held unmistakable authority, even if I was internally shaking. I had never acknowledged my place within my family, having always considered myself an outsider. A burden.

"From this point forward my sister and Silas will also be considered members of the Nightshade pack. They may come and go here as they please." The Commander looked dumbfounded but only nodded.

"If that is what pleases you, Lady Nightshade." I closed my eyes, allowing the title to hit me, wash over me, and pass. I breathed.

"Hikari," My head was clear, voice stable and commanding, "sweep the valley for fallen weaponry from the legion's army. Be careful when handling it. Akashi, go with him to retrieve any surviving Angels. I want them brought back here alive. Luna, set up a station for our own wounded– Kuma you're going to be treated there immediately. And Aengus," It felt wrong somehow, calling my somewhat father-in-law by name, "can I be assured you will communicate with the Hounds about the changes I plan to make?"

Aengus stood taller, prouder, "Undoubtedly, my Lady." We would definitely need to work on him becoming less formal, but for now I just nodded.

Hikari and Luna transformed, the latter radiating pride as the two disappeared out the double doors. Akashi hesitated only to place yet another kiss on my temple before following their lead. Aengus transformed and approached my side. The large red Hound threw his head back releasing a deep signal howl which echoed out the crack in the stone to travel across the valley.

Hounds below snapped to attention, their eyes finding us where we stood. I was confused at first when one by one they began to bow, before I noticed Aengus had done so by my side.

"That really isn't necessary!" I blurted, my face flushing in embarrassment.

"We have not willingly bowed to a Master for centuries." The Commander said, green eyes searching mine, "Please accept our sign of loyalty and faith, in the sincerest way we know how to show."

I was about to continue to protest but Becca started cackling from behind me. Annoyed, I turned to see her seated next to Silas, literally slapping her knee as she laughed.

"It's not supposed to be funny." I muttered and she waved her hand apologetically.

"Oh, I don't know. If I had a field full of men kneeling at my feet, I'd be eating that shit up!"

"Yep, I'm right here too." Silas released a dramatic sigh, pulling a laugh from me this time as well.

Outside the Hounds all began to howl and yip, their voices rising in a joyous symphony and erasing the dread of the day. There would still be tears and heartache. There would still be danger. But a flicker of something long dead flared to life in my chest which reassured me that for now, we would be okay.

Hours later, I sat before the largest bonfire I'd ever seen in my life. I was utterly exhausted by the time the Hounds asked me to light it, only managing a few sparks but none of them expressed any negativity. They took what I could give, and just kept building upon it. I was half convinced at this rate the flames would reach the ceiling of the cave.

Upon Hikari's return, now in the company of a dozen other Hounds pulling sleds piled high with Holy metal, I had them lead me to the dungeons. Once all the metal was accounted for, I sent them out, not wanting to risk anyone getting scratched while I molded the metals together to replace half of the old brimstone bars with new cells of silver and gold.

I also fashioned a set of hand and ankle cuffs, each set connected to the other with a thick chain. These would be for Finn. My stomach rolled, the image of him pinned to that wall flashing through my mind. I felt guilty, but I was newly awoken, risen, and craved blood. And seeing how close to death he had pushed his brother, the flash of power that exploded out of me was unstoppable.

Silas popped out of nowhere, yanking me from my thoughts and giving me such a fright, I nearly chucked an unused arrow in his direction. He only laughed before suggesting fashioning a headpiece for Finn as well. It was a good idea, and in the meantime would ensure he couldn't use his mental gift to paralyze anyone again. I wound a few more pieces of metal together, the creation disturbingly looking like a halo.

Ignoring that fact, I asked Silas to find a few Hounds to carefully clean the place up and light a few torches. Put an actual mattress in the cell Finn would be in. He was dangerous yes, but I didn't want him locked in a miserable pit unless he forced that kind of fate upon himself. Silas said nothing but seemed grateful for the consideration on his brother's behalf.

I was as gentle as I could while removing the flaming vines from Finns body. He didn't wake, not even when he fell. I was shocked to see a young Hound step forward to catch him before he hit the floor, giving a nod of thanks at their fearful glance. I didn't know what we would do with him yet, but I was not torturing him. The Hounds were so keen they picked up on that memo without me even needing to clarify it.

Once cuffed with his halo in place, he was carried downstairs to his cell. Silas looked on the verge of following him, but Becca's hand slipped into his rooting him to the spot.

I turned to the gaping hole in the wall, hands throbbing with heat as magic pulsed from me. Dunes of sand outside lifted, carried on an invisible breeze to fill the gap. Using the hell fire in my veins I melted the sand down, molding a ribbed mosaic of orange and blue glass to fashion a window for the room rather than the bleak cave it was before.

The last thing I did was obliterate my father's hideous throne. I sank the obsidian down, expanding it into a long oval table. I created one high backed chair for myself in the center but surrounded the table on all sides with velvet covered benches, an invitation for conversation rather than dictatorship.

Then and only then did I collapse against Akashi, half asleep and in need of water and a shower. When I awoke, I had been cleaned from head to toe, and Becca was still by my side smoothing some type of balm across my wings.

"That stuffs heavy." I'd muttered, the wing she was touching pulling away.

"It should help relax the new muscles. Aengus said they use it on newly shifted pups to ease the shock, and the pain." Whatever I groaned out made her laugh, nonetheless she'd helped me dress and led me outside to where I currently sat on a pile of furs before the bonfire.

Some of the Hounds were dancing. Others were drinking. Small groups huddled together to shed some tears or stories about those who died. I felt a knife twist in my gut as some of their voices carried words of praise for Anzens sacrifice.

"What did they do with the bodies?" I asked quietly, leaning closer to Luna so no one else heard. She paused, glass halfway raised to her lips.

"A burial ground was prepared above the cliffs outside this cave. You'll like them, full of wildflowers through the warm seasons and just as breathtaking during the cold." She glanced at me, "We did lay him to rest, but left a space for his headstone for you to fill if you'd like."

"Thank you." I mumbled, eyes drifting back to the Hounds before us. There were thousands of them, the overwhelming majority male. The few females I did spot were either huddled close to one another, or glued to the side of what I assumed was their mate.

"There's not many female Hounds, are there?" I asked, unable to help wondering aloud. Luna looked momentarily perplexed but shook her head.

"No. A female Hellhound has always been a rarity."

My eyes landed on Becca in that moment, and I couldn't help but grin at the irony. A place where females had been historically stifled and bred, now was crawling with two new half breeds with little to no tolerance. Lord help us all.

She caught my eye mid-sentence, her lips widening to a bright smile that I'd only ever gotten glimpses of before. Silas was by her side, an arm swung over her shoulders.

I caught his eye while Becca went back to whatever story she was very animatedly telling. I wanted to go see how he was doing, how he was processing, but the bastard sent a wink in my direction before I could overthink. I flipped him the bird and he grinned, leaning into whisper something to my sister that made her blush.

"What do you think he told her?" Akashi's breath swept over my neck seconds before his mouth left a short trail of hot kisses. I leaned back into him, more than happy to let him hold the weight of me as I was still adjusting to the wings.

"I'm supposed to believe you didn't catch it with your super hearing?" I asked, sarcasm dripping off of every word.

"Oh, I might've heard something about your sister I'd rather not repeat." He laughed, and the sound beat through me, warm and reassuring.

"Are the two of you, okay?" I asked, shifting to look at him as best I could with the wings. His eyes were distant, but he tried to sound reassuring.

"I watched her slice your neck open. She didn't even hesitate. I'm going to need a minute to forgive her for that."

"If it makes you feel better, I only didn't ask you because you would have hesitated."

"It does not," he mumbled, arms snaking around my waist and sinching me closer. "Is this okay?" He asked, pointedly kissing the arch of my wing. I felt heat that had nothing to do with the fire blooming through me and I nodded, not trusting my voice. He grinned, undoubtedly taking a mental note of my response but pushed for nothing further.

Together we sat, taking in the celebration of life before us. Occasionally Akashi would mumble some history to me, of the Hounds ways before Lucifer became a Devil. Luna chimed in, her eyes aglow with a longing for that long ago life.

Eventually Aengus pulled her to her feet. Some reason or other to dance with him tumbled from his lips as he drew her with him into the growing crowd. Silas and Rebecca were already dancing, the smile on her face as bright as it was when we were kids.

Kuma and Hikari eventually wandered over to where we were seated, the former sporting bandages over his shoulders and clearly intoxicated as he threw himself down on the fur beside us. True to form, Akashi slid out from under me, unable to resist the rare opportunity to best our beast of a brother.

I shimmied over to Hikari as the two of them began to mock-wrestle, the two of us whooping and clapping. The fire popped in time with the soaring music, and Hounds young and old danced and sang.

As Hikari and I counted down the seconds to Akashi's victory, that wonderful foreign feeling from earlier once again bloomed inside my chest. This time I was able to identify it for what it was:

Hope.

EPILOGUE

If Gabriel could wield fire, he would have burned this room in the temple long ago. Blindly he shredded his way through the scrolls, searching and finding nothing on the existence or demise of any demonic angel within known history. This room was an entity in and of itself, recording all God saw by its own power and will. If there was any information, he could find to use against his newest threat it would be buried in these godforsaken texts somewhere.

Enraged, he ripped the scroll in his hands to pieces, letting the withered pages sink to the floor. He didn't watch as it seamlessly repaired itself, just grabbed another scroll from the shelf, his desperation growing rabid.

Thousands of Angels had been lost this day, to either death or hells prison. The latter was a fate he didn't entertain to imagine, a place designed for sinners holding the purest as captives.

That's what this whole thing had always been about. Ridding the world of the impurities Lucifer left spotted in humanity since his appearance in Eden. He had taken the beautiful creation of Life and dirtied it. All Gabriel wanted to do was purify it again.

"Will this war never end?" He bellowed, shredding the new scroll in his hands in frustration.

It will.

Gabriel froze, the parchment slipping from his fingers. The blood in his veins pounded ruthlessly through his body as the presence of his Lord washed over him.

Your actions today have guaranteed that my child.

"But I don't understand," Gabriel turned, pleading with the faceless presence, "That half devil is just as dangerous as–"

I have recited it many times my child. Be not afraid. Your fear shall be your end.

"I am not afraid my Lord I am driven!" Gabriel clasped his hands before himself and fell to his knees, "I have pledged and will continue to do so: I will rid your Earth from its impurities. Your creation shall be whole once more!"

His Lord remained silent for so long Gabreil thought he had departed, but when the thundering voice shook through him again it was a sound of warning, not praise.

Be not afraid. Your fear shall be your end.

A flash of powerful light engulfed the room, causing Gabriel to shield himself with his wings and cloak. When it retreated, the Angel gaped at the now barren library. Each and every scroll, book and shred of history had been erased. Taken.

The only other thing in the room besides himself was a single black feather, drifting to rest on the table before him.

<u>*ACKNOWLEDGMENTS*</u>

The first and most important person I would like to thank is my husband. For 7 years you have dealt with the obsessive episodes, emotional breaks, chaotic ramblings, and trauma responses happening both in and outside of this book. I don't know where I would be today without you. Thank you for always lending a listening ear, encouraging me when I get scared and accepting both versions of me with open arms.

Next, my soul sister, Rebecca. Without you Raven would have never evolved beyond a catalyst for my anger. Though we've had our ups and downs (as sisters do) you've been here every step of the way. Thank you for offering your feedback on my ideas and sticking with me through our crazy lives!

Mom. First, I want to say thank you for reading this, I know it's long and doesn't have a single picture! This book probably made you emotional at many points and that's okay. Consider it a trophy or a medal, I know I certainly do. It's tangible proof that I'm okay– and came out on top!

And to the readers, who put in just as much time and emotion as authors do to support our work, thank you. You rock!

With grace, love, and respect,
NIGHTSHADE